"Let yourself go...tell me what comes to mind."

"A beach," Julee said without hesitation. "White sand. Moonlight on the water."

Cain's eyes drifted shut as well and he saw himself on the beach with a woman...the waves licking the shore, his tongue licking the salt from her neck....

She shivered and he drew her closer, warming her body with his. When their lips touched, he knew it wasn't the air that made her quiver like a leaf in the chill wind. It was the passion....

Julee's sharp intake of breath shattered their shared mental imagery. She stared up at him, her eyes wide with wonder and fear.

"What are you doing to me?"

Willing her pulse to normalcy, Julee struggled to make sense of what had just happened between her and Cain. Could Cain be the man who had haunted her dreams?

Dear Reader,

Welcome to Silhouette **Special Edition**...welcome to romance.
Spring is here, and thoughts turn to love...so put a spring in
your step for these wonderful stories this month.

We start off with our THAT SPECIAL WOMAN! title for
April, *Where Dreams Have Been...* by Penny Richards. In this
story, the whereabouts of a woman's lost son are somehow
connected to an enigmatic man. Now she's about to find out
how his dreams can help them find her missing son—and heal
his own troubled past.

Also this month is *A Self-Made Man* by Carole Halston, a tale
of past unrequited love that's about to change. Making the
journey from the wrong side of the tracks to self-made man,
this hero is determined to sweep the only woman he's ever
truly loved off her feet.

To the West next for Pamela Toth's *Rocky Mountain Rancher*.
He's a mysterious loner with a past...and he wants his ranch
back from the plucky woman who's now running it. But
complicating matters are his growing feelings of love for this
tough but tender woman who has won his heart. And no visit to
the West would be complete without a stop in Big Sky country,
in Marianne Shock's *What Price Glory*. Paige Meredith has
lived with ambition and without love for too long. Now rugged
rancher Ross Tanner is about to change all that.

Don't miss Patt Bucheister's *Instant Family*, a moving story of
finding love—and long-lost family—when one least expects it.
Finally, debuting this month is new author Amy Frazier, with a
story about a woman's return to the home she left, hoping to
find the lost child she desperately seeks. And waiting there is
the man who has loved her from afar all these years—and who
knows the truth behind *The Secret Baby*. Don't miss it!

I hope you enjoy these books, and all the stories to come!

Sincerely,

Tara Gavin

Senior Editor

Please address questions and book requests to:
Silhouette Reader Service
U.S.: 3010 Walden Ave., P.O. Box 1325, Buffalo, NY 14269
Canadian: P.O. Box 609, Fort Erie, Ont. L2A 5X3

Penny Richards

WHERE DREAMS HAVE BEEN...

SPECIAL EDITION®

Published by Silhouette Books
America's Publisher of Contemporary Romance

This book is for Audrey Mire, my new friend and pen pal in Thibodaux. Thanks for the cards, the articles and the kind words of encouragement.

 SILHOUETTE BOOKS

ISBN 0-373-09949-5

WHERE DREAMS HAVE BEEN...

Printed in U.S.A.

PENNY RICHARDS

of Haughton, Louisiana, describes herself as a dreamer and an incurable romantic. Married at an early age to her high school sweetheart, she claims she grew up with her three children. Now that only the youngest is at home, writing romances adds an exciting new dimension to her life.

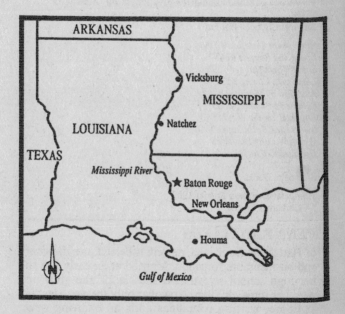

Prologue

The breeze coming off the sea was warm and moist and smelled of salt and adventure. It toyed with her dark hair and stroked her heated skin with caresses that, even in their whisper softness, couldn't compete with those lavished on her feverish, wanting flesh by the man who lay at her side.

The gentle lapping of the waves was a muted and mesmerizing sound...a siren's song that told of aged battles and legends of long-lost treasures buried in empty hulls and guarded by ancient superstitions and legions of colorful, finned swimmers. Its primal pulse fell on her ears, keeping time to the beat of her heart and fanning the passion provoked by the stranger's touch.

Desire was a live entity inside her body, a body left barren by the loss of love. A body left too long untended by a caring, loving touch. Now, incredibly, her aging sorrows seemed as faraway as the sound of a distant gull's cry, no longer holding the power to hurt... holding instead the bit-

tersweet melancholy of a favorite song. Now need flour-
ished, fed by the brush of the man's mouth, nourished by
the wet sweetness of his kiss that tasted of wine and hope.
She ached with the craving to partake of that offering of
hope. Was drowning in it.

An acceptance she didn't understand, but welcomed
nonetheless, guided her every response, and she forced him
to his back with a desperation and urgency that surprised
her. Excitement ordained the words of encouragement and
entreaty she whispered into his ear. Impatience governed the
hands that tore at his clothes with no thought to decorum or
shame or fidelity to her past love. Zeal dictated the eager
kisses she scattered across his face and chest and be-
yond....

His groan of pleasure was an aphrodisiac. Recovering the
initiative, he tumbled her onto her back. She cradled his
weight between her thighs, the obvious differences in their
physicality making her acutely, thankfully, aware that she
was a woman. She took him deep inside and gasped at the
combined pain and pleasure ... so deep that he touched her
very soul.

For a long moment, as he lay poised above her, there was
no movement, no sounds but those of the night and the un-
mistakable rasp of their breathing. Wisps of cloud drifted
across the face of the moon, and shadow-dapples danced
across a visage obscured by the silhouette cast by the rag-
ged thatch of a nearby date tree. She felt, rather than saw,
the urgency in his eyes, an urgency transmitted by the brush
of his thumb across her bottom lip. If there were any lin-
gering doubts, they were banished with the gentleness of his
touch.

She felt the simultaneous opening of her heart and body,
both ready to embrace his presence. Alert to the subtle nu-
ance, satisfied that she was wholly accepting of his mascu-

line invasion, he began to move against her in immeasurable, soul-shattering strokes.

She strove with him to reach that place where rationalization died, thought ceased, and the promise of tomorrow paled beneath the promise of the moment ... a place devoid of everything but the taste and feel and sound of mating flesh and kindred souls.

They found the promise together.

The crooning of the sea accompanied their cries of fulfillment. Even then, she clung to enough of her sanity to acknowledge that this was good and somehow destined to be.

Chapter One

The sound of three-year-old Brice's voice demanding "c'real" dragged Julee Sutherland from her sleep, though not without considerable reluctance.

The Dream, as she called the erotic fantasy that left her feeling restless and troubled and acutely aware of the length of her sexual abstinence, had taken her off to some faraway place again last night.

The Dream had insinuated itself into her life soon after she'd moved into the house in August, and invaded her nights at least once a week. While it was disturbing to experience such a total sexual capitulation to a nameless, faceless man, it was more disturbing to wake up with all the symptoms of having indulged in a night of hungry sex.

She traced her tongue over lips that felt swollen from too much kissing. Beneath the sheet, her fingers touched the tips of her breasts under her soft cotton T-shirt. Strange that they felt as if they'd actually come into contact with the rasp of a man's beard. Her entire body throbbed with a curious, pleasurable ache. She sighed. Until a few months ago, she'd thought only men were plagued by the kind of dreams she'd been having.

"Wake up, Mama."

With a groan, Julee opened her eyes, rolled to her side and encountered the somber features of her only child. Tad's son. Coming hard on the heels of a dream where she'd experienced a depth of surrender she'd never reached with her husband, the reproach in Brice's eyes filled Julee with shame. How could she possibly imagine a dream lover more satisfying than the passion she and Tad had shared?

"You awake?"

The question was asked with a serious expression, another reminder of Tad. Julee smothered a stirring of sorrow. Though the pain of her loss was manageable after almost four years, sometimes the similarity in Brice's and Tad's actions was disconcerting. She smiled and reached out to riffle her son's blond hair. "Barely."

"I'm hungry."

"I know. Why don't you go turn on the TV?" Julee suggested. "I'll be there in a minute."

The child's brown eyes brightened, and a mischievous, heart-stopping grin curved the mouth so much like Tad's before Brice bolted from the room. In a matter of seconds, the muted sounds of Power Rangers battling the Putties filtered into Julee's pink-and-moss-green bedroom.

Freeing another sigh, she pushed back the crisp floral sheet. She supposed it was too much to expect that Brice would let her sleep in just because her construction crew had been rewarded with the weekend off.

Tad would have said there was no rest for the wicked, but it wasn't wickedness that kept Julee's nose to the proverbial grindstone. She was a widow with a child to raise: Working long hours was a necessity, just as keeping her husband's dream alive by putting all her energies into a business she knew nothing about had been a necessity after his death.

When they'd first met, Tad's driving ambition had been to become not only a successful New Orleans architect but also a successful housing contractor. By combining both, he could have it all. His determination and enthusiasm had made it her dream, too.

When he died—she still couldn't think of his death as murder—it seemed imperative that she do everything within her power to hold on to Sutherland Construction, despite the fact that she didn't know a slide rule from a T square, and despite all the warnings about the advisability of clinging to a business that had cost Tad his life, and her almost everything they had accumulated during their marriage.

With a determination that bordered on desperation, Julee had ignored the concerned counsel of her friends and Tad's family and bulldozed ahead. So what if she didn't know anything about building houses? She wasn't afraid of hard work. She was smart; she could learn. Besides Brice, Sutherland Construction was all that was left of Tad, and she had vowed to make the business a success if it killed her. There had been many times since she'd undertaken her quest, she'd feared it would.

The sound of a karate cry emanated from the living room. Julee pushed the memories of Tad to the back of her mind and pushed the tousled hair from her face. She'd better check on Brice before he demolished the house.

The *slap, slap* of Cain Collier's running shoes against the cracked sidewalk of the old, genteel neighborhood kept a syncopated rhythm with the heavy beating of his heart. He hoped the run would chase away the fuzziness caused from lack of sleep. He'd been up until the wee hours, trying to finish a painting of an Italian villa. Because he seldom missed his five-mile morning run, he was considered a health freak by his associates at the high school in Houma where he taught the unlikely combination of Louisiana history and art.

Cain never bothered to correct them. How could he explain that his long strides not only distanced him from the neighborhood where he lived, they also distanced him from the pain and guilt he'd suffered every waking moment since he'd lost his wife and daughter nearly four years before? How could he make anyone understand that pushing himself to the absolute limits of what his physical body could bear was his punishment as well as his salvation and his sanity? Running blocked out the memories, shut out every noise, every thought. Cleared his mind of everything but the necessity of putting one foot in front of the other.

Sweat sheened his arms and legs and soaked the headband that bound back the hair his uncle said was too long for a man of Cain's age, a statement Cain refuted with a resigned smile and the observation that, as an artist, he was not only allowed, but expected, to be out of step with the rest of the world.

Being out of step was something he'd grown used to, if not comfortable with, through the years. Getting in step was a goal he'd set for himself five years earlier, before he lost his family.

Hurry, Cain. Hurry. Hurry. Hurry.

Cain wasn't sure where he picked up the goading litany that filled him with an inexplicable and urgent need to get back home. He shook his head to clear it and glanced around, aware of his surroundings for the first time since he'd stepped out his front door. Strange. Even though he wasn't halfway through his usual course, his subconscious had set his feet back toward his house. Irritated, he rejected the impulse to quicken his pace. What he ought to do was ignore that taunting voice, turn himself around and finish his run.

Hurry. Hurry. Hurry.

To hell with it. He might as well go back, even though reason told him there was no real need. The house he'd bought five years ago had nothing inside its four walls to make it a home. The single-story structure was just a place to lay his head and submerge himself in his painting. There was no wife waiting for him with his breakfast ready, a list of Saturday "honey do's" in hand, no woman waiting for him to come and kiss her awake and while away the morning in bed.

The random thought conjured a sudden, vivid memory, one he'd been trying to forget ever since he'd opened his eyes and found himself in a tangle of sweaty sheets.

His dream.

He offered a dark curse to the bright spring morning. He'd had the dream again last night, the same dream he'd experienced sporadically for several months. He had no idea why he had it or what triggered it, but it was always the same. Over and over, he made love to a woman whose face was hidden in shadows while the sea crashed and rolled around them.

He had no idea who the woman was or what the dream meant.

You could know if you wanted to. The nagging voice inside him was right. If he pressed the tiniest bit, he could see the woman's face and ferret out the deeper meaning of the dream. That there was a deeper meaning was a certainty, but Cain had no intention of trying to figure it out. All that had ever done was raise new questions...create more problems.

Besides, it didn't take a psychic to know what the dream meant. He was a healthy thirty-four-year-old, and he hadn't had sex since the accident that had taken Amy's life. No big mystery there. And it didn't take a clairvoyant to know that the woman in his dream was his neighbor, Julee Sutherland. Thoughts of her had filled his mind since he'd met her back in August. And since he'd filled several canvases with her likeness, it was safe to assume his interest in her exceeded minimal.

Hurry. Hurry.

"Yoo-hoo! Young man! Can you give me a hand?"

The sound of the woman's shrill summons penetrated Cain's thoughts and halted the compelling melody that urged him on. He drew to a halt and planted his hands on his hips, turning toward the sound of the querulous entreaty, his breathing harsh, labored.

An elderly woman, a vision straight from the forties in her Sunday dress, flower-bedecked straw hat and white gloves, waved at him from the driveway of a two-story Victorian house. She was standing next to the open trunk of an ancient Lincoln that sported a spit-and-polish wax job and four whitewall tires, one of which was flat.

"I'm so sorry to disturb your run," the woman said with a plaintive smile, "but I'm going to a ladies' luncheon, and I seem to have a flat tire. Would you mind terribly changing it for me? I'll pay you for your trouble."

Hurry.

Cain tamped back the urgency gnawing at him. Of course he'd change the tire. Though he might not look the part, he'd been raised a Southern gentleman. There was no way he could leave the woman stranded. "I won't take your money, but I'd be glad to change your flat."

"Oh, thank you!" the woman said, beaming. When he acknowledged that, yes, he was thirsty, she bustled into the house to fetch him a glass of iced tea. While she introduced herself as Hattie Carlisle and extolled the beauty of the spring morning, Cain took the jack and spare tire from the cavernous trunk and set about fixing the flat.

Hattie Carlisle's pleasant chatter fell on his ears with no more impact than a raindrop on stone while she lauded him for his kindness, bemoaned the sad state of the country and lamented over the pitiful lack of morals and courtesy found in a goodly portion of today's youth—all, she was certain, the result of too little supervision and too much pampering. Her views reminded him a lot of Trixie Guidry, the seventy-going-on-twenty-year-old widow who lived next door.

Cain worked as swiftly as he could—*hurry, hurry, hurry*—adding a rare observation to her comments and answering her questions. Her curiosity—or maybe it was loneliness—made her desire to know about him insatiable, and she demanded to know his name, what he did for a living, where he was from and where he lived. Being his usual personable, if somewhat quiet, self, Cain answered every query.

Ten minutes later, he slammed the trunk shut, suggested that the woman have the spare fixed as soon as possible and again waved aside her offer of payment. He just wanted to get home. *Needed* to. Doing his best not to be rude, but anxious to be on his way, he bade Hattie Carlisle goodbye and took off down the sidewalk. Her thanks followed him all the way to the corner.

Brice had decided to forgo his cereal for a breakfast of bacon and scrambled eggs. After wolfing down his food, he'd abandoned the television for the freedom of the backyard. From her vantage point at the kitchen window, Julee watched him kick his black-and-white soccer ball in a reasonable facsimile of the game while she cleaned up the remains of their breakfast.

It was a perfect morning for a little boy to play outside. Though the mid-May day already showed promise of becoming a scorcher, the grass in the shady backyard was still damp with dew, and the caladiums she'd planted in the windowbox and along the patio edge danced prettily beneath the early-morning sun. The hammock where she often stretched out to watch Brice play swayed between two oak trees and beckoned with the possibility of at least a few moments' rest before she started on her weekly housecleaning chores.

Cain Collier's kitchen light was on. Julee smothered a small sigh. She didn't want to think about her aborted, barely begun relationship with the man who lived behind her.

The clang of garbage cans and the grinding roar of the huge truck compacting refuse alerted Julee to the fact that she'd forgotten to take out her trash the night before. Grumbling at her absentmindedness, she tugged the plastic bag out of the can and tied it shut. Then she hurried out the back door and across the yard to the side of the house.

A gate separated the backyard from the sidewalk that ran alongside the garage to the front. She set down the bag and fumbled with the knotted piece of clothesline that secured the chain-link closure. She'd soon have to see about some kind of a lock, but for now, the rope kept Brice from venturing onto the street.

With a smile and a "thanks" for the trash collector who met her halfway down the driveway to relieve her of her burden, she started back. She was almost to the gate when she heard the pealing of the telephone.

"Phone!" Brice called unnecessarily.

Julee broke into a slow jog. "It's probably Grandma Sutherland. She wants to take you to the movies this afternoon."

"Yeah!" Brice cried, giving the ball a hard kick.

Julee was closing the latch on the gate when the phone rang the third time. Her hurried steps faltered when it occurred to her that the call might be from the unidentified male who had started phoning her on Saturday mornings about five months earlier. The calls weren't lewd in any way, unless she counted the low and sinister tone of his voice as obscene. They *were* threatening, and the message was always the same: "I know where you are, and I'm gonna make you pay."

She had the caller pegged as one of the workmen she'd used in the past. A giant of a man, Mel Dunning was crude, rude and obnoxious, not to mention married and the father of four children. He was, however, a darn good carpenter, and she'd hated to let him go.

She'd stood his particular brand of sexual harassment until the situation had become unbearable. The morning she'd fired him, he'd rammed a fist through the Sheetrock wall of the house they were building. "You'll be sorry, bitch," he'd muttered. "'Cause I'm gonna dog you till the day you die."

She had Mel figured for a blowhard coward. Anonymous calls were right up his alley, and his attitude had just underscored a prevalent fact: Being a woman boss in a male-dominated field was harder than she'd ever imagined.

Mel had kept his word. His cousin was involved in city politics, and there was always some sort of inspector checking to see that things were up to code at her job sites. She also had a recurring problem with materials coming up missing. A couple of light fixtures here, a dozen two-by-fours there. Enough to irritate, but not enough to make an issue over. Unfortunately, though she believed Mel to be the culprit, there were plenty of other light-fingered workers.

The phone pealed again. Julee rushed across the patio and through the back door, grabbing it in the middle of the fifth ring.

"Hello!" she said in a breathless voice.

"Carla?"

She didn't recognize the light, friendly voice. Julee felt the tension drain from her body. "I'm sorry," she said in genuine relief. "You have the wrong number."

"Is this the Magee residence?"

"No, it isn't."

"I'm sorry."

The masculine voice held regret. "That's all right," Julee assured the caller before she recradled the receiver. She'd taken no more than three steps when the phone rang again. She grimaced but answered with measured courtesy.

"Uh-oh," the caller said. "I guess this isn't Carla, huh?"

"No, it isn't."

"Is this 555-6799?"

"No."

"Gee, I'm really sorry." Contrition laced the apology. "I thought maybe I just dialed wrong the first time, but Bob must have given me the wrong number."

Julee's irritation gave way to understanding. She'd done the same thing herself. "That's okay. Maybe you should try information."

"Good idea. Thanks."

"Don't mention it." Shaking her head, she hung up again. She hoped the caller took her advice before he tried reaching the elusive Carla again. Julee started back outside and paused. She should just call Tad's mother and see what time she planned on picking up Brice. That way, the answering machine could catch the rest of her calls and take the stress out of her day.

The pressing need to hurry increased with every step Cain took, filling him with a mushrooming sense of doom. By the time he reached his street, the perspiration that dripped from him was the clammy sweat of fear instead of the healthy perspiration of exertion. He passed his house without stopping, not understanding what drove him, but knowing that whatever it was lay just around the corner.

Hurry.

Julee bade her mother-in-law goodbye, replaced the receiver and poured herself another cup of coffee. Taking a cautious sip, she went to the back door so she could check on Brice, letting her gaze pan the backyard. Brice wasn't on his swing set. He wasn't in the sandbox beneath the live-oak tree. He wasn't in the hammock.

She felt a smile tug at her lips. The little beast was hiding from her again. Hiding was his newest way to drive her insane. He liked jumping out at her from behind doors and out of closets.

"Come on out, Brice," she called in a singsong voice, pushing through the screen door and stepping out onto the wooden deck.

No answer.

Her smile faded. It wasn't like him not to respond when she called. Unwittingly, she remembered that she'd been so anxious to get to the phone that she hadn't retied the gate. Alarm quickened her heartbeats.

"C'mon, Brice. Mommy isn't in any mood to play games," Julee said as she headed toward the side of the house.

As she feared, the gate was wide open. The sound of squealing tires stole her breath and brought her footsteps and her heartbeats to a sudden stop.

Brice!

The mug in her hand fell from her nerveless fingers and shattered on the concrete of the sidewalk. Scalding coffee splattered her bare feet. If there was pain, it didn't register. An image of Brice's small body crumpled and bleeding beneath the tires of some phantom vehicle filled her mind.

Screaming his name, Julee sped down the sidewalk to the driveway, her frantic gaze sweeping the street to the left and then the right. There was no stopped vehicle, no prone body bleeding on the black asphalt. A wave of relief slowed her racing pulse and her headlong pace.

Then she saw him.

Not Brice. Cain Collier. He'd been out for his morning run. The waistband of his shorts was soaked. Sweat matted the hair splashed on his bare chest and stained the headband that held back dark blond hair.

But it wasn't his too-long hair that caught her attention. It wasn't the bold grooves slashed at the sides of a mouth that she truly believed to be one of the sexiest she'd ever seen. It wasn't the magnificence of his lean-muscled chest that heaved with his labored breathing or his powerful arms that she'd once foolishly imagined might hold her. It was the glazed expression in the smoky blue gaze he lifted to her.

And Brice's soccer ball clutched in his hands.

Cain gripped the ball so tightly his knuckles hurt. A little boy's ball. A boy, maybe two or three, with dark hair and brown eyes. Freckles ... *Brice!*

No! The denial came from somewhere deep inside him and went unheeded by the forces that made his body an unwilling prisoner of his mind.

Somehow, he *was* Brice Sutherland.

On some level, he was aware of Julee standing several yards away, staring at him, but his focus was on the emotions that controlled his body.

A man scooped him up from the side of the street. A big man. Strong. Maybe stronger than a Mighty Morphin Power Ranger. He reeled from a fear so powerful that blackness threatened to pull him under. So powerful he almost choked on it. He dropped his ball.

"Let me go!"

He didn't scream it—the man's hand held back the sound. But he wanted to. He thought it.

"Mama... Mama... Help me."

He fought. But he was so little. Weightless, almost, in the hands of the giant. The man wrenched open the car door and got in, slamming it shut behind them. Cain—the boy—fell back as the car shot forward. Tires squealed as the brown sedan took the corner.

He was crying—screaming—but all he could hear was the strangled sound of his sobs that were muted by the stranger's hand.

"Mama!"

"Give me that!"

The command was sharp and angry and brought Cain out of his trance with a suddenness that left him confused and disoriented. Even so, the underlying fear in Julee's voice was as clear as the green of her eyes.

Dazed, Cain looked down at the ball still in his hands and back up to the woman who, for a brief couple of days, he'd thought might possibly fill the void in his life. Though nothing but chain-link fencing and a few shrubs separated their backyards, they were separated by a past that would never permit them a future, except, perhaps, in his dreams.

"Where did you get that?" Julee asked, a jerk of her head indicating the ball.

Cain looked down at the ball, and held it toward her. He didn't remember picking it up. "It was lying in the street."

She made no move to take the ball. "Have you seen Brice?" she demanded.

Cain shifted his gaze from her worried face to the corner. *Had* he seen the boy? No. Not really. He shook his head, and when he turned to look at her again, his voice was as bleak as the expression in his eyes.

"They took him."

"Can you think of anyone who might have a grudge against you?"

Julee lifted her shocked gaze to the policeman Cain had insisted she call. Until now, she hadn't thought of Brice's disappearance as anything more than a random incident. Detective Dylan Garvey's question raised the possibility that Brice's disappearance might have been a deliberate deed. The prospect cast a sinister shadow over the whole episode.

"You'll pay, Sutherland. Damn it, you'll pay for killing my babies. The words had been spoken by Lanny Milligan the day Tad and his construction company was found innocent in the deaths of Lanny's two children, his sister-in-law and her daughter. Lanny had meant what he'd said, and Tad had indeed paid.

"I can't think of anyone who hates me enough to take my child," she volunteered at last.

"But?"

Julee met Dylan Garvey's direct blue gaze. She knew that the way to find Brice was to keep her wits about her and leave no stone unturned. She also knew that dredging up the incidents that precipitated Tad's death would be like opening a Pandora's box of old memories and emotions, wounds that had healed but whose scabs could be easily ripped away, exposing tortured, bleeding flesh.

She blinked back the sting of tears. No matter how much it hurt to resurrect the past, she knew she had to do whatever was necessary to find Brice.

"You're very observant, Detective Garvey."

"It's my job," he said with a slight smile. "Now, why don't you tell me who you think might want to get back at you by taking your little boy?"

"The only person I can think of might be Lucy Milligan."

The detective recorded the name in a small spiral notebook and brought his gaze back to Julee's. "Why don't you tell me why Lucy Milligan might do something this desperate?"

Julee took a deep breath. "About four years ago, four members of her family died in a house fire. My husband's construction company built the house."

No emotion crossed Detective Garvey's face. "Go on."

Julee told him about Tad's dream to be the architect and builder of beautiful houses, to be the head of the most successful construction company in New Orleans, and how that dream was coming to fruition when tragedy struck.

"We were very much in love, and as the company prospered, Tad began to delegate more and more to his foremen so we could spend time together. We were out of the country when the fire occurred. In a nutshell, the electrical contractor the foreman subcontracted the work to had a bad gambling problem. He shorted the job so he could make a bigger margin of profit."

"Wasn't the house inspected?"

"It was out in the country, outside the city limits." She shrugged. "You're a law officer, Detective Garvey. You know the play. If you know the right people there are ways to get around the rules."

The policeman nodded, his pen darting over the small page. "Who were the victims?"

"Two of the Milligan children. Lucy's sister and her eight-year-old daughter."

"The Milligans blamed your husband."

It was a statement, not a question. Julee nodded and drew in a deep breath. "It went to court. Ultimately, Sutherland Construction was acquitted of any wrongdoing, and the electrical contractor was found at fault, but Tad still blamed himself. He felt that if he'd been paying closer attention to business, the tragedy might have been averted."

"What about the other woman's family?"

Julee chose her words with extreme care. "He didn't make any trouble."

"I'd like to talk to Mr. Sutherland. Is he here?"

Julee felt the blood drain from her face. "Tad's dead."

The harsh statement stopped Dylan Garvey's pen. "How?"

The faraway look in Julee's eyes and the dispassionate note in her voice belied the tension evident in her tightly knotted fingers. "Lanny Milligan gunned him down with his deer rifle as we were coming out of a restaurant." A fleeting, sickly smile quivered on her lips. "We'd gone out to celebrate the acquittal and the fact that my in-home pregnancy test was positive."

The detective swore softly.

"The Milligans felt cheated, I guess."

"How's that?"

"The electrical contractor committed suicide a few days after he was found guilty, and when the dust settled there wasn't much left for a cash settlement. When the court found Tad innocent, Lanny Milligan was dragged from the courtroom yelling that Tad would pay. That's when he decided to kill Tad, I guess.''

"I assume he went to prison."

Julee nodded. "Angola."

"And you think his wife might be behind all this?"

Julee shrugged. "Unhappy people sometimes do desperate things."

"It's worth checking out. Can you think of anyone else? Someone you might have angered? A client? A worker? Someone who might want ransom money?"

She thought a moment. "Everyone knows I'm struggling financially," Julee said. "Maybe Mel Dunning," she said at last. "It's pretty farfetched, but I fired him about five months ago. He's made my business life hell ever since."

"How's that?"

Julee explained his connections to the city bigwigs and how the various city departments had kept close tabs on her construction jobs.

"What makes you think he might be capable of something as overt as kidnapping?"

"I don't know that he is. Actually, I always considered him a conceited blowhard. But I've been getting a phone call every Saturday morning ever since around the time I fired him."

"What kind of call?"

"The man says, 'I know where you are, and I'm going to make you pay.' The only person I can think of who might say that is Mel."

The detective asked a few more questions and told Julee to go down to the station and fill out a missing-persons report later that afternoon. He offered her a warm handshake and said he understood what she was going through. Something in his eyes told her that he did.

She watched him and his partner drive away and closed the door behind them. If only she could close the door on her memories as easily. If only the past would stay buried. But it was beginning to look as if that was wishful thinking.

After Tad was killed and she'd paid off the outstanding debts, there had been precious little money in Sutherland Construction's coffers. Most of Tad's clients had drifted away during the trial, and when Lanny Milligan gunned him down, the rest hurried to find someone else to build the home of their dreams.

Pregnant, alone, with no one to turn to, there had been several occasions she came close to swallowing her pride and calling her father, but somehow, she never could. Her gene pool had contained too large a dose of Eldridge pride. Instead, she faced the fact that, except for the child she carried in her womb, she was alone.

Determined to salvage Tad's business, she'd sold the house he'd designed especially for her and used the money to try to reconstruct the company. Through some smooth talking, she managed to convince a couple of the few remaining clients that she could build the houses Tad had promised them.

Unable to afford a foreman, and armed with nothing but her stubborn determination and a book titled *How To Be Your Own Building Contractor,* she'd gone out every morning to battle not only the world's prejudice against a woman doing a man's job, but the crude passes and innuendos from the men she hired.

To further complicate her life, Brice had been born six weeks early and had gotten off to a rocky start. The hospital bills mounted. After a month, Brice was declared well enough to go home, and as soon as was physically possible, she had packed up what was left of her life and moved lock, stock and air guns to Houma. Tad's parents were the closest family she had, and Brice deserved the love of his grandparents.

Then, late the previous summer, she'd moved from across town to this house, drawn by something she couldn't explain....

Julee shook off the recollections and went to collect the cups the policemen had used. She'd been in Houma for more than three years and felt that the move had been a positive experience. She'd begun to feel her life was leveling out. The pain of losing Tad had lessened to a dull ache in her heart, and Brice was healthy and happy.

While her small company couldn't compare to Tad's— after all, she wasn't an architect—she was proud of her public image. And though she was an unlikely candidate for a segment of "Lifestyles of the Rich and Famous," she made enough to live comfortably. Her personal life was limited to Brice and the Sutherlands, an occasional workout at a local gym, and an infrequent date. But she had been happy in Houma. She'd felt at home. Safe. Now she wondered if she'd ever feel safe again.

There were no erotic dreams for Cain that night. Instead, he lay staring up at a ceiling he couldn't see, trying to come to grips with what had happened that morning.

In spite of his determination to leave the past behind, it had caught up with him. The whimsical psychic ability that had failed to warn him of the danger to Amy and Holly, and had been noticeably absent from his life since their deaths, was back.

The damnable gift—or curse—had returned from wherever he had banished it four years ago, and it had returned with a vengeance. If he lived to be a thousand, he'd never forget the feelings he'd experienced when he picked up the soccer ball and relived Brice's terror during the kidnapping.

Nor would he soon forget the look on Julee Sutherland's face when he'd told her her son had been taken.

"What do you mean, they took him?" Her voice was hardly more than a whisper. "*Who* took him?"

Cain shook his head. "I don't know," he said honestly. "I was running. I saw the car turn the corner, heard the tires screeching." He shook his head again. "I don't know."

Tears sprang into Julee's eyes and she covered her mouth with her hand, as if the gesture was the only thing that held back a keening wail of sorrow. He watched her square her shoulders and take one deep breath and then another in a feeble attempt to hang on to her composure. He wasn't fooled. The slightest tug on her emotions would unravel the fragile thread of her self-control like a kid pulling on the loose string of a crocheted doily.

"What kind of car was it?" she asked.

"A brown sedan. A Pontiac of some sort, I think."

"Did you actually see Brice in the car?"

Another loaded question. "I . . . heard him calling," he offered in a cautious voice.

Julee swayed. Cain reached out and gripped her upper arm. "Why don't you let me take you inside so you can call the police."

"Police?" Though Cain wouldn't have thought it possible, her face grew even whiter. Her breath caught on a sob. "Dear God! Why would anyone want to take Brice?" she choked out. "Why would anyone take my baby?"

Cain hadn't been able to dredge up a single reason that might lessen her pain. Now, after more than sixteen hours, he still couldn't.

His offer to call the authorities had been met with a stoic look and a steely determination that she could handle it, that she had to call Brice's grandparents, too. Knowing he'd been dismissed, Cain had left her standing in the middle of the street and gone back home. He hadn't seen her since, except from a distance.

The police had arrived shortly after he'd urged her to make the call. He hadn't been surprised when they knocked on his door and asked if he'd tell them his version of what he'd seen that morning. Cain told the dark-haired detective how he'd been running, how he'd seen the car take a left at the end of the block and how he'd found Brice's ball in the street.

Dylan Garvey asked if Cain had managed to get a license plate number. Cain gave it to him, but didn't mention that the car was stolen. Revealing that information would just complicate things and open up his life to the very notoriety he shunned.

Though he'd told the truth—or as much as he could while omitting the psychic incident—it had taken just one look into the sharp eyes of Dylan Garvey to know that the detective suspected he was hiding something.

Later in the day, an older couple arrived at Julee's. The grandparents. More attuned to her emotions than he wanted to admit, Cain knew Julee wanted them to go so that she could give in to her own grief, but they hadn't left until after the incident was related on the six-o'clock news.

He was fixing himself a sandwich when he saw Julee wandering around her backyard, trailing her hand down the curve of the slide, sitting in Brice's swing and scuffing the toe of her sneaker in the bare patch of ground where the child's shoes had worn away the grass. Even though he'd known what she was going through, she hadn't cried. After a few moments, she went inside, and a few minutes later, she drove off.

Cain watched her speed down the street. Knowing first-hand how grief blinded a person to danger and could set them on a streak of self-destructive recklessness, he had willed her to be careful. He hadn't drawn an unworried breath until he saw her pull into the driveway during the ten-o'clock news.

Her lights had gone out soon after that, and he assumed that she had gone to bed.

Now, lying in his own bed, Cain's mind was filled with images of Brice's smiling face and memories of his little-boy curiosity. Cain also recalled every terrifying, sordid headline and remembered all the kidnapping horror stories he'd ever seen on television. He conjured up troubling, half-remembered pictures of toddlers and teenagers on milk cartons and in post offices and grocery stores...photos of smiling children who'd been taken by strangers who robbed them of their innocence. And their lives.

Unable to stand the turn of his thoughts, Cain threw back the sheet and sat up, resting his elbows on his knees and burying his head in his hands. It didn't help. Instead of visions of nameless children, he saw the anguish in Julee's eyes and heard Brice Sutherland's silent cry for help.

He gave a low groan and pushed himself to his feet, his movements as stiff as those of an old man. Swearing, he headed toward the kitchen. Maybe a beer would help him relax enough so that he could get some sleep. Maybe two or three would help him forget the psychic experience that had overcome him that morning.

And maybe the sun will come up in the west tomorrow.

Cain knew he was only postponing the inevitable. In time—soon—he would have to examine what had happened and deal with what it meant to the new life he'd constructed so carefully. Soon, but not now.

He was about to reach for the light switch inside the kitchen door when he noticed a shaft of luminescence slicing through the darkness from the Sutherland house. He crossed the room, finding comfort in the anonymity of the darkness.

Julee's kitchen blind was up. She sat at the small kitchen table, her profile turned to him, a mug cradled between her palms. She was staring at some point across the room, but he suspected that her gaze was focused inward, on images of the child who'd been taken that morning.... On memories.

As he watched, she lifted her hand and made an angry swipe at the crest of her cheekbone. She was crying. Somehow, he knew that these were the first tears she'd shed. He also knew that she'd had no more luck finding rest than he had. He watched as she brushed at the tears again. And again.

Giving up on stanching their flow, she covered her face with her hands. Cain saw her shoulders shake. His fingers tightened on the edge of the countertop. Grief had been a close companion of his for so long that he knew exactly what she was feeling. The emptiness. The loneliness. The helplessness.

He closed his eyes and pictured himself entering Julee Sutherland's kitchen and kneeling at her side. Sliding his arms around her and pulling her close. Offering her what comfort he could. And knowing that even if things were different and she were free to accept that comfort, it would never be enough....

A pleased smile crossed the man's face. Everything had gone off without a hitch. She would learn that he meant what he said. That he was a man of his word. The boy was his. He shook his head. It never ceased to amaze him how easy it was to find people willing to break the law . . . for the right price.

Money. It was, indeed, the root of all evil.

Chapter Two

Child Abducted From Backyard!

The headline screamed across the front page of the Houma paper. In a town of thirty-odd thousand, an abduction was big news. News that was important enough to override Julee Sutherland's need to grieve for her loss in private. Past experience had taught Cain that the media weren't noted for their sensitivity. Allowing emotion to keep them from getting a story was unthinkable.

The article gave the usual cut-and-dried version of what had happened the previous morning, but unlike the six- and ten-o'clock television reports, the newspaper account mentioned the scandal involving Tad Sutherland's construction company and his death at the hands of the man whose two children had died in the fire. It also related that Julee now headed her own construction business in Houma and mentioned that the only lead the police had was that a neighbor, a high school art teacher, had seen the getaway car.

A frisson of apprehension quivered through Cain. He refolded the paper. Now that the vultures knew he'd seen something, they would descend on him like a plague of locusts in an attempt to satisfy their voracious hunger for any morsel of news. The idea that they might ruin lives in their quest caused them little concern.

Cain rose, poured himself another mug of coffee and added a spoonful of sugar to his chicory-laced brew. The clanking of the spoon against the sides of the cup was the only indication of his irritation.

He wondered what Julee was doing on a Sunday morning after her son's abduction. As he watched, she stepped through the back door, a cup of coffee in hand, almost as if his thoughts had conjured her up. Even with the distance of two backyards between them, the weary slump of her shoulders was obvious.

He considered going over and offering her his support by mouthing the meaningless platitudes: *They'll find him. He's all right.*

But after the way their tentative friendship had ended, he was hesitant. Besides, the banalities were just that. Meaningless. No one—not even he—knew if Brice would be found, and even if he was, even if he hadn't been harmed in any physical way, the incident would impact his life and Julee's forever, just as the events surrounding Tad Sutherland's death would forever color her view of the world.

What if Brice wasn't all right? Cain knew firsthand that the old "time will ease your pain" adage was true to a point, but you never forgot. He hadn't, anyway. "Life goes on" was the only truism he'd found one hundred percent correct. Life did go on, but he could tell Julee from experience, it was never the same.

* * *

Carrying her coffee, Julee strolled through the backyard, doing her best to keep her mind off Brice, even though she already knew it was an exercise in futility. The previous day had taught her that.

Memories lurked in every nook and cranny of the house, in every piece of furniture. Brice was a part of every mundane task she undertook. She folded clothes and choked back a sob when she saw his Ninja Turtle underwear. She vacuumed and found a Hot Wheels car and a Lincoln Log hidden beneath the cushions. She opened the pantry to get some bread and saw his favorite cereal sitting on the shelf. She ate some, hoping it would make her feel closer to him, but all the sweet, fruity stuff did was make her stomach queasy.

Filling out the missing-persons form had been the worst part. Only sheer willpower had kept her from going to pieces. She'd forced herself to stay calm...to hang on to her control and not to dwell on all the horrible things she knew could happen to missing children.

"Dwelling on negative things is like inviting them to happen."

How many times had Tad said that? A dozen? A hundred? All Julee knew was that she couldn't allow the bad thoughts to gain a toehold. Brice was all she had. Nothing bad had happened to him. It just couldn't.

Clinging to the persona she'd adopted when Tad died, the persona of a woman who knew how to cope with whatever problems might come her way, she had filled out the papers and come back home. Only she knew that her behavior was a farce, a facade that would crumble like a stale cookie left too long in the humid, Louisiana air.

When Tad's parents had arrived, she longed for nothing more than to let the Sutherlands hold her while she cried out her grief. But Loretta Sutherland, who kept Brice while Julee worked, was almost incoherent with weeping, and Gene, who had suffered a recent heart attack, didn't need the stress of two hysterical women on his hands. She had forced back her own needs and offered them what comfort she could.

When they'd left, edginess had driven her outside. There, like the inside of the house, memories of Brice abounded. She heard his squeals when she pushed him on the wooden swing set she'd had built for him. She saw his smile in the happy face he'd drawn in his sandbox that morning. She tasted his sweetness in the honeysuckle blossom she picked and put to her lips... one of his favorite things to do.

Anger—at herself for being so careless, and at whatever monster had taken him from her—forced her into her Explorer and away from the house. She left the driveway like a competitor in the Indy 500, but she'd gone no more than a mile or two when she became aware of some inner voice cautioning her to slow down.

A few minutes later, she rounded a curve and saw a stray dog standing in the middle of her lane. Her heart leaped into her throat and she wrenched the wheel to the right. The truck's wheels slid off the asphalt and skidded in the soft dirt of the shoulder, bumping through the ditch and coming to a stop bare inches from a pine tree.

She had murmured a prayer of thankfulness for heeding the voice that had cautioned her to slow down, and chided herself for her childish, reckless behavior. Still trembling, she'd eased the wheels back onto the highway.

Reluctantly, she'd come home and gone to bed, but even sleep was denied her. Still awake after midnight, she'd toyed with the idea of calling her father but decided that calling him would be futile. If he hadn't acknowledged his grandson's birth, he certainly wouldn't care that someone had kidnapped him.

Knowing she couldn't sleep, she'd gotten up to brew a cup of tea. A few minutes later, she had settled down at the table with her hands wrapped around the steaming mug.

She had given in to her grief then. The tears that had threatened her composure all day had slid down her cheeks, and no amount of wiping would stop them....

Now Julee squared her shoulders against the memories and let her weary gaze roam the backyard. There was no escaping the reminders of Brice, so she'd just have to deal with them. Dealing with what life threw her way was something she'd had a lot of practice at.

She blinked back the threat of tears. The hardest part was the uncertainty. Who had taken Brice? Why had they chosen *her* child? Would they ask for a ransom?

Contemplating the alternatives she hadn't been able to face in the darkest hours of the night made her heart pound and her stomach churn. She wasn't stupid. She watched her fair share of television and had a sketchy knowledge of the statistics about kidnapped children. She also knew that the more time that passed, the less likelihood there was of the child being found.

A movement from across the way diverted her attention from her troublesome thoughts. Cain was in his kitchen. Though she couldn't actually see him, she knew he was standing in the window, watching her. She could feel it.

Maybe she should call Detective Garvey and ask him to have another talk with Cain Collier. She couldn't shake the nagging feeling that her reclusive neighbor knew more than he was telling.

The phone rang, interrupting what Cain thought was his surreptitious observation of Julee. He reached for the wall phone hanging near the sink.

"Hello."

"Can't stay out of the limelight, I see."

The gravelly voice belonged to his uncle, Phil Rousseau, a policeman in nearby Thibodaux.

"What makes you think the paper is talking about me?"

"I'm a detective, ergo, I'm smart. I read in the newspapers that the local art teacher saw the getaway car. I know my nephew teaches art, and figured the odds were in my favor that it was you."

Cain couldn't help smiling. "Brilliant deduction, Phil. Your talents are wasted in Thibodaux."

"Flattery will get you an offer to dinner tonight," Phil said with a chuckle. "Spaghetti. My place at seven."

"I accept."

"Great." There was a lull in the conversation before Phil asked, "So what the hell happened? I thought that was a nice, quiet neighborhood."

"It is. And what happened is exactly what the media said."

"Uh-huh. My friend Detective Garvey thinks you're hiding something, and he's a little ticked off. So ticked off he's doing a background check on you, even though I told him you're my beloved sister's boy, an upstanding citizen, wonderful teacher and one helluva good artist."

Cain's knuckles whitened on the receiver. If Garvey did a background check on him, it would bring out everything he'd tried so hard to put behind him.

"That hardcase Yankee is your friend?" he asked Phil, more to change the turn of his thoughts than because he really cared.

"Yep. One of the best."

"How'd that happen?"

"He met a nice Thibodaux girl who was working up in New Jersey. They had a baby boy. Some woman snatched him out of the hospital. I worked the case. He and the girl got married, and he moved down here. We hired him, then when the city cut back, he was the first to go because of his lack of seniority. So now he works for the Houma P.D. Their gain. Our loss."

"That good, is he?"

"That good," Phil said. "So when he says he thinks you know more than you're telling, I'm inclined to believe him."

"Do you really think I'd hold back information about the kidnapping of a two-and-a-half-year-old kid?"

There was a slight pause before Phil answered, as if he was searching for the right thing to say. "Let's just say I think there's a possibility that you could tell him more if you wanted to."

Cain leaned against the bar. Phil knew him too well. "I told him everything I saw at the time." Almost everything. Everything but that the car was stolen, and if Garvey was as good as Phil claimed, he'd find that out soon enough.

There was another lengthy pause. "But you know more now, don't you?" Phil pressed. "Because it happened again."

Cain didn't have to ask what "it" Phil was talking about. "What makes you say that?"

"Because you're basically honest and forthright, and despite your reservations you believe you are your brother's keeper. If you knew something that would help, you would tell. So if you came across as secretive to Dylan, it's because you're protecting yourself."

"Get to the point, Phil."

"All right. The only thing that's ever made you feel vulnerable is your psychic ability. It isn't information you're hiding. What you're trying to hide is that it's back."

Cain chuckled, but the sound held no mirth. "You are good, Phil. Too good."

Phil ignored the sarcastic compliment.

"Did you tell your buddy Detective Garvey that I'm a pseudo-psychic?"

"No. I thought I ought to confirm that it was back with you first. Besides, when he does the background check, he'll find out everything."

Though Cain didn't voice his concerns to Phil, it was exactly what Dylan Garvey might find out that had him worried.

"So when did it happen?" Phil asked.

"Yesterday morning," Cain said, knowing that to deny the episode was useless. "Before...or during the kidnapping."

"Are you serious?"

"Yeah." Cain let out a long sigh. "I was out running, and I got this funny feeling that I should hurry back. I didn't think anything about it, but I did cut my run short. I got there in time to see the car turn the corner. Then I saw the ball lying in the street. I picked it up, and—"

"Abracadabra—presto chango!" Phil supplied.

Cain pinched the bridge of his nose, recalling the strange sensation that had overtaken him at that moment, a feeling that he actually *was* Brice Sutherland. "Something like that, yeah."

"There's no doubt in your mind that someone took the boy?"

Cain closed his eyes. A picture of the child fighting his captor played relentlessly against the backdrop of his mind. The boy's silent screams rang in his ears. "None."

"What did they look like?"

"I don't know. They slipped up behind me, and—" Cain caught himself, but there was no need to explain what he meant. Phil knew how the gift worked. "I mean, they slipped up behind Brice. He never got a good look at them. All I—he—could see of the driver was the back of his head.

He was scared spitless, Phil. He kept trying to call out to his mother.''

"Damn." Phil's voice held weary impotence.

Like his uncle, Cain was well aware of how few stolen kids were ever found, and how, often, when they were located, it might be better off for everyone if they hadn't been.

"What about the car?" Phil asked.

"I gave a description and the license number to Garvey."

"But you know something else, don't you?''

Cain expelled a harsh breath. "The car is stolen. I knew that yesterday. They've already dumped it."

Cain heard Phil mumbling and knew he was taking notes.

"Are you going to pass this on to Garvey?"

"You know I have to."

"Along with the fact that your upstanding nephew has some sort of limited psychic ability. Just enough to screw up his life."

"It isn't limited."

The same humorless laugh escaped Cain again. "Then why didn't I know Amy and Holly were going to be killed before it was too late to do anything to help them?" His voice held the anger of a person who knows his best wasn't good enough.

"I don't have an answer for that. But if I had to wager a guess, I'd say it's because you won't give your talent free rein. You never have—not even when you were helping us. That's why I think it seems limited."

It was a theory Phil had put forth before, one Cain suspected was closer to the truth than he wanted to admit. Neither spoke for several seconds.

"I don't suppose you'd consider helping us out on this one—look at a map—or something?" Phil asked.

"A map?"

"Yeah. There's a guy on the West Coast who can touch maps and can get locations of... bodies and stuff."

Cain grimaced. "I've never tried that one."

"And you won't, right?"

"I've helped the police out before, and look what happened."

"Yeah. Look what happened. They solved most of the cases—thanks to you."

"It also ruined my marriage."

"Amy was narrow-minded."

"It's unkind to speak ill of the dead," Cain said in a tired voice. "Amy wanted a regular family, an ordinary life. As a matter of fact, so do I. I've told you everything I know about Brice Sutherland's kidnapping, honestly."

"Okay," Phil said, the finality in Cain's voice prohibiting any more questions about the case. "How's she taking it?"

The sudden shift in the direction of the conversation caught Cain off guard. "Julee? How would I know?"

"I thought your interest in the widow Sutherland was more than neighborly when she first moved in."

"For all of five minutes or so, it was." When Phil didn't reply, Cain added, "As sharp as you are, you should know it was an impossible situation."

"That's a shame."

"Yeah, well, so's pollution and the high crime rate."

Phil's sigh filtered through the phone line. "Speakin' of crime, I'm going to give Dylan a call and tell him about the stolen car. May I also assure him that you'll cooperate by coming forward if you remember anything else?"

Cain pushed away the guilt he felt for denying Phil what he wanted. Damn it, who said he was his brother's keeper? After everything he'd been through, he deserved some privacy, some peace of mind. He deserved to live a normal life—or whatever normal was for a person like him.

"If I remember anything, I'll be glad to come forward." *But I won't go looking for answers.* It was a compromise, the best he could do.

"Good enough. Don't forget dinner."

"Will it be a question-and-answer session?"

"No. We'll just eat and watch the Cards on ESPN."

"Then I'll see you at seven."

"Seven," Phil chanted. "Oh, and Cain. Bring the Chianti, will you?"

Cain hung up, a residual guilt nagging at him. There was a time he'd been glad to offer his services—for whatever they were worth—to the police.

The gift of psychometry—his apparent ability to obtain information about places, persons or objects just by coming into contact with them—had first manifested itself when Cain was six, though prior to that, there had been other incidents his parents had ignored or chalked up to coincidence. As a child, Cain had assumed that everyone received images about things or people by touching them.

That particular day, he'd hugged his grandmother as a thank-you for making his favorite birthday dinner, and had known instinctively that she was very ill. When he asked her if she felt all right, she'd smiled and said she was fine, just a little headache. He had urged her to go to the doctor.

His parents had tried to calm him, but he had begged, growing incoherent with his crying, telling his grandmother that he didn't want her to die. To quiet him, she'd called and made an appointment for that very day. A visit to the doctor had revealed that her blood pressure was dangerously high. Cain's insistence and prompt medical attention had averted a massive stroke and possibly death.

When they looked back, his parents were able to point out countless other occurrences that could be linked to his uncanny ability, things they could neither deny nor explain. They sought counsel from doctors, ministers, psychologists and finally, at their wits' end, a local palmist, who just smiled and said that their son had the gift of psychometry.

Rather than ease their minds, the news raised more questions and caused more concern. Cain soon learned that his gift made him different, and that difference caused no end of trouble between him and his friends. Though it was an integral part of their lives, at Cain's request, the Colliers made as little of his ability as possible. They understood that the last thing a child wanted was to be unlike his friends.

He was in his last year of college when he first inadvertently used his gift to help the police. He would never forget sitting on the edge of Phil's desk, waiting for his uncle to come back from an impromptu meeting with the chief. As he waited, Cain poked through some items that had been dumped from a woman's purse.

When Phil returned, he'd been furious—at Cain and himself. He should never have gone off and left the purse and contents lying there, and Cain had no business messing with it. Both transgressions violated the rules concerning chain of evidence. Then he saw the look on Cain's face, and his anger had turned to anxiety. He'd later told Cain that he'd seemed to be in some sort of trance, his eyes glazed, his breathing heavy, his sight turned inward toward some scene that only he could see.

When someone in the hall slammed a door, Cain had snapped out of the spell and held out a compact. "This isn't hers," he'd said.

"Isn't whose?" Phil had asked.

"The dead woman's."

"Whose is it?"

"It belongs to the killer."

Phil had been working under the assumption that the killer was the dead woman's husband, who'd caught her in an affair with one of his best friends. The man had boasted in a drunken rage that he'd "kill the bitch for what she did to me." He'd already been charged with first-degree murder. Though the case was circumstantial, he had motive and opportunity. Ballistics proved that the slug that killed his wife had come from his 30.06 deer rifle.

Phil faced a real problem. First, he had to convince the chief that Cain wasn't a crackpot. Second, he had to rethink the whole crime. The first part was relatively easy. When Cain held the chief's cigarette lighter and described what had happened when the chief had left for work that very morning, he made a believer out of the crusty old cop. Unfortunately, he couldn't tell them anything else except that the killer was a woman with dark hair.

It was only later that Phil learned that the shooter was the wife of the man the dead woman had been having the affair with. A peroxide blonde, she'd donned a dark wig and used the deer rifle to kill her one-time friend.

The victim's possession of her killer's compact was strictly accidental. When the two couples had been out together shortly before the crime, the victim had borrowed the compact to check her lipstick and forgotten to return it. If Cain hadn't picked up the compact by chance, an innocent man might have spent the rest of his life in prison or sentenced to death.

Following the close of that case, Phil had asked for Cain's help on a regular basis. His unwelcome fame spread, and a couple of New Orleans cops had come to him for help, looking for anything that might aid them in breaking the cases they were working on. Sometimes he was able to get impressions; sometimes, no matter how hard he tried, it was useless. He wasn't always right, and often the impressions he received were skimpy at best. To him, the whole thing was hit or miss, but Phil maintained that more often than not, Cain helped.

As was to be expected, the media got wind of his ability, and Cain became the subject of TV and newspaper interviews. The calls started then, and his life became a circus. At twenty-three, basically a private person, he found himself in the limelight. Whether he was considered the devil's cohort or a godsend, his notoriety was something he wasn't at all sure he liked.

Even now, he didn't know which were worse: the believers or the skeptics. Those who didn't believe made fun of him, taunted him, made him feel like a sideshow freak. Those who did were always wanting him to see if their mate was involved in an affair or asking for the winning horses at the fairgrounds.

Even though he'd told Amy about his gift before they married, and she'd assured him it wouldn't make a difference, it had. Privacy was at a premium; their lives were scrutinized and intruded upon by everyone who came into contact with them, grist for every gossip mill in the city.

Amy begged him to quit, to move away and start over, but even though he felt the same pressures and suffered the same feelings she did, he also felt on occasion that what he was doing was good. In retrospect, he knew there had been a small part of him that had reveled in the fame.

Pride goes before a fall.

To try and appease her, he'd had their unlisted number changed a dozen times, and moved to different parts of the city several times during the next three years. Even then, the most determined found him.

The more his fame grew, the more his marriage deteriorated. Five years ago, in a bitter argument, Amy threatened to leave him if he didn't agree to move away from New Orleans, where they could start over with a clean slate. Cain had accused her of selfishness.

A few days later, a man he'd helped send to prison threatened him and his family. Cain had never considered the possibility that his helping the police would put him or his family in jeopardy. He began to see that maybe he was the selfish one.

He never told Amy about the threat, but he agreed to move to Houma and stop helping the police. Unfortunately, the decisions he made to change his life didn't stop the perceptions that came at awkward, unexpected moments. And, though he didn't help the New Orleans police anymore, he'd continued to help his uncle on occasion. Though Phil guarded his source as only a cop can, Amy resented even that.

Cain and Amy toughed it out in Houma for almost a year—she wouldn't go to counseling with him—but when Holly was four, Amy had packed up their belongings, filed for a divorce and moved in with her sister and her husband until she could get on her feet.

The strange thing was that as soon as Amy moved out, the psychic perceptions had stopped. No matter how hard he tried, he couldn't get any vibrations from the people or things he touched. Cain considered it the height of irony that the very thing that ruined his marriage disappeared as soon as his wife walked out the door.

With the exception of the erotic dream he'd experienced with increasing frequency the past few months and the episode with Brice's ball the day before, Cain hadn't received anything that remotely resembled a psychic manifestation in the four years since the dream that had been sent to warn him that Amy and Holly were in danger.

As far as he was concerned, neither counted for much since both had come too late to avert the tragedies. Still, knowing that he was once again in tune with the psychic forces was unsettling.

He didn't like it one bit.

Cain left the kitchen and went into his studio. As with his running, he often found forgetfulness in his work. He studied the painting of the villa he'd finished and set it aside. Taking a new canvas, he started sketching a woman and a man on a beach....

Lanny Milligan lay in bed in the infirmary, pale and hollow eyed beneath the fluorescent lights. A sharp pain speared his stomach, and he drew up his knees in agony.

The aspirin he'd taken the day before had his bleeding ulcer giving him hell. As a matter of fact, he was beginning to think he'd overdone it. His plan had been to rig the whole thing so that the warden would transfer him from the prison to the hospital, where his chances of making an escape and settling his old score with Julee Sutherland were better. He hadn't intended to kill himself, but if the amount of blood he'd vomited up was any indication, that might be a definite possibility.

Lanny gritted his teeth against the pain. No. He had no intention of dying. Not just yet. Tad Sutherland might be dead, but his wife and kid hadn't suffered nearly enough—a state of affairs he intended to fix...real soon.

He'd lost everything. First the kids, and most recently, Lucy. Six months ago, Lucy's grief had finally gotten the best of her, and she'd taken her life rather than live it alone.

Tears filled Lanny's eyes, and a giant knot of emotion choked him. He scrubbed at his eyes. He couldn't start thinking about Lucy, or he'd lose his own mind. He was getting out of here, and then Julee Sutherland and her kid would be sorry.

Another pain ripped through him. Lanny groaned and buzzed for the nurse, hoping she could give him something for the agony. In a matter of minutes, the RN stepped through the door, a hypodermic needle in her hand. The guard came in with her, but he needn't have bothered. Lanny knew he wasn't going anywhere just yet.

When Julee heard the doorbell chime later that evening, she peered through the peephole before opening the door. She'd been bothered all afternoon by a deluge of sensation-seeking reporters, both in person and on the phone. She'd finally turned on her answering machine so she could monitor her calls. She didn't want to talk to anyone, but this visitor was different. It was Dylan Garvey, the handsome detective who'd been there the day before.

With her heart racing, she unfastened the locks and swung the door wide. Her heart slowed when she saw an attractive chestnut-haired woman standing next to Dylan, outside the peephole's parameters.

"Hello, Detective," Julee said, her surprise obvious. She noticed that he seemed a bit nervous, an emotion she would have imagined alien to him. The faint hope she felt turned to apprehension. "Have you found out anything?"

He shook his head. "Nothing yet." He indicated the woman. "I'd like you to meet my wife, Chantal. Chantal, Julee Sutherland."

Julee's perplexity grew, even as she extended her hand to Chantal Garvey. "It's very nice to meet you. Won't you come in?"

The couple looked at each other and stepped inside. Julee ushered them into the living room, with its wide plank floors, massive stone fireplace and abundance of glass.

After they had declined anything to drink, Dylan met Julee's gaze with the straightforward look she recognized from the day before.

"I suppose you've gathered that this isn't an official visit," he said. "I guess we should have called, but we decided to come on the spur of the moment."

Chantal reached for her husband's hand, gave him a loving look and turned to smile at Julee. "We came because we thought we might be able to offer you some support and to give you some information."

"What kind of information?" Julee asked.

"Material supplied by the National Missing Children's Hotline," Chantal explained. "It's a wonderful organization, and they offer a wealth of information about different things parents of missing children can do in addition to the police investigation."

Seeing the question reflected in Julee's eyes, Chantal glanced at her husband and turned her gaze back to Julee. "When our oldest son was born, a woman took him from the hospital," she said. "We didn't get him back for more than a week."

Chapter Three

Julee went back to work the next day. The Sutherlands had suggested that she stay at home until Brice was found, but she reminded them that she had obligations not only to Rocky Melancon, who expected his house to be finished by a certain date, but to the men who relied on the weekly paycheck they received from Sutherland Construction.

Besides, she'd experienced two days of pacing the floor, worrying, praying and crying, and she knew that keeping busy would help fill the aching emptiness of her heart.

As she expected, she was the recipient of several pitying looks. What came as a surprise was the genuine concern she received from the men, many of whom were accustomed to taking her orders with barely concealed resentment. Even the few who had aggravated her life with their innuendo and flirting wore looks of sincere contrition as they expressed their regret over what had happened. All in all, there was a subdued aura to the crew as they went about their work.

Julee directed the men and solved the problems that arose, but a part of her mind was focused on Brice's disappearance and her visit from Dylan Garvey and his wife the evening before.

The Garveys' story was as heartbreaking as it was heartwarming. Their little boy, Brady, had been taken from a Thibodaux hospital when he was just a few hours old. Chantal wasn't married to Dylan at the time, but she had called him, and he'd come down from New Jersey to assist the Thibodaux police in the search.

Chantal claimed that it was her husband's bulldog tenacity that had eventually put him on the trail of the guilty party, a woman with a history of multiple miscarriages. Chantal and Dylan had married soon after they got their baby back and now had another child, an infant daughter named Larissa. It was obvious to Julee that the Garveys were crazy about each other and their kids, which made for a happy ending.

Since their marriage, the Garveys had become involved with several organizations that offered support for the families of missing children. After explaining the available services and help, they'd told Julee to call if she decided she wanted to contact any of them.

Julee had been so surprised by the Garveys' unexpected visit and so impressed by their story and their devotion to each other, that they were probably halfway back to Thibodaux before she realized she hadn't mentioned her uneasy feeling about Cain Collier.

"Ms. Sutherland?"

The feminine voice scattered the troubled thoughts that had chased through Julee's head all day. She turned to see a middle-aged, red-haired woman in a too-tight dress and spike heels regarding her with a bright smile. The face was familiar in a vague way, but Julee couldn't put a name to it.

"Yes?" she replied in a wary tone.

The woman's smile widened. "I'm Mavis Davenport from the Thibodaux paper. I was wondering if I might have a word with you?"

Julee's heart sank. She knew the woman by reputation, which wasn't the most sterling. Mavis Davenport was known for twisting facts and lacing her columns with innuendo, never for writing the truth. She was a sensationalist, more interested in stirring up controversy and making people miserable than in reporting the news.

"I thought you were the society writer," Julee said.

"Well," Mavis said with a lift of her penciled brows and a smirk that bore a slight resemblance to a smile, "I am, but no one's been able to have a word with you, and I was wondering if I could interview you about your child's disappearance."

"No." She turned and stalked away and then whirled, almost knocking the reporter down. As if she sensed Julee's hostility, Mavis backed up a few steps.

"How did you find me, anyway?" Julee asked.

Mavis shrugged. "I always did want to be an investigative reporter," she said, as if the confession was explanation enough. "I won't take up much of your time, Ms. Sutherland. I just want to get your views on how the police are doing, how you feel about what's happened...that sort of thing."

Julee put her hands on her slim, jeans-clad hips. She was appalled by the woman's insensitivity and her chutzpah. "Obviously, Ms. Davenport, you've never had a child, or you wouldn't need to ask that question," she said, not bothering to hide her disgust.

"I feel as if someone has ripped out my heart and shredded it into little tiny pieces. Now, I suggest you get into your car and drive back to your desk and fabricate some dirt about someone else."

Pivoting on her heel, Julee marched away toward Luther Mabry, her job foreman, a man old enough to be her father, a man she'd often wished were her father. Luther slid a comforting arm around her shoulders and pointed toward the crew, who was busy nailing cedar strips to the outside of the house. She didn't look back once. A few minutes later, she heard the roaring of a car's engine.

"She's gone," Luther said.

"Thank God."

"Wasn't that biddy from the Thibodaux paper?"

Julee nodded. "I can't believe she had the gall to come and harass me on the job."

"That kind has no sense of decency," Luther told her. He glanced at the cheap watch circling his brawny wrist. "It's only an hour till quittin' time. Why don't you go on home for the day. I can handle it."

"I know you can," Julee said. "But—"

"But you're paranoid about watching over every step of the job so that history doesn't repeat itself. I understand, but you've got to learn to trust me."

Luther hadn't worked for Julee long before she realized that she *could* trust him with the story of her past, and confessed her fear of it ever happening again. He was the only one of her workers who knew what she'd been through, the only one she felt she could call a friend. "I do trust you."

"Then go home. This is all routine stuff. You know I'll call if anything comes up."

Knowing she was beaten, Julee nodded. "Okay. I'm out of here."

A wide grin creased Luther's whisker-stubbled face. "Good. See you in the morning, boss."

* * *

Trixie Guidry came out of her house as Julee pulled into the driveway. Julee heaved a sigh. Trixie had been out of town since Friday evening, sparing Julee her opinions about what had happened to Brice and her advice about what to do.

Trixie was pushing eighty and tried to look forty. She was a firm believer in tarot cards, horoscopes and tea leaves, a busybody and an inveterate gossip, but Julee would be the first to admit that the old woman's heart was good and that, despite her eccentricities, she loved Julee dearly.

"Hey, darlin'!" A remarkably spry Trixie, who claimed to stay in shape by working out with Max Something Or Other on television, sailed across her front yard, a casserole dish clutched in her mitted hands. Her wide, toothy smile pushed her rouged cheeks into little knots resembling wrinkled crab apples. "I've been watchin' for you."

Julee forced a smile and unlocked the front door. "Hi, Trix. Come on in." She looked at Trixie's offering and raised her eyebrows. "Dinner, I presume."

Trixie beamed. "I made some lasagna, and since—"

—*you always make enough for an army, you thought you'd bring some over*—Julee mentally supplied, having heard the statement countless times.

Trixie finished Julee's thought verbatim, and a look of sorrow filled her pale blue eyes. "I figured you might not be up to cookin'."

"Lasagna sounds great, thanks," Julee said, pulling off her boots in the entryway. "Come on into the kitchen. I made a pitcher of spiced tea before I left this morning."

"Sounds wonderful," Trixie said, following Julee through the house. She settled her skinny behind onto a bar stool with a sunflower cushion and leaned an elbow on the forest green Formica.

"So how was your day?" she asked, watching while Julee took two frosty mugs from the freezer.

Julee poured the glasses full and added sprigs of mint plucked from the plant growing in the greenhouse window above the sink. "Not bad, other than getting cornered by a reporter a little while ago."

"Humph! No respect, those newspeople. No respect." Trixie punctuated the comment with a loud slurp from the glass. "Mmm, tasty."

"Thanks." Julee sat down beside the older woman. Neither spoke for several minutes, content to sip her tea in the comfortable silence of good friends.

"How are you holdin' up?" Trixie asked at last.

"Pretty well, I guess."

"You don't look so hot."

Julee's lips curved into a weary smile. "Give me a break, Trix. I just got home from work. The humidity is so high you can ring out the air. I need a bath."

"You *need* someone to share your worry."

"That's your job," Julee said with a fond smile.

Trixie place a withered forearm on the countertop and leaned toward Julee. "I mean, a man."

Julee groaned. Ever since she'd moved into the neighborhood the past summer, the old woman's primary goal in life had been to find Julee a husband. "Not now, Trix, please. I have other things on my mind."

"You always have other things on your mind. Mark my words, woman. You're goin' to wake up one day and look in the mirror and see an old woman standin' there instead of the young sprout you are now. Don't pine for your man the way I did for Euwell. Get on with your life before it's over."

The admonition was familiar. "I will, Trix, I promise. As soon as we find Brice."

"And then it'll be as soon as you feel like the business is better established," Trixie said, pointing a bony finger with a red-lacquered nail at Julee. "I know you, missy."

In spite of herself, Julee laughed.

"It's not funny. You've got to face the facts." As soon as she said the words, the old woman began to squirm in her seat.

"What?"

"Nothin'," Trixie denied.

"Look, I know you as well as you know me," Julee said. "Now, spit it out."

Fixing Julee with an earnest look, Trixie sighed. "You know I'd rather cut off my pinkie than hurt you for a second, don't you?"

"Of course I do."

Trixie reached out and covered Julee's hand with hers. "Then you know that what I'm about to say is for your own good."

Oh, Lord, what now?

"I think you should really think about what you'll do if...if..."

"If they don't find Brice," Julee supplied when Trixie's voice faltered.

Trixie's head, covered with a mop of Sparkling Sherry curls, bobbed up and down on her scrawny neck. "I don't mean to be negative, darlin'," she hastened to say, "but I do believe in bein' realistic. If whoever took Brice was goin' to ask for ransom money, surely they'd have made some sort of contact by now. I don't want to worry you, mind you, but you ought to know the truth."

Trixie took a deep breath and with an apologetic look at Julee, plunged in. "I heard on 'Donahue' the other day that the big thing now is stealin' kids to adopt them out."

Julee felt the color drain from her face.

"Oh, dear!" Trixie cried. "I *have* upset you. Laws a mercy, I never meant to."

"It's okay," Julee assured her. "I'm not naive. Believe me, I know all the bad things that can happen, but I've tried not to think about anything happening to Brice. Tad always said negative thoughts draw negative vibes, just like positive thoughts draw positive vibes."

Trixie patted Julee's hand. "That's excellent reasoning, darlin', but your horoscope said to be prepared for the worst, that people and things aren't always what they seem. I just want you to be equipped to deal with whatever happens, that's all."

"I know, and I do appreciate it."

The doorbell chimed, and Julee felt she'd been literally saved by the bell. "I'll be right back," she said.

Trixie sprang up from the stool. "I'll follow you out. It's almost time for the six-o'clock news."

The first thing Julee saw when she opened the front door was a television news van sitting in her driveway. A team of reporters hovered nearby, minicams and microphones at the ready. Before she could gather herself, Trixie pushed past her, flapping her apron like a farmer's wife herding livestock.

"Shoo!" she cried. "For shame, having the nerve to harass a brokenhearted mother! Now, get yourselves out of here and let this poor woman alone!"

"We just want to ask her a few questions," the newscaster, a pretty dark-haired woman, said.

"I'll answer them for you," Trixie told her. "No, she hasn't heard anything. No, she doesn't have any idea who would do such a thing. Yes, her heart is broken." Beaming, Trixie turned to Julee. "How was that?"

Julee compressed her lips in an effort not to burst into hysterical laughter. "Thanks, Trixie. I couldn't have done better myself." She looked at the newswoman and added, "No further comment."

With a last wave at Trixie, she closed the door, slid the dead bolt shut and went into the living room. In a few moments, she heard the van's engine start. From behind the blinds of her front bedroom, she watched in relief as it sped down the street and turned the corner...the same corner the kidnappers had taken when they'd snatched Brice....

Should he or shouldn't he? Cain wondered. Going over to offer his support was the neighborly thing to do. On the other hand, being in the same room with Julee Sutherland had a way of making him very aware of how lonely he was and how long it had been since any woman had interested him in more than a passing way.

Julee was everything he liked in a woman. Short and shapely, her petite body curved in all the right places. Her chin-length, red-brown hair was thick and threaded with sun-lightened streaks from the hours she spent working outdoors. Her eyebrows flared at the outer corners over eyes as green as the moss growing around the oak trees in his backyard. Her mouth was full lipped and as curvy as the rest of her, the kind of mouth every woman dreamed of having and every man dreamed of kissing.

Cain pushed that idea away. Thoughts like that were about as welcome as his occasional bursts of psychic awareness. And, he thought with a wry smile, about as effective. He went to the kitchen and checked her backyard. There wasn't a sign of her.

The first time he'd seen her was when she'd come to check out the house with the idea of buying it. Her jeans and work boots seemed incongruous with her distinct femininity. Intrigued despite himself, he'd introduced himself and answered her questions about the neighborhood. He'd been pleased that there was no Mr. Sutherland, and when Julee told him what she did for a living, Cain had marveled that anyone who looked so womanly could ramrod a crew of rough-edged men.

It wasn't that he had any chauvinistic leanings; he was all for equality and women's rights. On the other hand, he was a man who genuinely liked women. And he'd been brought up the old-fashioned way, believing that they were special and whenever possible they should be protected from the ugliness life often doled out.

According to some of his students, his feelings were dated and often not appreciated, but old habits died hard. He had to remind himself that women like Julee Sutherland didn't want or need protection. They were perfectly capable of fighting their own battles and anxious to do so. From what he'd observed so far, Julee was coping with the situation just fine. Still, going over and telling her he was sorry and asking if the police had any leads was the least he could do.

He could also tell her that the barracuda from the Thibodaux paper—Mavis Somebody—had actually had the gall to come to the high school and try to get him to make a statement. Thank God they'd intercepted her at the office, and he hadn't been forced to meet her face-to-face. No doubt she'd be hounding Julee next.

His mind made up, Cain went into the extra bedroom he'd converted into a studio and grabbed a small, framed picture from the top of his drafting table. He dashed out the door and around the corner, knocking on Julee's door before he could talk himself out of the decision.

He rang the doorbell twice before he got a response. "Who is it?" Julee called.

"Cain Collier."

He heard the dead bolt click, and the door swung open. Julee stood before him, dressed in shorts that were almost entirely covered by a T-shirt that hung to mid-thigh. Unfortunately—or fortunately, he couldn't decide which—the soft cotton clung to her still-damp body, defining, rather than hiding, the soft womanly shapes beneath.

Cain's breathing accelerated, as if he'd run a couple of miles. With an effort, he dragged his gaze to her face. Julee wasn't wearing any makeup, and her wet hair was slicked straight back, revealing the delicate contour of her ears and the exquisite structure of her jaw and cheekbones.

It dawned on him that she'd been in the bath when he rang the doorbell. He also realized that he should say something instead of just standing there like a hunk of stone.

"Hi."

Julee crossed her arms over her breasts. "Hi."

He gestured toward the door. "You ought to use the peephole before you open the door. Anyone could be out here."

"I did," she said. "You must have been standing off to the side."

"Oh." Cain cursed the unusual nervousness that made him as tongue-tied as some of his freshmen students.

"Come in," she said, stepping away from the doorway.

He shook his head, preferring to keep the visit short. "I don't want to bother you. I just came to see how things were going."

"Okay, I guess," she said. "The police don't know anything new. And believe me, your coming is no bother. You may have saved me."

"From what?" Cain asked.

"Another solitary meal."

She pressed her lips together to still a sudden trembling. He noticed the slight straightening of her shoulders and the tiny lift of her chin before she spoke again.

"Trixie brought over some lasagna. There's plenty for two." Surprise sealed Cain's lips, and Julee rushed on before he could formulate a reply. "It's so quiet without Brice. Especially at mealtimes."

The aching loneliness he heard in her voice was something he understood all too well.

"Sometimes," she said in a thoughtful, considering tone, "I think mealtime is when I miss him the most." Despite the iron control she held over her will, moisture glittered in her eyes. She dashed away the tears and offered him an apologetic smile. "I guess single guys don't know how kids chatter during meals."

"I wasn't always single."

The innocent reminder hung between them like a spider's web suspended between branches, a small but ominous comment, rife with the potential to ensnare and inflict pain they neither wanted nor needed.

"I'm sorry." The apology was little more than a harsh whisper.

Anxious to make his escape, he held out the picture he'd brought; she reached for it automatically. The painting was a vibrant montage of watercolor done on a rumpled grocery sack, a scene Brice had remembered from the summer before when his grandparents had taken him camping at Lake Ouachita in Arkansas. The rectangle of brown paper was divided into a section of blue and one of bright orange, yellow and red—the water and the sky at sunset. Vertical brown lines protruded from the blue foreground. Those, Brice had said, were the dead trees sticking out of the water. Cain had been very impressed with the child's ability to transfer the memory to paper and had offered to frame it. Brice had been thrilled.

Julee seemed less so. She clutched the small painting in a white-knuckled grip, and Cain cursed the impulse that had prompted him to bring the picture. As usual, his timing was off.

Without stopping to consider the consequences to either of them, without any thought other than to offer her comfort, he took two steps and drew her into a loose embrace.

"I'm sorry," he said in a rough voice. "I thought the picture might please you."

Julee raised her head and looked up at him, her eyes swimming with tears. "It does please me," she choked out. "It's just—"

"What a great shot!"

The strident voice sent Julee stumbling back inside the open door a step. Cain spun around. Every molecule of his body told him that the woman standing there with a camera pointed at him and Julee was trouble with a capital *T,* and his feelings had nothing to do with psychic ability. The memory of who she was eluded him. Media, for sure. She had that look about her.

"I told you I didn't want to talk to you," Julee said, while Cain was trying to place a name with the face. "I thought you might have changed your mind." The woman lowered the camera and fixed Cain with a sly smile. "And what about you, Mr. Collier? You *are* Cain Collier, aren't you?"

Cain nodded, suspicion forming in his mind. "And you're—"

"Mavis Davenport," Julee spat out. "A reporter from the Thibodaux paper who won't take no for an answer."

Cain muttered a low curse.

"No need to get testy, Ms. Sutherland," the reporter said. "I'm just trying to do my job." Turning her quasi-smile on Cain, she asked, "May I ask what your relationship is to Ms. Sutherland?"

"We're neighbors," he said.

"Close neighbors, obviously."

"Yeah. Our backyards connect," Cain said, deliberately letting her think he'd misunderstood.

Mavis's shrill laughter rent the comparative quiet of the evening. "Clever. Very clever, Mr. Collier. I understand you saw the getaway car."

"No comment," Cain said, stepping inside the house and reaching for the door.

"You know, Mr. Collier, if you refuse to answer my questions, I'll just have to root out the answers for myself."

"You do that," Cain told her. "I understand digging up dirt is your specialty."

Mavis Davenport's smile disappeared, and the look in her eyes turned colder than an arctic January. "Let's just say that I'm very good at what I do."

The double entendre wasn't lost on Cain. Without giving her the satisfaction of another response, he shut the door in her angry face.

"You just made a powerful enemy."

Cain shrugged. "She won't be the first. Or the last."

Julee crossed her arms as if she was chilly. "Mavis came out to the job site earlier. I told her I wouldn't be interviewed, but I guess she thought if she kept on, I'd give in."

"She came to the school, too."

"You're kidding!"

He shook his head. "The office secretary got rid of her for me."

"I can't believe her gall," Julee said with a shake of her head. "I appreciate your handling her for me."

"No problem."

Awkwardness took control of the next few seconds before Julee asked, "How about some of that lasagna?"

Cain would have liked nothing better, but circumstances being what they were, sharing a meal, or anything else with his beautiful neighbor, was out of the question. "Thanks, but I can't. I have papers and final artwork to grade."

"Oh."

Was it his imagination, or was that disappointment he heard in her voice? "Maybe another time."

Her smile was quick, forced. "Sure." She peeked out the front window. "She's still sitting out there in her car."

"I'll go out the back. Maybe if she thinks I'm still in here, she'll give up and go home."

"I hope so." Julee led the way through the house and let Cain out the door that led to her large deck. He was almost to the fence when she called his name. He turned.

"Thanks for framing Brice's picture. It's great."

Cain nodded and, in a move that would have made his old track coach proud, vaulted over the fence like a pro.

Julee watched in admiration as Cain took the fence in a single, impressive leap. She couldn't believe she'd asked him to have dinner with her. Thank goodness he'd declined. They wouldn't have had ten words to say to each other. It had been nice of him to take up for her with Mavis Davenport, though. If he hadn't been there, she might have slugged the nosy reporter.

She took a last, lingering look at her neighbor before he disappeared into the shadows of his porch. He had the lean-muscled body of a man who took care of himself, and the type of rugged good looks she found attractive—even though his hair was a bit too long for her taste.

Julee turned away and locked the doors behind her. It wouldn't do for him to think she was desperate for his company...even though the thought was close to the truth. Already, the loneliness inside the empty house reached out for her.

Maybe if she got busy with something—like fixing a salad to go with her lasagna—she could forget the quiet of the house.

Several minutes later, when she sat down at the table to eat her solitary meal, she admitted that ploy to alleviate her loneliness and worry hadn't worked. Nothing had worked so far, she thought as she lifted a bite of salad to her lips. Why had she imagined Cain's company might banish her loneliness?

Did he really have papers to grade? Her woman's intuition told her that his refusal stemmed more from the fact that she made him uncomfortable than because he had commitments. Well, he made her uncomfortable, too, and had from the first. Was it that mutual awkwardness that left her feeling as if he was holding back? Or was the enigmatic aura surrounding him something more? *Had* he seen something he hadn't told the police? Had Brice said something? Maybe he'd called out....

She shook her head. She was really grasping for straws here. If Cain knew anything, surely he'd tell the police. Even though the vibrations between the two of them had been awkward from the first, Cain had struck up a real friendship with Brice, who made it a point to talk to Cain whenever he was outside.

When Brice had learned Cain was a painter, he made it a habit to show off his own artistic attempts. To Cain's credit, he hadn't put down Brice for his clumsy efforts, but had praised him for the boldness of his strokes and his vibrant use of color. Brice was thrilled when Cain offered to frame the picture he'd painted from his Arkansas vacation. It had broken Julee's heart to see how much he craved Cain's approval and how much he needed a man's influence in his life. Thankfully for Brice, Cain had never failed to be anything but patient and kind.

Lots of kidnappers are nice. Most of them, in fact.

The unexpected and unwelcome thought sent her fork clattering to her plate. An icy finger of fear sent a shiver down her spine. Was her uncertainty about Cain's truthfulness a mask for a deeper suspicion, the possibility that he really did have something to do with Brice's disappearance?

The pain in Lanny's stomach felt like a red-hot poker, but he felt better than he had the day before. Not good, but maybe he would make it. He had to make it. Time was getting short, and he wasn't apt to have many more chances. Soon, he'd make Julee Sutherland and her kid pay. He got a lot of satisfaction from the thought that the man responsible for his family's deaths would be watching from his place in hell, where he burned and burned....

Julee stood in the shower and let the tepid water beat on her weary body. It ran in torrents over the sensitive tips of her breasts, over the slope of her belly and between her thighs, where a curious ache lingered.

Exhaustion had finally gained her a night's rest, and she'd slept like the dead until just before dawn, when she'd dreamed of being with Tad at the hotel in Ladispoli, the little Italian town where, just days before their world crumbled beneath their feet, they had laughed, talked and planned their future with the supreme confidence of their youth. The dream had seemed so real she imagined she could smell the aromas of coffee and fresh-baked bread. Then, as dreams were wont to do, night came without rhyme or reason, and she found herself on the beach with the stranger. She wanted to believe it was Tad she was with, but a part of her had known it wasn't....

High above them, hills undulated away from the sea, and waves lapped against the white shores like the tongue of a huge cat lapping up spilt cream.

The man pulled her into his arms. She went eagerly, wanting him as much as he wanted her. The taste of urgency was sweet on his lips and in the way his body pressed against hers. She felt her limbs grow lax, and, sensing her complete capitulation, he eased them both to the sand.

Her breasts seemed to swell beneath the exquisite gentleness of his touch, and a languor distinctly at odds with the need spiraling inside her took control of her limbs, while her heart beat faster and faster.

Threading her fingers through springy hair that grew long down his neck, she dragged her lips free of his, letting her open, searching mouth sample the salty flesh of his neck and bare chest. His soft groan melded with the call of a night bird. Without a word, he pulled back, whispering her name. It wasn't Tad. She knew that now. And she didn't care. It was him. Her dream lover.

Moist night air drifted against her heated flesh, but nothing could extinguish the flame....

With a soft moan, Julee closed her eyes and leaned against the wall of the shower while her soapy hands moved over her breasts. She recalled her helplessness to deny him or herself. There had been nothing to do but let him put out the fire....

She sighed and turned off the water. Even though her body felt as if she really had made love, she was left feeling unfulfilled. There were the tender little aches that went with possessing and being possessed, but the aching need deep inside her was left wanting.

Damning the man in her dreams to a fiery hell, she turned off the water, opened the shower door and reached for a towel. Maybe she needed to see a shrink. Her little boy was gone, stolen from his own yard, and she dreamed about strange men making love to her! What kind of mother was she, anyway?

By the time she'd pulled on her underwear, Julee had worked her way through her anger into a blue funk. She was pulling on her jeans when the doorbell rang. Zipping and buttoning as she went, she padded barefoot to the front door. When she looked out the peephole she saw Dylan Garvey's car in the driveway. Dylan himself stood on the porch, his back to her, slapping a rolled-up newspaper against his thigh. Wondering what he was doing out before 7:00 a.m., she unfastened the locks and opened the door.

He turned. His frown took her by surprise. "Good morning."

Dylan didn't return her smile. "May I come in?"

Julee stepped aside on legs that felt suddenly weak. "Sure. Is something wrong?" Apprehension made her voice quiver.

"I'm starting to think that a lot of things are wrong."

The cryptic statement made no sense. "What do you mean?"

"I thought I'd made it very clear that you had to be honest with me, Julee."

"I have been honest with you." Confusion sharpened her voice.

"Then why didn't you tell me about you and Cain Collier?"

Julee's confusion changed to exasperation. "What about me and Cain Collier?"

Dylan held out the paper. "Check out the front-page story. And then maybe you'd like to explain it."

Julee unfolded the newspaper. A color photograph that Mavis Davenport must have snapped the evening before took up the top half of the front page. Her heart sank. The picture captured her in that brief moment she'd sought comfort in Cain's arms. The bold black headline read: Bereft Mom Sleeping with the Enemy?

Julee wanted to scream and longed to throttle Mavis Davenport for sensationalizing her grief, but knew the futile feelings for what they were. Instead, she refolded the paper and handed it back to Dylan. "There's nothing between me and Cain Collier."

"Nothing between you! Damn it, Julee!" Dylan exploded. "How can you say that?"

"Because it's true!" she cried.

Dylan planted his hands on his hips. "Maybe there's nothing personal, but there's plenty enough." He pinned her with a hard, uncompromising look. "Why the hell didn't you tell me that Cain's wife and daughter were the other victims of the fire that killed Lanny and Lucy Milligan's kids?"

Chapter Four

"Well?" Dylan asked when Julee didn't answer.

"I don't know why I didn't say anything," she said truthfully. "I guess I didn't think it was important."

Pinning her with an intimidating glare, Dylan ticked off his comments on his fingers. "First, Cain Collier's wife and daughter were killed in a house built by Sutherland Construction. Second, his brother-in-law gunned down your husband to exact his own perverted sense of retribution. Third, Cain Collier is the last person who saw your son."

Dylan shook his head. "How could you not think it was important enough to mention? How could it not occur to you that he might be involved in some way?"

Julee shrugged. "He seems . . . nice."

"Damn it, Julee! That's what everyone says about serial killers and child molesters."

Julee flinched. Hearing her own thoughts put into words was terrifying. Dylan must have seen how his blunt statement affected her. When he spoke again, his anger was gone. "I'm sorry. Chantal says I have a bad habit of jumping in with both feet."

There was genuine regret in his eyes. Julee suspected apologies didn't come easy to Dylan Garvey. "It's all right."

"Look, can I come in and have a cup of coffee and start over?"

Julee stepped aside. "Sure. Let me call my foreman and tell him I'm going to be late."

After Julee made the call, she and Dylan went out to the deck and sat at a glass-topped table, cups of coffee before them. The backyard was shady, but the early-morning sunlight created lacy patches through the leaves and glistened on the dew-laden grass. Caladiums and begonias basked in the warmth and bobbed in the breeze that made an occasional foray through the branches.

"I know you've told me everything once," Dylan said, breaking the silence. "But now I've had a chance to read all the newspaper accounts about the fire and the trials and . . . your husband's death, I'd like to hear your version again, and don't leave out the slightest detail."

Julee nodded, and for the next fifteen minutes told him everything she remembered about those terrible days. Dylan listened and took down an occasional note in his small spiral tablet. "After Brice was born, I decided to leave New Orleans and start over," she said, wrapping up her tale.

Dylan picked up his mug. "What made you pick Houma?"

"Tad's parents live here. I thought Brice should have the opportunity to be around the only family he has left."

"Your parents are both dead, then?"

Julee's mouth tightened. "My mother died before Brice was born. My father and I have been estranged for several years. He thought Tad was after my money." Seeing the question in Dylan's eyes, she added, "My father is Cyril Eldridge."

When there was no response from Dylan, Julee laughed. "I'd give a year's wages to have my father see that look on your face. You don't know who he is?"

Dylan rubbed his chin with his palm, his embarrassment clear. "Obviously, I should."

"He owns several hotels in New York, Chicago and L.A. Not to mention a bank or two, a winery in the Napa Valley and large chunks of real estate around the world."

Dylan grinned that knock-your-socks-off grin that had no doubt helped capture his wife's heart. "Thanks for enlightening me. Cops don't exactly travel in the same social circle."

"Neither do building contractors," Julee said.

"So you don't see him much, then?"

"Not once since my marriage," she said with a shake of her head and a twist of her lips that passed for a smile. "When I married Tad against my father's wishes, I burned my bridges. We were just back from our honeymoon when I got a letter from his attorney, telling me that Cyril considered me as good as dead and that he was cutting me not only out of his life but out of his will."

Dylan whistled.

"Yeah," Julee concurred. "Then, that afternoon, he sent a driver to pick up the new Porsche he'd given me for my birthday a few months earlier."

She hardly paused for Dylan's pithy comment. "I honestly expected him to get over it, but when a year passed and he made no move to reconcile, I realized that he probably wouldn't." The gaze she turned to Dylan was filled with old sorrow. "If it hadn't been for Tad loving me as much as he did, I don't know if I'd have been able to get through it."

"So your father doesn't know Brice is missing?"

She shook her head. "He wouldn't care if he knew. I sent him a birth announcement when Brice was born, but Dad never even acknowledged it. He's a hard, unforgiving man."

"That's a shame."

"Yeah, well, Brice has a set of wonderful grandparents, so Dad's the real loser."

"I wasn't close to my father, either," Dylan said in what Julee sensed was a rare confession of an old pain. Then he leaned back in his chair and crossed his arms over his wide chest, the gesture implying that he'd said all he intended to say about himself. "Tell me how you came to live next door to Cain Collier."

"Coincidence, I guess. When I first moved to Houma I lived across town, closer to my in-laws." Her lips curved into an embarrassed smile. "It's crazy, I know, but one of my favorite pastimes is driving around, looking at houses. The first time I saw this place I fell in love with it. Something about it just...drew me. I felt as if I belonged here." She shrugged. "I can't explain it."

"Go on."

"So," Julee said, giving a self-conscious laugh, "even though I knew I couldn't afford it, I gathered my nerve, knocked on the door and asked the owners if they'd sell. Unfortunately, they loved the house, too. They'd done most of the work themselves and weren't about to part with the place.

"Then, the man called me last August. He was getting transferred and wondered if I was still interested in buying. My business was growing, and I was thinking about getting something bigger. I jumped at the chance to live here."

"It's a great house," Dylan concurred, looking around the lofty room.

"Thanks. Brice and I have been happy here."

"And you didn't know Cain Collier was your neighbor?"

She shook her head. "He introduced himself when we were moving in...carried in some boxes and things. He was friendly, and helpful—"

"Attractive?" Dylan asked.

"Yeah," she admitted with a chagrined smile. "I did find him attractive, and I liked him."

"His name didn't ring any bells?"

She shook her head. "Why should it? There are a lot of Colliers in the world. The newspaper accounts gave the names of the woman and child who died in the fire and said she was from New Orleans. How was I to know Cain was connected to them?"

"What about his reaction to your name?"

Julee stared in the direction of Cain's house for several seconds before bringing her gaze back to Dylan's. "I've asked myself that question a hundred times. I don't remember. If there was a reaction, it wasn't noticeable."

"When did you finally put two and two together?"

"A day or two after we moved in. Cain and I were just talking, getting to know each other. You know—are you married? Divorced? What kind of music do you like? Do you like Mexican food? That sort of 'is this going anywhere?' ritual singles go through. He asked what I did for a living, and when I told him, it was like a door being slammed shut in my face.

"I knew something was wrong, but I didn't know what. I tried to pick up the conversation by asking if he was married, and that's when he told me about his wife and little girl dying in a fire at his sister-in-law's."

The bleakness Julee had felt at that moment was reflected in her green eyes. "I knew it wasn't a coincidence that they had died in a house that Sutherland Construction had built. Of course, it meant that whatever attraction either of us felt was out of the question. We just...backed off by some sort of mutual, unspoken agreement.''

''Why?''

Julee's surprise was obvious. ''His family was killed in a house my husband was responsible for building. That sort of thing isn't easily forgiven, and even if it were, overcoming it in a relationship would take a mighty big person.''

Dylan jotted something down in his notebook. ''You feel guilty for what happened, even though the courts found your husband innocent?''

''Yes.'' The admission was a harsh expulsion of air.

''Take it from me, life's too short to carry around any unnecessary emotional baggage,'' Dylan counseled.

''I tell myself that all the time, but I can't seem to help it,'' Julee said.

''So once you realized you were—how'd that newspaper woman put it?—sleeping with the enemy, that was the end of it.''

Julee's face flamed. ''We were a long way from the sleeping-with stage,'' she told Dylan, thankful the detective couldn't read her mind. Sleeping with Cain was something she'd thought about several times when she was tired and lonely and her body longed for a man's touch....

''Are you still attracted to him?''

''He's a handsome man,'' she said, compromising her position.

''How would you describe your relationship with him now?''

''We're just neighbors. The picture in the paper was a... misrepresentation of a situation. Cain brought me a picture he'd framed of Brice's, and I broke down for a minute. He was comforting me—that's all. His concern about Brice seems genuine, but...''

Her voice trailed away and Dylan finished for her. "But you have some reservations about him despite the fact that you're attracted to him."

"It's hard to say what I feel. There's a part of me that says Cain could never be a part of anything dishonest or hurtful, but on the other hand, there was something wrong with him when I found him holding Brice's ball. It was almost like he was in a...trance or something, and then, when I spoke to him and asked him what he'd seen, he seemed to be holding something back."

"I thought so, too," Dylan said. "Do you think it's reasonable to assume that it's these mixed feelings you have for Cain that kept you from confiding your reservations to me?"

Julee hoped she didn't look as guilty as she felt. "Maybe."

Dylan's smile was fleeting. "An honest answer. Well, for what it's worth, even before this story broke I was having Cain checked out. Even without Mavis Davenport's conjecture, it was just a matter of a few hours before I'd have drawn the same conclusions."

"Do *you* think Cain had something to do with the kidnapping?"

Dylan shrugged his massive shoulders. "He's about the only suspect we have, unless we go on the assumption it was a random act. Of course, there's the off chance that the kidnapper found out who your father is and plans to hit him up for a huge ransom."

"Fat chance," Julee said. "What about Lucy Milligan?"

"After Lanny's trial, she was transferred to a mental hospital out in New Mexico where she could be close to her brother. She hanged herself in her room about six months ago, which more or less lets her out as a suspect." Seeing

Julee's shock at his callous comment, he said, "You'll have to excuse the morbid humor. It's an old police trick that keeps us from going over the edge ourselves."

"I see," Julee said, but she didn't.

"With Lucy out of the way, I asked myself who else could want to get back at you," Dylan said. "The only person besides your buddy Mel—who's being investigated as we speak—is Lanny Milligan, who's doing a very long time in Angola prison.

"I have to be honest with you. It is possible to arrange this kind of thing from a jail cell, and it happens more frequently than any institution cares to admit, but I doubt Lanny Milligan has the kind of money or the outside contacts to pull off something this big."

"And that brings us back to Cain."

Dylan shrugged. "No cop worth his salt would overlook the fact that Collier lost his wife and child in a fire your husband was indirectly responsible for. You said it yourself on Saturday. Desperate people sometimes do desperate things."

"But why now?" Julee asked. "Why wait four years?"

"You haven't forgotten or forgiven yourself in four years," Dylan reminded. "Why should he?"

After Dylan left, Julee called Luther and told him she'd be a while longer. She needed some time to try to come to terms with the feelings and memories Dylan's visit had unearthed...like the knot in her chest that threatened to choke her when he'd asked about her father. Like the attraction she'd felt for Cain from the first moment she'd seen him. An attraction they both knew could never be acted on.

She refilled her coffee cup and went back outside. Almost simultaneously, Cain walked onto his wide covered porch. Julee wondered if he'd been watching her as she'd felt him doing on other occasions. The thought made her hands tremble, but she wasn't sure if it was with fear or anticipation.

Cain wore fawn-colored cotton slacks and a watermelon-hued shirt for one of the last days of school. The clothes fit him well, and he looked stylish and handsome, even though he still needed a haircut. In spite of herself, her heart turned a little flip. He was a *very* good-looking man, she thought with a despairing sigh.

He started across the dew-wet grass. Her stomach churned with alarm at the thought that he might have had something to do with Brice's disappearance. Strangely, the feeling was balanced by a despicable but heady exhilaration at the prospect of talking to him. Julee started across her deck, cursing Dylan Garvey for making her admit to her ambivalent feelings for Cain.

She met him at the fence.

"Hi," he said, his smile tentative.

His hair was still damp from his shower, his lean cheeks were smooth shaven, and the breeze sent a whiff of a peppery masculine cologne her way. "Hi."

"I thought you'd already be on the job."

"Detective Garvey paid me an early visit." Julee didn't miss the shadow that darkened Cain's blue eyes at the mention of the policeman. But there was no mistaking the glimmer of hope in his eyes, either.

"News?" he asked with a lift of his eyebrows.

"Of a sort." She took a deep breath. "Have you seen the morning paper?"

Cain shook his head. "I usually read it in the teacher's lounge during my free hour." The wrinkles in his forehead smoothed as comprehension dawned. "Mavis ran the picture."

"Yes," Julee said. "And an article. You'd better be ready to face the questions."

"What kind of questions?"

"About your relationship with me."

She wanted to tell him that he should be ready for questions from the police detective, as well, but the same uncertainty that had kept her from revealing her concerns about him to Dylan now forced her to keep silent about the fact that Dylan considered Cain a possible suspect.

"We have no relationship." The finality in his voice seemed to add, *and we never will.*

"That isn't what the photo and headline imply." Julee lifted her chin and met his irritated gaze with a steady one of her own. "She dug deep enough to ferret out all the details about the... fire, and our... association to it."

As soon as she spoke the words, she wished she could call them back, but they hung suspended between them, both irrevocable barrier and undeniable bond. Cain's eyes mirrored a montage of transitory emotions. Anger. Guilt. Sorrow. Resignation.

The same resignation she felt when she'd read Mavis Davenport's article. Though they'd both known the truth for months, today was the first time either of them had openly conceded that they were bound together by a tragedy that would never set them free.

"Hi, darlin's!"

Trixie's cheerful salutation pulled Cain's and Julee's attention toward the yard next to Julee's. They both waved. Trixie, wearing an exercise outfit better suited to a teenager than a woman in her seventy-ninth year, pranced to the point where the three yards converged. She beamed up at Cain. "Hello, you good-lookin' thing."

"Hi, Trix," Cain said with a fond smile that brought the crinkles at the corners of his eyes into play.

"Have you heard anything?" Trixie asked, her gaze moving from Cain to Julee.

"Not really."

"Mmm. Too bad. Your horoscope doesn't have anything much promising today. Just some nonsense about finding answers to a lot of questions, and healing old wounds." She gave Julee an arch look. "Considering the picture in the paper, I thought for sure there'd be something about romance."

The embarrassed look on Julee's face brought a throaty laugh from Trixie. She wagged a bony finger at Cain. "And you! I read all about you in the paper this morning. You've been holding out on us, you naughty boy. A psychic! Right here on the block, and us not knowin' it!"

Julee could see that Trixie's comments made Cain uncomfortable. She'd read the comment about his supposed ESP powers herself, but hadn't thought much of it. That sort of thing wasn't her cup of tea. Still, like Trixie, she wondered why no one had known about it.

Cain glanced at his watch, obviously anxious to make his getaway. "I gotta run, ladies. I'm going to be late for school."

At that moment, Julee would have loved to be a psychic herself. She'd have given anything to know what Cain was feeling before Trixie interrupted them.

"Settle down!" Dylan said as Phil Rousseau stalked past him for the fourth time in the past thirty seconds.

At the window of his small office, Phil turned. "Settle down? You sit here and tell me in all seriousness that you think my nephew had something to do with a kidnapping and you expect me to settle down?"

Dylan held up his palms. "Look, I told you Saturday that I thought he was hiding something, and now that I've found out he has motive and opportunity, his behavior is starting to make a lot of sense. By the way, why didn't you tell me about the connection between Julee Sutherland and your nephew, so I didn't have to spend the time finding out for myself?''

''Because he's my nephew.''

''I think that's called obstructing justice,'' Dylan reminded.

''Damn it, Dylan, Cain isn't a kidnapper, and if all this makes such good sense, how about explaining it to me? Did Cain force Julee Sutherland to move into a house behind him? And if he wanted revenge, why did he wait for four years to make his move?''

''I don't have any rational explanation for how she wound up being the guy's neighbor. I guess it was just one of those weird stranger-than-fiction flukes. But maybe he decided to do something when he saw how well she was doing, how happy and healthy her little boy was. Maybe it started eating him that she had everything and he had nothing.''

''Oh, yeah, she's got life easy, all right,'' Phil said in a sarcastic tone. ''She's a widow with the responsibility of providing physically and emotionally for her son. Yeah, that's a real piece of cake. Anybody would be envious.''

Dylan felt his face turn red. ''But her child is alive. Cain's isn't. If you think he's innocent, why don't you explain why Julee and I both feel like he's hiding something about what happened Saturday morning.''

Instead of answering, a grim look entered Phil's eyes. He scraped a hand through his thinning hair and turned away.

''Well?''

''I swore I wouldn't do this,'' Phil muttered, almost to himself.

''Do what?''

''Break my word to Cain.''

"If you don't tell me whatever it is you know, your nephew might wind up in the slammer."

"What is this?" Phil asked, turning on Dylan angrily. "First you accuse me of obstructing justice and now you're threatening to pick Cain up? You don't have any evidence. All you have is a cockeyed notion."

Dylan saw the hurt and fury in Phil's eyes and regretted that he and his best friend had come to words. But he had a job to do, and Phil knew that better than the next guy.

"Look," Dylan said in a conciliatory tone, "I didn't mean anything personal, and I didn't mean to make you mad. But if you know something that will help clear Cain's name, you'd better tell me. A child's life is at stake here, in case you've forgotten."

"I haven't forgotten anything!" Phil barked. He stared at Dylan thoughtfully for several seconds and then said, "Cain is a psychic."

"And I'm the Queen Mother," Dylan said, rolling his eyes toward the ceiling. "Look, I read all the old stories. I know that two of the fire victims were the estranged wife and daughter of the psychic detective who had previously helped the New Orleans police—Cain. I made it a point to go back and read all the articles in the *Times-Picayune* about his supposed psychic gift. What a crock!" When there was no reciprocal laughter from Phil, Dylan sobered. "Come on, Phil, surely you don't believe all that mumbo jumbo is for real."

"I *know* it's real," Phil said. "Remember when I told you Sunday that I bet the kidnappers used a stolen car and had already ditched it? Well, it was the truth, wasn't it?"

"Yeah."

"Cain gave me that information. I just . . . presented it to you as if it was something I came up with myself."

Dylan nodded in a considering way. "I might be inclined to believe you if Cain had told us where to find the car, but we both know it doesn't take a psychic to figure out that anyone who commits a crime in a getaway vehicle is crazy if he uses one that's registered in his name or keeps driving it around for very long. The greenest rookie on any force can figure that one out."

"What can I say?" Phil said, resignation in the set of his shoulders. "You're right."

"If you want to make a believer out of me, you've got to give me more than a bunch of coincidences. Anyone can look at a police report and make a few educated guesses. Does that mean they're psychic?" Dylan asked. "It's the law of averages. Like the weatherman going outside on a cloudy day and predicting a fifty-fifty chance of rain."

Phil gave an emphatic shake of his head. "I've seen it work too many times for it to be the law of averages or coincidence," he said, his stubborn nature refusing to abandon his beliefs. "And Cain has never seen any police reports. He never wanted to see one. All he needs is something that belonged to the victim or to visit the crime scene to pick up on any lingering vibrations."

"*Lingering vibrations?* For cryin' out loud, Phil, would you listen to yourself?"

"Okay, you don't believe, that's fine. But I'm telling you, he had nothing to do with it. Cain has a logical explanation for his suspicious behavior that morning."

"And what's that?"

"When he picked up Brice's ball, he experienced his first psychic episode since the dream that warned him about his wife and daughter's deaths four years ago. It shook him up."

"He dreamed they were going to die in the fire?"

"Yes, but the dream came too late for him to get word to them."

Dylan nodded. "And did he dream Brice was going to be kidnapped in front of his house?"

"No, but Cain said something kept telling him to get back home...to hurry. When he got there, he saw the car turning the corner. He was too late."

"It sounds to me like his gift needs a little fine-tuning to do anybody any good," Dylan said, mockery lacing his voice.

Phil's eyes were filled with conviction. "I know him, Dylan. He's a decent, hardworking guy. He's lived in a special hell all of his life because his aptitude for knowing things either makes him a target for people like you, or for those who want to use him for their own gain. It ruined his marriage, and he still blames himself for not knowing about the fire sooner." Phil pointed a blunt finger at his friend. "Don't persecute him."

Dylan stood. At the door, he turned. "I don't intend to persecute him. I do intend to find out the truth."

When Cain got home from school, he was tired, angry and filled with a feeling of futility that was all too familiar. As usual when his emotions were churning, he knew he needed a physical outlet. It was too hot to run, and the only other hope of solace available was to immerse himself in his painting. He changed into a T-shirt and disreputably worn cutoffs and went straight to the bedroom that held his painting paraphernalia.

Standing across the room, he regarded the painting he'd started the evening before. It was a woman walking along a rocky shore. The sunlight glinting off the water was so bright Cain could almost feel its heat. The sand was so white and the sky so blue that the hills and the church on the rocky hill stood out in stark relief.

As with everything he'd painted lately, he'd dreamed about the place and the woman walking along the shore for two nights running. And both nights, the dream had melded with the other dream, the dream of him making love to a woman while night birds called and the sea frolicked on the edge of the world.

He'd awakened both mornings aching with a fierce need. His morning run had lessened his desire and the cold shower he'd taken had helped cool the intensity of his feelings, but neither fully eradicated the dream, which was still uppermost on his mind when he'd talked with Julee earlier in the day.

Maybe it was the aftereffects of the dream that had made him so conscious of the way her breasts thrust against the soft cotton fabric of her chambray shirt and the way the faded blue denim of her jeans hugged her thighs and shapely bottom. Maybe it was that lingering memory that drew his gaze to her mouth.

The news Julee had given him about Mavis Davenport's story hadn't been much of a surprise. Neither was the fact that the reporter had delved into his past. What had surprised him was the pain that shot through him when Julee had put the reality of the fire into words.

It was funny, maybe even childish, but until he'd heard her say it, he'd managed to convince himself that her drawing away last August was based on something else—like the fact that she was a rich man's daughter and he was a lowly schoolteacher.

But her mention of the fire brought everything into sharp focus for her—Amy and Holly's deaths as well as the fact that Lanny Milligan, his brother-in-law, had cold-bloodedly shot down the husband she adored. Cain knew that he could never act on his feelings. How could there ever be anything between them?

He'd thought about the things she'd said during the drive to school. Maybe getting it out in the open was for the best. Now he wouldn't have to come up with flimsy excuses not to share a meal with her. Now maybe he could put aside his misplaced fascination and move on with his life. Maybe.

At school, he'd headed straight for the lounge and the newspaper. The photo was as provocative as he'd been led to believe. Anyone not knowing better might think the embrace was the real thing. The article rehashed the story of the fire, Cain's loss, Tad's death at Lanny Milligan's hand, and told how Cain had once used his psychic powers to help the police. It ended with the possible libelous implication that Cain had insinuated himself into Julee's life for the sole purpose of seeking revenge.

Furious at the Davenport woman's audacity, Cain refolded the paper and tossed it into the wastebasket. He wondered how anyone who tried as hard as he did to lead a so-called "normal" life could spend so much time in the limelight.

Throughout the day, he found himself the subject of many a questioning look and several pointed questions from his students that ranged from "Can you tell my fortune?" to "Do you know who did it?" Every class had been a fiasco.

At noon, he was called into the principal's office and subjected to a lengthy questioning that ended with the principal casually suggesting that Cain sit out the remaining week of school—with pay, of course. The publicity involved was stirring up a lot of comments from students and parents alike. The school didn't need the publicity or the speculation about his involvement with the kidnapping.

Cain reminded the principal that he was innocent until proven guilty. Mark Hightower had suggested in a gentle voice that if Cain truly had the students' best interest at heart, he would go along. After all, there was only another week of classes.

Mark knew damn well Cain cared about the students. That's why he'd become a teacher. Cain had no choice but to agree. The school year was officially over for him.

Shoving the incident from his mind, Cain went to the kitchen and poured himself a massive glass of iced tea. He took his palette from the freezer, where it kept the paint from drying out. Then he put on a CD by the Crash Test Dummies. In fifteen minutes, he was immersed in his painting while he listened to songs about people who were different and didn't know why and how Superman kept trying to save the world even though he got no pay.

The music changed through the course of the evening, from the Crash Test Dummies, to Eric Clapton, to Yanni. Everyone had always commented on his eclectic taste in music, and Cain could truly say his likes ran the gamut from classical to new age to country.

Rachmaninoff's soothing, romantic *Rhapsody on a Theme* filled the air as Cain's brush caressed the canvas with careful, loving strokes.

The sound of the doorbell barely penetrated the passionate, creative fog that surrounded him when he really got into his work. The bell chimed again. Uttering a mild curse, he put down his palette and the brush he was using and glanced at his watch. It was almost six. He'd been working more than two and a half hours, and realized he was starving.

The doorbell chimed the third time, and, with a sigh, he headed for the front of the house. He knew before he opened the door that his caller was Dylan Garvey. He greeted the policeman with a grim smile. Dylan's face was somber, watchful.

"Come on in, Detective. I've been expecting you."

For the space of a heartbeat, Dylan looked nonplussed. Cain's smile bordered on wicked. Let the cop think his psychic powers had told of his imminent arrival.

"Can I get you something to drink?"

Dylan took his notebook and pen from his pocket. "No thanks, I'm still on duty."

"After reading the newspaper article, I assume you came to ask if I had anything to do with Brice Sutherland's kidnapping."

Like Cain's saying he was expecting Dylan, the statement took the detective off guard.

"You have to admit Mavis Davenport had a point, and you also have to admit you were less than open during my previous questioning," Dylan said.

"I guess her theory makes some sort of perverted, twisted sense," Cain said with a thoughtful nod. "I'm sorry you don't think I was giving my full cooperation."

Dylan looked skeptical.

"I was in no way involved in the abduction of Brice Sutherland, Detective Garvey," Cain added. "He's a good kid."

"And how do you feel about his mother?"

Cain didn't like the speculative gleam in Dylan's eyes. "I like her just fine," he said. "Look, do all these questions mean I'm a suspect?"

"They mean I have some questions that need answering. I suppose you have an alibi for Saturday morning."

"I've already told you I was running."

"Did anyone see you?"

"How should I know?" Cain said. "I imagine a lot of people saw me, but who'd really notice?"

"You didn't talk to anyone?"

"It's a little hard carrying on a conversation while you're running." Cain didn't even try to hide his sarcasm. He could see that his glib replies didn't please the detective.

"The paper says you possess some sort of psychic power. Phil says so, too. What do you say?" Dylan asked.

"I say you don't believe it."

Dylan laughed. "You're right. But you do claim to be a clairvoyant or whatever?"

Cain shrugged. "I claim, Detective Garvey, to have more highly developed ESP skills than the average person, which means that if I open myself up for psychic flow, I usually receive something."

He leaned toward Dylan with a pseudo-earnestness that he knew would irritate the cop. "The part that drives me crazy is that I don't have any control over what I pick up on, and I don't know everything. Sometimes I don't know if what I see is in the future or has already happened."

"Phil says that your actions on Saturday are all tied up to the fact that you experienced some sort of psychic... flow or whatever and you were trying to hide it. Is that true?"

Cain blew out a disgusted sigh. "Yeah. It was the first time in four years."

"Tell me what you... felt."

Cain gave the policeman a dispassionate but thorough version of the emotions and visual images that had bombarded him the moment he picked up Brice's soccer ball.

"Did you actually see him in the car as it went around the corner?"

"No," Cain admitted.

"Did you hear him yelling or anything?"

Cain closed his eyes and for an instant the sound of Brice's impassioned "*Mama! Help me!*" filled his mind. He opened his eyes and fixed the detective with a steady look.

"His mouth was covered. I didn't actually hear him... except in my head. Inside himself, he was screaming for his mother."

Dylan jotted down a notation in his little spiral notebook and glanced up at Cain. "Is it fair to say that you aren't one hundred percent accurate."

"That's right."

"Is that how you explain dreaming of the danger to your wife and daughter too late to do them any good?"

Cain felt the color drain from his face. "I never claimed to walk on water, Detective Garvey."

"Can you pick up information on demand?" Dylan asked, backing off that line of questioning.

Cain shook his head. "If I'm not meant to have a piece of information, nothing can force it."

"What about dreams?"

"Sometimes my dreams have deeper meanings," Cain said with a nod. "But as you've pointed out, I don't always get it until too late."

Again Dylan recorded something in his little tablet. "How close were you to your brother-in-law?" he asked, switching topics again.

"Lanny?" Cain asked with a frown. "We weren't close at all. He was a little too weird for me, and I always thought he was a few bricks shy of a load."

"Have you seen or heard from him since the trial?"

"I haven't seen him. He called, though, after Lucy committed suicide."

"Do you mind telling me what he said? How he sounded?"

Cain thought a few seconds. "He was upset. Crying. For all his faults, he was crazy about Lucy and the kids."

"Did he say anything about Julee Sutherland?"

A contemplative look entered Cain's eyes. "As a matter of fact, he did. He said something like, 'I'm not finished with her yet. Her and her kid are gonna pay.'"

"Is that all?"

"Yeah. Look, Detective, do you mind telling me what all this is about?"

"We just got word that Lanny Milligan took a nurse hostage and escaped from a hospital where he was being treated for a bleeding ulcer. I find it a little coincidental that Lanny escaped from prison four days after Brice Sutherland disappeared from his backyard, don't you?"

Cain held up a hand. "Wait a minute. Let me see if I understand where you're coming from. You're saying that Lanny had someone snatch Brice—and you think that might be me—while he was making plans to break out of jail, so that he could hurt Brice when he got out?"

"You just admitted that he had it in for Julee and the boy."

"Yeah, but doesn't arranging something like that take money? Lanny's attorney's fees busted him."

"Maybe so, but we just found out he got a healthy check from the insurance company when Lucy died."

Cain swore.

"And then, there's still the possibility that you helped him."

"Are we back to that?" Cain asked, his lips twisted in disgust.

"Looks like it."

Cain squared his shoulders. Somehow, it seemed like the perfect ending to his day. "Are you taking me in?"

Dylan shook his head and rose. "I don't have a shred of evidence against you. But I think we'll keep an eye on you for a while."

Cain stared at Dylan, blue gaze probing blue gaze while two strong wills clashed. "You think he'll come here."

"I think there's a strong possibility that he'll come after Julee Sutherland and that he'll contact you, yes." Dylan put his notebook and pen in his pocket. "Keep in touch, Collier, and if I were you, I'd make sure nothing happened to your pretty neighbor." Without another word, he headed for the door.

"Detective Garvey."

Dylan turned.

"Mind if I use your pen?"

Dylan looked at him questioningly.

"I just thought of someone who can vouch that I was running Saturday morning. I'll write her name down for you."

Dylan took the pen from his breast pocket and tossed it to Cain, who caught it easily.

Cain wrote the name Hattie Carlisle on a scrap of paper. "I changed a flat for her," Cain said, handing the paper to Dylan. Instead of giving Dylan the pen, Cain clutched it in his fist and closed his eyes.

"You're named after your father," Cain said, in an even, hypnotic tone. "He was a policeman. A big man. Had a place on his side where he was cut in a struggle with a knife. He was gruff. Hard. Too hard. You loved and admired him, but at the same time, you hated him."

Cain opened his eyes and regarded Dylan. He looked shocked.

Cain handed the pen back to the detective.

"He never told you he loved you," Cain continued without flinching. "Not once."

Dylan appeared as if he'd taken a punch to the stomach, and a startled, wary expression leaped into his eyes.

"He never said the words," Cain said. "But he felt them."

The first thing Lanny did was go into a busy convenience store and buy some hair color with the cash he'd taken from the police guard's wallet. The lineup photo that would be splashed over television land and printed in the papers would be of a blond man who weighed a good fifty pounds more than he did now. The weight loss was deliberate, something it had taken him almost six months to do, something he'd started working on soon after Lucy's death.

Changing his looks was imperative. He couldn't afford to be picked up before he'd paid Julee Sutherland back for what she and her husband had done to him.

He owed Lucy and the girls that much.

Chapter Five

Dylan left Cain's house with mixed feelings, confusion one of them. He didn't believe in all that ESP stuff, but neither could he deny that what Cain had told him about his father was true. Chantal was one of the few people who knew about his relationship with his father.

Cain could have made a lucky guess about the Garvey father-son relationship, but there was no way he could have known about the long scar, a reminder of Patrick Garvey's run-in with a teenage kid who'd taken a measly twenty-three dollars from a neighborhood grocery clerk.

Dylan rubbed his hand over his forehead, as if the action might rid him of the uneasy feeling his encounter with the alleged psychic had left behind.

He hated breaking the news about Lanny Milligan's escape to Julee, but it would be the big story on the ten-o'clock news and *the* front-page headline the next morning. Besides, he thought as he got out of the car, even though it might frighten Julee, she needed to be aware so that she could take extra precautions.

When the doorbell rang, Julee looked out the peephole and saw Dylan's car sitting in the drive. Surprised to find him on her doorstep for the second time that day, she opened the door. "Is something wrong? Have they found Brice? Is he okay?"

The questions tumbled from her one after the other, like stones rolling down a steep embankment. The fear and panic threading her voice was countered by a tentative ray of hope.

Dylan shook his head. "There have been a couple of new developments I think you should know about."

Julee felt the tautness leave her body. She stepped aside. "Come in."

Dylan followed her to the living room and took his usual place on the wicker-and-floral sofa. Declining anything to drink, he said, "I had a talk with Cain Collier a few minutes ago. I confronted him about my feeling that he was hiding something."

"And..."

"He says that the hesitation you and I sensed is connected to the psychic vibrations he claims he experienced when he picked up Brice's ball."

"Psychic vibrations!" Julee scoffed. "I don't put much stock in that sort of thing, do you?"

"I never have."

"What did he claim to see?"

Julee listened while Dylan gave her a condensed version of Cain's account of the feelings he'd experienced from the moment he picked up Brice's ball until she demanded to know where he got it.

Brice had struggled. He had tried to call out to her.... Whether or not the story was true, Julee felt the sting of tears at the thought of Brice's fear. She laced her fingers together to still their trembling, but otherwise, she kept a tight rein on her emotions. She noticed that Dylan kept a close watch to see how she was handling the information and knew that the last thing he needed was a hysterical woman on his hands.

Hysterical. Brice must have been hysterical. He was leery of strangers, and— Julee's thoughts drew up short. Was she actually contemplating the idea that Cain Collier's account was true? A man who claimed to be a seer or clairvoyant, or whatever he chose to call it?

"That's a pretty vague scenario," she said. "I mean, anyone would naturally assume that Brice struggled, that he was afraid, that whoever took him had his hand over his mouth to keep him from crying out. It doesn't take a psychic to know those things."

"You're right," Dylan agreed. "But Collier did tell his uncle later that the car had been abandoned. It had."

"Coincidence."

"Probably." Dylan leaned his elbows on his knees, clasped his hands together and stared at the floor.

"What is it?" Julee asked, sensing there was something he wasn't telling her.

Dylan glanced up at her, a glimmer of humor in his eyes. "How do you know there's something?"

"ESP," she said, straight-faced.

He grinned. "It's great that you can keep a sense of humor."

"That isn't humor," she corrected him. "It's sarcasm. So tell me, what's so serious you're having trouble finding the right words?"

Dylan's gaze was steady, uncompromising. "Lanny Milligan broke out today."

Julee felt the color leach from her face. "How?"

"He was in the hospital being treated for bleeding ulcers. I don't have the details, but he overpowered a guard somehow and then took a nurse hostage until he could put some distance between him and the authorities. The doctor said he didn't know how he did it. He's in pretty bad shape."

Julee's voice was little more than a whisper. "Do you think he had someone—like Cain—take Brice so that he could...hurt him when he got out?"

"That would be my guess," Dylan said. "But I have to be honest with you. I don't have anything on Cain Collier. If all that psychic stuff is true—and just maybe it is—it explains his behavior on Saturday. But I'm from the Show Me state. Collier says he has an alibi, and I'll check it out first thing in the morning."

"Good," Julee said shakily.

"Look, I don't want you worrying. We'll be keeping an eye on both of you until this is solved."

"Me! Do you think Lanny will come after me, too?"

"I don't know," Dylan said. "I wish I could tell you no, but I just don't know. The man shot your husband down in front of dozens of people. I think he's capable of anything."

Julee shivered.

"Look, why don't you let Chantal come over and organize the neighborhood? If they ask enough questions they might be able to turn up something about Brice."

"I don't know," Julee said. "Won't that put the volunteers' lives in danger?"

"Most likely it'll keep Lanny from trying anything. And it might be a good idea to have someone in the house while you're at work. We'll have an unmarked car cruise the neighborhood to keep an eye out for any strangers in the area," Dylan said.

The phone rang. Julee excused herself and spoke into the cordless receiver lying on the end table. "Hello."

"Hi" came the familiar, malevolent voice. "I know where you are, Julee. And I'm gonna make you and your kid pay."

Julee gave a frightened cry, pressed the off button and clutched the phone to her breasts, unaware that she was shaking her head while she whispered a soft "No."

"What is it?" Dylan demanded, leaping to his feet.

She looked at him, a dazed expression in her eyes. "That was the man I told you about. The one who's been phoning me on Saturdays."

Dylan's lips tightened. "What did he say?"

"The same thing he always says," Julee told him. "That he knows where I am, and he's going to make me and Brice pay. It isn't Mel Dunning, Dylan," she said, conviction in her voice. "It's Lanny Milligan."

The next morning, Cain decided to run around the block in front of Julee's house before he finished his run. If he was lucky, he might catch a glimpse of her as he passed. Lord, he must have been hanging out with the fourteen-to-eighteen crowd too long, he thought, a wry smile pulling at the corner of his mouth. If that wasn't high school thinking, he'd eat his socks.

He was dog tired—not just from his five-mile run, but because he'd been up until past midnight the night before, mulling over what Dylan had told him about Lanny's escape, and working on his painting. He'd never considered himself obsessive about his painting before, but this project seemed to have a life all its own.

A life of his own. He hadn't been able to call his life his own since Mavis Davenport's article had come out in the paper. Not only had he been plagued with calls, no less than five people had actually come to his door, asking for an appointment, or just shoving something at him and demanding that he tell them what he felt from the personal article.

Cain had gotten rid of them as diplomatically as he could, damning the newspaper woman all the while. He should call the phone company and request a new, unlisted number. At the thought, a familiar feeling of déjà vu enveloped him. He didn't have to consult Trixie to know that another move was in the cards.

The sight of several cars in Julee's driveway shifted Cain's thoughts from his problems and momentarily slowed his pace. He wondered what was going on and decided to ask Trixie, who was pulling weeds from a patch of sunflowers taller than she was.

Sensing his approach, she looked up with a pleased smile. "Hi, handsome!" she said. "Have you seen your horoscope this morning?"

Cain shook his sweat-dampened head and planted his hands on his hips, slowing to a walk.

"It's a humdinger!" Trixie chortled, watching as he continued to cool down. She screwed up her wizened features. "Let's see if I can remember how it went. Oh, yes! Something like...your fondest dream is but a heartbeat from becoming a reality if you just let go of the past," she paraphrased with an arch look and a sly smile. "Romance blossoms tonight." She winked at him. "Got a hot date, or what?"

"No hot dates," he said, his mind going to his dream of being on the beach with the unknown woman, a dream that was quickly becoming his fondest dream. To even contemplate that the feelings of total mental and physical fulfillment could become reality was incomprehensible.

He scoffed at the very idea. What the horoscope probably meant was that he could live the normal life he'd dreamed of if he'd just let go of all the baggage left over from his failed marriage and accept the gift he'd been given.

"What's going on at Julee's?" he asked, his voice still a bit breathless.

"They're setting up a hot line where people can call with any information that might lead to Brice's whereabouts. They're printing up flyers with his picture on it, and they're going to be putting them out all over the state. Anyone who wants can volunteer to help."

It sounded like a good idea, and it also meant that someone would be in the house all day, which wasn't a bad idea, since Cain agreed with Dylan's theory that Lanny might try something.

"Are you going to offer your help?" Trixie asked.

"I don't know what I can do."

"You can use your psychic powers, that's what you can do!" Trixie said, her eyes wide.

Cain stopped his pacing, uncaring at the moment that his muscles might cramp up. "No one believes me, Trix," he told her with a nonchalant shrug and a self-effacing smile. "And besides, I don't help solve cases anymore. My *powers* are too unreliable."

"But it's true, isn't it? You really can pick up vibrations about people by just touching their things?"

"Sometimes," Cain said, unable to make light of things when the old woman's face wore such a look of sincerity. "Sometimes I can."

The furrows in her forehead smoothed and a beautiful smile creased her cheeks. "What a wonderful gift! I've been fascinated by the things the mind can do all my life, but the closest I've ever come is reading tarot cards and practicing numerology." She laughed, almost sadly. "My biggest problem with that has always been who the heck decided what the numbers mean, and how do we know he was right? But what you have..." She shook her head. "Now, that's truly marvelous."

Cain smiled. He'd never thought about his ability as wonderful.

She shook herself like a dog shaking off excess water, and her wrinkled face broke into her usual saucy grin. "I'll tell you one thing I do know for certain, and I knew it before I saw it in the cards."

"What's that?"

"You sort of...like Julee, don't you?"

Cain smiled. "How could you tell?"

Trixie snorted. "Well, it sure doesn't take any ESP to figure it out. You look at that woman like you want to kiss her senseless."

"So much for my poker face," Cain said. Inside he was seething with apprehension. If his feelings for Julee were that obvious to Trixie, were they apparent to everyone? Unable to tolerate the thought, he waved at Trixie. "I gotta go," he said, heading down the street.

"Cain!" she called, halting him once more. "If it's any consolation, darlin', Julee looks at you the same way."

Julee arrived home that evening at five-thirty. It was another thirty minutes before she got everyone cleared out so she could take a long shower, grab a bite to eat and hopefully fall into bed. As she showered, she thought about her day and wondered if there was anything else she could do to aid the police investigation.

Loretta Sutherland and Chantal Garvey had arrived early that morning, and three other women followed soon after, all hugging Julee and assuring her they'd do all they could to help locate Brice.

Julee had left her mother-in-law in charge while she went to New Orleans with Chantal to film a short spot to be aired during both segments of the nightly news. The piece would show several snapshots of Brice, explain where, when and how he'd been taken, and end with a plea from Julee to please bring her little boy back unharmed. The police number and the number of the Missing Children's Hot Line would be on the screen the entire time. She didn't know if making the tape or any of her other efforts would pay off, but sitting around doing nothing wasn't accomplishing a thing, and working herself and her crew at the breakneck pace she'd enforced on them the past few days wasn't doing anything but driving a wedge between her and her men.

To make things worse, she'd lost two crackerjack carpenters—one who quit without notice because he claimed she was working them into the ground, and another who'd gone to a better job.

Luther was her only port in that particular storm. He'd told her not to worry; they'd find more help. She supposed he was right, but she didn't need to fall behind. Getting Rocky Melancon's house finished by the date she'd promised involved a nice bonus.

She sighed. With everything that was going on, it was no wonder she lay awake at night, listening to the monotonous drip-drip of her shower and fighting both her sorrow over the loss of her child and her worry and depression, as well.

Despite the disbelief she'd voiced to Dylan, she'd spent a goodly portion of the night pondering Cain's claim that he could pick up vibrations from objects and places. She wouldn't be the first. Obviously someone in the New Orleans police department had bought into the story, and whatever Cain did he did often enough to give him some sort of credibility. She wished she did believe, *could* believe. She wished she had no uncertainties about his gift... or his involvement. Then maybe she could ask for his help.

Julee paused to give that last thought consideration. Did she really believe Cain was involved with Brice's disappearance? In spite of certain bits of evidence that pointed to his possible involvement, she didn't think so. Yet, just as Dylan had no concrete reasons to suspect him, she had no concrete reasons for believing him innocent. Her feelings were based on nothing more than the fact that her heart beat a little faster in his presence, and her body grew as taut as a bowstring when those penetrating blue eyes met hers.

In spades, her waffling emotions and her refusal to seriously consider Cain a suspect were based on nothing more than the fact that the man caused her hormones to riot, and everyone knew they couldn't be trusted. It was a proven fact that rampaging hormones had contributed to more chaos and wrong decisions than anything, and hers were certainly working overtime lately, as the recurring dream proved.

The Dream was beginning to concern her. Until this week, her forays into the erotic dreamscape had been confined to weekends, but she'd had the dream twice since Saturday, and each morning when she awakened, she couldn't rid herself of the notion that she could smell the salty air on her skin... skin that still tingled with the remembered touch of the stranger's hands and lips. It occurred to her that if Cain was a psychic, maybe he could tell her what the dream meant and who the man was. But even if Cain's claims were true, Julee knew she could never ask him. She would be too embarrassed. Even if he told her the man in the dream was Tad, or some other man she had yet to meet, she knew that deep in her heart, she wanted it to be him....

The doorbell rang as Julee stepped out of the shower. She wrapped herself in a terry-cloth robe and went to answer it. The peephole showed a man on the doorstep. Cain. Her heart kicked into a higher gear. Had he picked up on something else?

Don't be ridiculous, Julee! Surely you aren't considering the possibility that Cain really does have ESP?

She didn't know. She just knew that seeing him there sparked an irrational hope. With her heart pounding harder than the situation warranted, she undid the locks and opened the door for him.

His gaze, warm and blue and a bit reckless, roamed from the pink-tinted tips of her toes to her wet, slicked-back hair. He plunged his hands into the pockets of his khaki shorts. "Hi."

A heat that rivaled that of the sandy beaches of Folégandros, an island in Greece where she'd spent many a sunlit day as a child, warmed Julee's cheeks and made her insides feel as soft and malleable as melted wax. She clutched the lapels of the robe.

"Why are you here?"

"A couple of reasons," Cain said. "But first, just so you'll feel more comfortable, I need to tell you that the illustrious detective in charge of the case called a little while ago to tell me that my alibi checked out."

When Julee didn't reply, he continued. "Hattie Carlisle, the woman whose tire I changed, remembers me well. I know that doesn't put me in the clear, but it's at least an indication that if I was involved with the kidnapping, it was only indirectly."

"And that's supposed to make me feel better?"

"It makes me feel better," Cain said.

"So what does your alibi checking out have to do with your coming to pay me a visit?" she asked, using coolness to hide the fact that her heart was racing.

His smile was friendly...beautiful. "I thought that since you had no reason to be suspicious of me now, I might be able to help."

"I don't believe in ESP, Mr. Collier," she said in a voice that held an unmistakable chill.

A strange look filled his eyes. A look of hopelessness and pain and regret. "You used to call me Cain."

That was back before I knew your wife and little girl were killed in a house Tad built. Back before I knew that Lanny Milligan was your brother-in-law. A bittersweet feeling of having lost something precious pierced the heart Julee had worked so hard to harden.

"Cain, then."

"I didn't come to offer my psychic services to you, Julee," he said in a gentle tone. "There are things in my life I'd like to forget about, and that's one of them. I came to volunteer to put out flyers...or whatever."

The tenderness in his voice sent shame coursing through her. Her rudeness was uncalled-for. If he did have a psychic gift—or thought he did—and it *had* failed him, it was natural that he would want no more to do with it. It occurred to her that, viewed in that light, his claim of being upset when he'd experienced Brice's abduction on Saturday made a lot of sense.

"I'm sorry," she said quickly. "I appreciate your offer." She stepped aside. "Come in. I'll run and get you some flyers."

Embarrassment sent her fleeing from the entryway to the spare bedroom, where Loretta and Chantal had set up their mini command post. How could she have been so cruel? she wondered as she picked up a stack of flyers emblazoned with Brice's picture and carried them back to where Cain waited near the door.

Forcing her eyes to meet his, she handed Cain the stack of loose paper. Their fingers touched, and an electrical arc of awareness sizzled through her. She sucked in a small breath of air.

"I'm sorry," she said again, and she was, though if he'd pressed, she couldn't have said what she was sorry for. For her callousness? Her disbelief? For jumping to conclusions? Or for things she didn't dare put into thoughts, much less words?

"So am I."

Julee's gaze clung to his, searching...searching. Across the room, the relentlessly funny sitcom broke for a commercial extolling the virtues of one car over the competitor's. Julee was too busy processing the almost tangible undercurrents of emotion swirling around her and Cain to notice.

They'd gone past a simple apology for her misunderstanding and her bitterness. Somehow, she knew that Cain understood exactly what she was sorry for, that he'd somehow heard the words she was afraid to say, that he was somehow in tune to the feelings she was afraid to feel.

A part of Julee's mind registered that the television had cut to a local affiliate, but it wasn't until she heard the sound of her own voice that the tension binding her and Cain snapped.

She turned and saw her face filling the television screen. She didn't listen to the message she was delivering to the public. Instead, her attention was focused on the woman staring out of the television screen. Even wearing the thick makeup the station had applied so she wouldn't look washed out beneath the harsh studio lights, she looked sallow and colorless. While concealer went a long way toward hiding the dark circles and puffiness beneath her eyes, nothing could alleviate the weariness reflected there or the hopelessness in her voice.

Her plea to the kind folks of Louisiana ended, and three pictures of Brice flashed onto the screen, one after the other. The sight of his smiling face bombarded her heart with a rush of fresh grief that brought a flood of tears. She brought her hands to her mouth to hold back a cry of anguish.

The movement behind her barely registered. It wasn't until moments later, when the sitcom returned to the screen and she'd regained control of her shaky composure, that Julee remembered Cain. She turned to see what he thought of her histrionics, and wasn't all that surprised to find that he'd gone.

Cain sat at the kitchen table nursing a bottle of cold beer and staring at the picture of Brice that graced the flyers he'd tossed onto the table moments before. Frustration ate at him. He wanted so badly to ease Julee's pain, and he knew that he had neither the skill nor the right even to try.

He would be a long time forgetting the sound of her cry of grief, and even longer forgetting the agony etched on her face as she asked for help from the television viewers.

It wasn't fair that she should be suffering this way, not after the pain she'd already borne. It was no fairer than for Mavis Davenport's article to have thrust him into the limelight after he'd struggled so hard for anonymity.

Just thinking about the sudden influx of calls and people wanting to avail themselves of his services made his blood boil. Even some of his students had dropped by just to see what he could tell them. Mark Hightower had called, too, telling him that the school board had held an emergency meeting and had voted not to renew his contract for the next year. Furious, he'd considered a lawsuit against Mavis

Davenport and the newspaper, but that would only make him more visible to the public.

Cain lifted the bottle to his lips. Well, as the old adages went, there was no use crying over spilt milk; the die had been cast and there was no going back. All he could do was deal with the situation, just as he had in the past.

Setting down the bottle, he looked at the picture of Brice's smiling face and fought back the unmanly sting of tears. He, more than most, knew what it was like to lose a child. He stared down at the image of Julee's son and saw instead her tortured face superimposed over it . . . a trick of the mind's eye.

"To those who know to do good, and doeth it not, to him it is sin."

The Biblical verse—one of his grandmother's favorites— came from somewhere deep inside him. In his mind, there was no contradiction between his belief in God and the gift he believed the Almighty had given him. It had nothing to do with religion, nor was there anything mystical about it.

Scientists claimed most people used one-tenth of their mind's power. He believed that everyone had some psychic ability, just as a lot of people had pleasing singing voices. The difference was that some people developed their talents; some didn't. Few people were agreeable or able to put aside their own wills and let their minds become receivers for thought and sound waves, the same way few people with good singing voices were willing to work and sacrifice to become stars.

Cain tipped back the bottle and let the last of the yeasty brew slide down his throat. There was no use kidding himself. He knew exactly where all his mental justification was leading—he was actually considering helping Dylan locate Brice.

If you can, bozo, he reminded himself. What he'd told Dylan was true. Even though he might be willing to help, it didn't necessarily follow that he could. There was no forcing what he wasn't meant to know, just as there was no stopping the reception of information when his mind was in tune to acquire it.

What can it hurt to try? Cain finished the beer and wondered exactly what he should do. He had nothing of Brice's to hold. Suddenly, he recalled Phil saying that the West Coast psychic used maps. He shrugged. It was worth a try.

He rose and put his empty bottle into the trash can. Still, he needed something of Brice's if he was going to make this work. Debating whether or not to call Julee and request a toy or a favorite article of Brice's clothing, Cain reached out to straighten the stack of flyers he'd scattered onto the tabletop.

"Yellow hair."

Startled by the sound of his own voice, and staggered by the strength of the audio message, Cain sat down hard. What on earth did it mean? Brice didn't have blond hair. His hair was dark, like Julee's.

Pondering the dilemma, Cain let his fingers move slowly over Brice's still, photocopied features, the childish nose...the laughing eyes.... His hand stilled on the crest of Brice's chubby cheek. There. Right there. Warmth. Warmth beneath his eyes. Did that warmth indicate tears?

Cain shook his head. Who the heck knew? This trick was too new and untried for him to make an educated guess. Still, suppose it did mean something? Suppose it meant emotion or, as the man in California claimed, the presence of something connected to the case.

Rising again, Cain went into his closet and dragged down a leather-bound atlas he used when he traveled. He flipped over to a map of Louisiana and put his hand on it, letting the tips of his fingers trail over the picture of the state from the Arkansas line to the Gulf. Nothing.

He tried it again. And again. Frustration set his teeth on edge. He flipped to the front of the atlas, where a picture of the whole United States filled the page. Slowly, so slowly that there was no possibility of missing the slightest hint of warmth, Cain's fingers skimmed the map. Twice. From left to right. Top to bottom. There was nothing. Not so much as a tingle. Nothing but the slick feel of paper.

Irritation warred with another, new feeling. Fear.

What if the reason he couldn't locate Brice on the map was because his body was no longer giving out vibrations to be picked up?

What if Brice was dead?

The first thing Lanny did when he arrived in Houma was stake out Julee Sutherland's house. All the activity piqued his interest. He'd asked around and found out that the influx of people was a concerned-citizens group who aided parents in locating missing children. His first reaction was pure, unadulterated fury. How could he get his revenge with the house full of people?

Later, after he'd calmed down, he was able to step back and reevaluate the situation. Having all those people swarming the house was just a little glitch. They made his job harder, but not impossible.

He'd decided that forcing his way into her house was out, but there were other ways. He'd think about it. He was a resourceful kind of guy, and he couldn't afford to mess things up. When they sent him back to Angola the next time, there'd be no second chance to seek his revenge on Tad Sutherland's family. No, he'd bide his time, and something would turn up.

It had.

When he'd seen Julee leave with the other woman earlier that morning, he'd followed them in the car he'd stolen from a supermarket parking lot. He hadn't been at all surprised when they drove to a construction site. The same source that kept him apprised of Julee Sutherland's whereabouts had informed him that she'd managed to keep her husband's business going. What surprised him was how easily he'd been led there.

From an inconspicuous spot in a copse of woods, he'd watched her get out and talk to a man, obviously the job foreman. Then she got in the car and drove off.

He had watched her go, a plan already forming in his mind.

Even now, he smiled at the beauty of it. He had simply marched himself up to the man and asked if they had an opening. Even though the foreman hadn't liked that he didn't own any tools, luck had been with him. They were shorthanded.

Lanny laughed, a grating rusty sound, and crossed his arms over his burning stomach. He'd done a little carpenter work through the years. He ought to be able to fake it, at least until he figured out a way to corner Julee Sutherland and make her pay....

Chapter Six

After Cain tried unsuccessfully to locate Brice on the maps, he called his uncle. Before he could tell Phil about the outcome of his experiment, the older man said, "I hear your alibi checked out."

"Yeah."

"So you're not a suspect anymore?"

Cain gave a dry laugh. "I think I'll be a suspect in Garvey's mind until he brings in the real perpetrator."

"Dylan doesn't give up easily," Phil said. "But he isn't stupid, and he keeps an open mind."

"Could have fooled me."

Phil laughed. "You really rattled his cage this evening. I don't know what you said about him and his dad, but you must have come pretty close to the truth."

They chatted for a few more minutes, and Cain recounted how he was being inundated with calls and visitors. When he told Phil about the school board's decision not to hire him the following fall, Phil said, "Call a lawyer."

"I thought about it, but that would be defeating the purpose, don't you think?"

"Guess you're right," Phil agreed.

Finally, Cain got around to telling his uncle about his offer to help Julee and his attempt to locate Brice the way the California psychic had done.

"I knew you wouldn't be able to keep from trying," Phil said. "Not with a kid involved."

Cain heard the smile in his uncle's voice. "Yeah, well, I wish I hadn't," he replied, pinching the bridge of his nose between his thumb and forefinger.

"Why?"

Cain sat down at the kitchen table and rested his elbows on the tile surface, fighting a depression that had become all too familiar since his failure to pick up the danger to Amy and Holly in time. "The maps were cold, Phil. Stone-cold. I tried the Louisiana map and one of the United States, and got nothing...*nada.*"

"Don't beat yourself up. Maybe that's just one trick that doesn't work for you," Phil said.

"Yeah, I guess."

"Okay, what is it?" Phil asked. "There's something bothering you besides the fact that you didn't get a reading."

"You're right. It occurred to me that there could be another reason it didn't work."

"Like?"

"Like maybe I'm not picking up any vibrations or warmth because Brice is...dead."

Phil swore. "Do you think that's a possibility?"

"C'mon, Phil. You're a cop. You know it's a possibility—even a probability—and it has been from the very beginning."

"Yeah," Phil said in a weary voice.

"There was something else," Cain said suddenly. "Something that happened when I touched Brice's face on the flyer. I heard a child's voice say, 'yellow hair.' "

"What does that mean?"

"I wish I knew. Brice's hair is dark like Julee's. Maybe it means one of the kidnappers has yellow hair, I don't know."

Cain heard Phil's troubled sigh. "I don't know, either. Ask his mother if it means anything to her, and just keep passing on the information as it comes. I'll try to make Dylan swallow it."

"I will, Phil. Thanks."

"No," Phil said. "Thank *you.*"

If anyone had asked her, Julee would have been hard-pressed to explain the depression that settled over her after Cain walked out without a goodbye. She told herself the feeling was understandable. The constant strain of not knowing where Brice was, knowing he was frightened, perhaps hurt...or worse, would take its toll on anyone.

Then there was the added stress of having a houseful of people around and making sure there were colas, cookies and plenty of sandwiches for them—not to mention her increasing worry over Gene Sutherland, who was again experiencing an occasional twinge of angina and was losing weight by the day. Since his forced medical retirement, Brice had become the sun in Gene's universe.

Stop trying to fool yourself, Julee. What's wrong with you is that even though you know it's hopeless, Dylan

*Garvey has forced you to admit that you're more than a lit-
tle taken with your handsome neighbor.*

"All right," she said to the nagging part of her psyche. "I
admit it. Satisfied?"

But the inner voice was far from satisfied. It demanded
that she face every feeling she had for Cain, asked her to
reconcile those feelings with the love she'd felt for Tad and
the residual guilt left over from the fire.

Even though she didn't really believe Cain was involved
with Brice's disappearance, she couldn't see her feelings for
him ever amounting to anything. Simply put, Cain had
made it pretty obvious that he wasn't interested.

She wondered if his indifference was based on guilt and
the same feeling of wrongness she felt. Or was it more? Was
it because he found her lacking as a woman?

The doorbell's chiming ended her self-inquiry. When she
opened the front door, she found Trixie standing there, a
plate piled with pork chops, mashed potatoes and fresh
green beans in her beringed hands.

"Hey, Trixie," Julee said with a sigh that mirrored her
disappointment. Had she really expected Cain to come
back?

"Mmm-hmm," the old woman said, nodding her vibrant red head with its faux designer scarf tied in a gaudy
bow over one ear. "Just as I thought. Down in the mouth
because you're doing too much. Thought you might need a
hot meal and some scintillating company."

Trixie could always be counted on to make some outra-
geous comment or another, and Julee had a feeling that
what she needed was just what the old woman said—some
conversation that was uplifting instead of a rehash of Brice
and the investigation. She smiled in spite of herself.
"Sounds like just what the doctor ordered. Come on in."

Trixie followed Julee into the kitchen and set the plate down on the countertop with a loud thud. "Eat."

"Yes, ma'am. As soon as you hand me a fork."

Trixie's pleasure at being allowed to wait on Julee was apparent as she fetched the necessary utensils and busied herself pouring them both a glass of iced tea. When she was satisfied that Julee had everything she needed, Trixie sat down and rested her pointed chin in her hand.

"What gives?"

"Nothing," Julee said, unwilling to expose her feelings of inferiority to anyone, even the woman who'd become her dearest friend.

"Don't give me that hogwash. You're depressed, and I'm not leaving here until you tell me why."

"Okay, okay," Julee grumbled good-naturedly. "Since you put it that way, I guess I'll tell you." She pinned Trixie with a challenging look. "Am I still attractive?"

Trixie grinned, baring a mouth filled with snowy white dentures.

"Trixie...don't start," Julee commanded.

"Start what?" Trixie asked, fluttering her fake eyelashes with pseudo-innocence.

"Don't start with that old so-that's-what-this-is-all-about look."

Trixie placed a manicured hand over her heart. "You cut me to the quick," she said. "How would I know what this is all about when you haven't told me?"

"I want to know if you think I'm still attractive."

"That's an interesting question coming from a woman who comes home at least once a week with a new tale of some creep on the job making a pass at her."

"That's different!" Julee said. "That's just a bunch of guys trying to make my life miserable."

"And doing a darn good job of it for the most part," Trixie said with a wry twist of her lips. She reached over and covered Julee's hand with hers. "You listen to me, darlin', and you listen real good. You aren't just attractive. You're downright gorgeous."

Julee blinked. Gorgeous? The idea was startling. "But I don't ever fix up anymore."

"No sense gilding the lily, as my mama would have said. Trust me. You're beautiful—inside and out."

Julee felt the sting of tears in her eyes. She squeezed the hand covering hers. "Thanks, Trixie."

"What are friends for?" Trixie asked. "You know, young lady, your problem is that you're so busy you never take time for yourself. You need to get a little selfish and pamper Julee Sutherland every now and then."

"I know, but there's never enough time."

"Take time." Wearing a suddenly thoughtful expression, Trixie cocked her head to the side and tapped her cheek with a bloodred nail. "All of this self-inventory wouldn't be because of our good-looking neighbor, now, would it?"

Julee felt the heat of a blush spreading over her features. "Not really. I mean, he's attractive, but I keep telling you I don't need a man in my life. Not now."

"And like *I've* told you before, you ain't gettin' any younger."

As Julee hoped, Trixie's visit lifted her spirits. But even her friend's reassurances didn't fully allay her fears. It was true that the last thing she needed was a man in her life, but she wasn't hypocritical enough to deny that Cain's blatant disinterest caused her some concern. In a typical feminine gesture of uncertainty, she went into her bathroom and gave herself a critical once-over in the mirror.

She seldom bothered to fix her hair in anything but a ponytail, and she was so exhausted when she got home that her skin care consisted of sunscreen during the day and creaming off the dust and grime from work in the evening. She considered herself fortunate that maintaining the natural arch of her eyebrows took nothing more than the occasional tweezing of a stray hair.

Was Trixie right? Had she relegated herself to the bottom of the list while pursuing Tad's dream and trying to be a good mother to Brice? Was Cain's apparent disinterest rooted in the fact that she'd lost her looks and maybe her whole feminine aura while trying to put her life back together?

When was the last time she'd soaked in a hot tub of sweetly scented water instead of hurrying through a shower? When was the last time she'd indulged in a manicure? A facial?

After Tad's death, she'd been smart enough to know that she couldn't make Sutherland Construction a success without the carpenters and other men who worked for her. She'd also realized that she would be a single woman working at a job typically considered a man's. In an effort to minimize the differences, she'd forgone wearing makeup to the job and made jeans and oversize shirts her everyday apparel.

It had helped, though there would always be those few men who tried crossing the invisible line she'd drawn. Even so, she understood that the catcalls and whistles and occasional crude comments were harmless for the most part, just men asserting—or maybe trying to bolster—their masculinity. God knows, she'd suffered through more sexual harassment than most women would encounter in a lifetime, but for the most part, she'd learned to tune it out. If she couldn't tune it out, she'd dealt with it.

Strangely, it wasn't the benign harassment that made her blood boil. It was the assumption that she didn't know what she was doing and would never make it in the construction business because she was a woman who'd infiltrated a man's world. It had taken a while, but she was proving them wrong.

But at what cost, Julee?

Tonight was the first time she'd considered the possibility that she'd denied her femininity for so long that she was no longer attractive. It wasn't a situation she liked.

Filled with a sense of failure and fear, she started a tub of bathwater and dumped in a generous dose of expensive bath salts Tad had bought her on their last trip to Paris. While the tub filled, she cleansed her face and plucked her eyebrows. And all the while, a part of her mind told her she was foolish.

An hour later, she'd finished a pedicure and put a hot-oil treatment on her hair. She patted herself dry and spritzed on a generous mist of Hologram—"the ultimate scent for a woman with an ever-changing mood." Then she let her hair dry naturally, rolled it in hot curlers, and slathered her body with lotion. She considered putting on makeup, but talked herself out of it, since bedtime was just a couple of hours away.

Satisfied that she'd pampered herself enough for one night—though certainly not enough to make up for the four-year lapse—she donned shorty pajamas of fine, sheer cotton lawn.

The tap-pant leg was flattering, and the sleeveless, scoop-neck top, hand embroidered with tiny pink rosebuds, revealed the swell of her breasts—not that there was anyone to appreciate that her breasts were firm and well shaped and—

Stop it, Julee! she chided herself. *What's gotten into you, anyway?*

Feeling better, but unaccountably restless, she went into the kitchen, poured herself a glass of sangria and put Kenny G on the CD player. By the time the glass was empty, her feelings about herself and the world in general were much improved. So much improved, she poured herself another glass of wine.

The last lingering light of day cast shadows on the backyard, and the hammock swaying in the evening breeze called to her with the promise of rest.

She was so lured by the serenity and the anonymity of the coming night, she slipped on her sandals and out the back door, the threat of Lanny Milligan and his vendetta far from her mind.

By the time Cain finished his conversation with Phil, darkness was beginning to settle in. Cain went to the refrigerator for another beer, carried it out onto the patio and lowered himself into a lounge chair. A few precipitate stars twinkled in the purple twilight sky. A mockingbird sat in a nearby tree, belting out its stolen songs with brash moxie. A soft breeze whispered through the trees. The rustling of the leaves sounded like a lady's starched petticoat. From the next street, a child's laughter wafted on the breath of the night.

This somnolent, waiting time before night's approach and the day's last lingering had always been a favorite of Cain's mother. Evening, she'd said, was a time to take stock. A time to admit and accept defeat as well as to plan tomorrow's strategies. A time to count victories and pat yourself on the back for the good you'd accomplished. It was a time to make peace with yourself for any mistakes you'd made and to plan a way to fix any hurts you'd caused.

A smile claimed his lips. It had been years since he'd thought of his mother's homespun philosophy, but now he admitted that it was a sound one, one more people should try, including himself.

He lowered his gaze from the darkening sky to Julee's house. Her kitchen light was on. If his mother was right, he should forgive himself for not being able to locate Brice's whereabouts. He should take the initiative and go back over and ask Julee what—if anything—"yellow hair" meant. And he should try to explain why he'd left her alone with her misery when she'd lost control earlier.

Explain? How could he explain his actions when he didn't know himself why he'd left. No, that wasn't true. He did know, but the reason wouldn't be acceptable to her. He wasn't even sure it was acceptable to him.

The truth was that if he'd stayed another second, if he'd stayed long enough to draw another breath, he'd have pulled her into his arms and offered her whatever comfort she might have found there, and the consequences be damned. Even though Julee Sutherland was off-limits, he suspected that the forbidden, once tasted, would be not only unbearably sweet, but highly addictive.

The truth was that no matter how hard he'd tried to stay away from her, no matter how foolish it was for him to dare to feel anything for her, he did. In the short nine months he'd known her, thoughts of her had taken control of his waking hours and, he suspected, his sleeping hours, as well.

Deep in his heart, Cain knew that the woman in the dream was Julee Sutherland. Maybe because the nighttime excursion into erotica was an extension of the fantasies that drifted through his mind while he filled canvas after canvas with her image....

Cain shook his head and raised the bottle to his mouth for a long pull. This was crazy. Julee wasn't interested in him in any form or fashion, so the best thing he could do was concentrate on being a good neighbor and help her find her son.

As he sat there in the gathering darkness, the object of his thoughts stepped out onto her deck. She took no more than half-a-dozen steps when she stopped. She was looking right at him.

Without a word, he set the bottle next to the chair and rose, drawn to her like a bear to a honey pot. She crossed the deck to the fence.

As they stood there, not speaking, several impressions crossed Cain's mind. She smelled divine. Looked even better. And she was wearing nothing but a short cotton robe over matching pajamas. His body responded in familiar masculine appreciation.

The encroaching darkness all but hid the apology in her eyes. "I didn't mean to run you off with my emotional...display," she said, breaking the silence.

"You didn't," Cain assured her. "I just...had to go."

Julee curled her fingers around the top of the fence. "I'm sorry for being so rude about your offer to help."

One corner of Cain's mouth hiked up in a half smile. "No problem. A lot of people don't believe in psychic phenomena."

"Seeing is believing, huh?" she asked, smiling back.

"Yeah," Cain said, a picture of a struggling Brice flashing before his eyes. "Seeing is believing." When she didn't reply, he said, "Julee, can I ask you something?"

"About Brice?"

"I don't know. I think so."

"Sure," she said with a shrug. "Why not?"

"Do the words 'yellow hair' mean anything to you?"

"Yellow hair..." she mused, a thoughtful expression on her face. "Yellow hair..." She shook her head. "Why do you ask?"

Cain's smile bordered embarrassment. "You wouldn't believe me if I told you."

"Ah..." she said with a nod of comprehension. "You got it through some vibrations or something, right?"

"Or something."

"Look, I don't want to offend you, but can we talk about something else?" she asked. "It's a beautiful night, and it's been a long, grueling day, and I'd like for five minutes not to have to talk about Brice or think about Brice...where he is, who has him...what's happened to him." Even as she spoke, a pained expression crossed her face. "Does that make me a terrible person, a terrible mother?"

Cain responded as if there were no gruesome happening in their past to separate them. He responded like a man who wanted only to comfort the woman who had somehow worked her way into his heart despite his best efforts to keep her out. Reaching out, he curled his hands over her fingers that clutched the fence top.

Julee grew very still. For a second, he wondered if she even breathed.

"No," he said in a soft voice. "I think it makes you very human."

She shook her head. "Well, when I said as much to my mother-in-law earlier, she looked at me for a second or two as if I'd sprouted another head. By the time she said she understood, it was too late. The guilt had already set in."

"There's no need to feel guilty," Cain told her, his thumb sweeping across her fingers in a gentle caress. "No one could doubt your love for Brice, especially your mother-in-law. Sometimes our stress levels reach overload, and we've got to release the pressure before we explode."

"Better stand back," she said. "I think I'm getting close."

Cain laughed. His fingers tightened over hers. "So what do you think would give you a little peace of mind?"

"A full night's sleep with no dreams?" she said with a shrug. "I don't know."

"Sleep? You can do better than that. C'mon. Close your eyes and just let yourself go...tell me what comes to mind."

"This is crazy," she said, even as her eyes drifted shut.

"What do you see?"

"A beach," she said without hesitation. "White sand. Moonlight on the water."

The words, each spoken a little softer than the last, brought a sharp image to Cain's mind. His eyes drifted shut, and immediately he saw himself on the beach with a woman...the waves licking the shore, his tongue licking the salt from her neck....

"What else?" He hardly recognized the passion-thick voice as his own.

"A bird's cry. Some night bird. The scent of sea air."

The bird called; a gust of wind sent a fine mist of salty spray over him and the woman. She shivered and he drew her closer, warming her body with his, warming her mouth with his lips. But the moment their lips touched, he knew it wasn't the air that made her quiver like a leaf in a chill wind. It was the passion.

Her mouth parted, and, as their tongues danced in an age-old ritual of desire, she threaded her fingers through his hair to hold him close. His hands drifted up over her arms to her shoulders...and dragged down the silky fabric of her dress...baring her breasts to his touch...to his mouth.

Julee's sharp intake of breath shattered Cain's mental imagery. She jerked her hands free, and his eyes flew open. The ocean scene had vanished. There was no sand, no sea air, nothing left of the moment but an uncomfortable throbbing in his groin and the certainty that his suspicion was right. Julee was the woman in his dreams.

She took one step back and then another, staring up at him, her eyes wide with wonder and something akin to fear.

"What are you doing?" she asked in a harsh whisper. "What are you doing to me?"

Cain reached out to stop her and grabbed a handful of the night. "Julee! Wait!"

His plea fell on deaf ears. She was already halfway to her house.

Julee wrenched open the back door, dashed inside and clicked the dead bolt into place. Breathing heavily, she leaned against the door and squeezed her eyes to shut out the vivid picture still lurking in her mind. Willing her pulse to normalcy, she struggled to make sense of what had just happened between her and Cain. It didn't take more than a moment to know she couldn't make sense of it, because it simply didn't make sense.

She had been holding on to the fence, her hands imprisoned by his. But when he had told her to close her eyes and describe what she saw, she'd begun to feel as if she was reliving one of her dreams. For a moment she could feel the damp, salty air and the weight of the man's body pressing her into the sand... *Cain's* body fitted against hers in the most intimate way, *Cain's* mouth on hers, on her breasts....

Julee gave a tormented moan and covered her face with her hands. It seemed so real she'd actually believed Cain had touched her intimately, had practically accused him of it. But she knew that he hadn't, because all the time the Cain in her mind was touching her body with his hands, she could feel the real Cain's hands clutching hers on the fence.

What did it mean? Was it possible that there was something to this psychic stuff after all?

Don't be ridiculous, Julee. Stop making excuses for what amounts to nothing but the plain and simple fact that you felt something sexual for a man for the first time since Tad died.

There was nothing wrong with that, was there? As Trixie said, it was time she started thinking of herself and her needs.

But not with Cain.

No. Not with Cain.

Hot tears filled Julee's eyes. She turned off the kitchen light and went into her bedroom, longing only for sleep, praying for a brief respite from the problems plaguing her life.

To drown out the irritating dripping of the shower, she put a Yanni recording in the CD player and crawled between the cool sheets. But the usually soothing music did nothing to calm her; instead, the haunting melodies filled her with a heart-deep loneliness and the guilty, irrefutable knowledge that her body ached for Cain Collier's touch.

For the first time since Brice's birth, Julee fell asleep with tears in her eyes and Tad's name on her lips, to sleep and perchance to dream....

But this time the dream had a terrifying twist.

Sleep was impossible. Cain didn't even consider trying it. Instead, he got another beer and set to work on his painting with a frenzy that surprised even him. Yet even though he was centered on his work, there was a part of his mind that was able to think along another plane. A part that relived the scene with Julee.

Her shocked reaction implied that she'd experienced similar, if not the same, emotions he had while he relived his dream in exquisite, seductive detail. Was it possible? he wondered. Had he actually made love to her with his mind?

When he added the finishing touches to the painting at 3:00 a.m., he was no nearer an answer to his questions than when he started. He was, however, very drunk. Without bothering to clean his brushes—a blatant and unforgivable act tantamount to desecration—he fell into bed with his clothes on and promptly passed out.

The dreams started almost at once.

First, there was The Dream. This time there was no doubt the woman was Julee. The setting had become so familiar he might have picked up where they left off out by the fence. There was the moonlight, the sea, the driving, rhythmic passion that carried them ever nearer to fulfillment.

Cain was nearing satisfaction when something bright drew his attention. He looked up and saw flames dancing on the face of the water, and on the far shore of the sea—that had somehow become a pond—a house was blazing against an evening sky.

Part of him recognized that Julee was gone and he was alone. Not a single remnant of that dream remained. Someone cried out for help. Two voices. One, a child's; the other, a woman's. Amy. Holly. They were in the house, and it was burning... burning....

"No-o-o-o!" Cain screamed, the sound ripping up through his tight throat from his very soul. He started to run... through the brush and around the edge of the pond, his feet crunching on leaves and snapping dead twigs. But no matter how hard he ran, the house seemed farther away than ever.

"I know where you are," a voice taunted from the shadowy darkness of the woods. "And I'm going to get you and your family...."

The voice spurred Cain to a faster pace, even though he thought he was running as fast as he could. Suddenly he found himself a few short yards from the blazing house. A woman's silhouette appeared at the window, and he heard Amy call out his name.

He sprinted closer, so close the heat beat against him in blistering waves. And then it seemed that the house was melting, sinking in on itself. It wasn't until he saw Julee's face at the window and heard her say sorrowfully, "Too late . . . too late again," that he realized the house was collapsing beneath its own weight.

Disbelief swept through him with the force of a back draft. He couldn't lose them. Not again. He couldn't lose Julee. "No-o-o!" he howled, flailing his arms and forcing himself nearer the disintegrating house. "No!"

The sound of his voice penetrated the dream and Cain fought his way up through the layers of sleep. A harsh, frightening noise filled the room. It took him a few seconds to realize the sound was his own labored breathing and that he was sitting in his bed, drenched with perspiration, his chest heaving like an old-fashioned bellows.

Outside his window, dawn was a gray opalescence, and the first awakening birds twittered in joyous communion with Mother Nature. Their cheerfulness was a macabre jest contrasted to the horror he'd just experienced.

A dream, he thought, his body twitching in a nervous reaction. *Only a dream.* Relief spread through him, leaving him feeling like a stick of melted butter. He let the weakness claim him and sank back against the pillow, throwing his forearm over his face while his body struggled to regain its equilibrium.

Why had he dreamed about the fire again? Was this thing with Julee and Brice and the sudden return of his psychometry dredging up old memories as well as tantalizing him with inconclusive bursts of information? And what, if anything, did dreaming about the fire mean?

Cain squeezed his eyes shut and brought back the moment when he'd lifted his head and seen the fire across the lake. His breath caught at the sudden awareness that the burning house wasn't the same house he'd dreamed about before Amy's and Holly's deaths. But the rest was the same.

The blaze of the flames against the darkening sky, the sounds of their anguished voices calling out to him for help...

Why was the house different, and what was Julee doing in the fire that had destroyed his family? Cain didn't have a clue. Nor did he have any idea to whom the threatening voice in the woods belonged.

He dreamed about Julee. About finally having the chance to get back at her for ruining his life. He'd show her and her money-grubbing husband that revenge went beyond the grave. He already had the boy, but he wasn't finished yet. If it was the last thing he did he'd make her understand exactly how it felt to lose a child....

Chapter Seven

When Julee woke up Thursday morning, her head throbbed from the wine she'd drunk the night before, her eyes felt swollen and her nose was stopped up from her crying.

Sometime during the night, when her roiling thoughts had settled down and exhaustion had finally overcome the monotonous, nerve-racking dripping of the shower, she'd had The Dream again, but somehow, that dream had vanished and she'd found herself alone in a room filled with smoke and the frightening, crackling sounds of fire. She'd called out—to Cain, instead of Tad—and when she'd looked out through the flames licking at the window, she'd seen him running toward her before the house gave a mighty groan and started to collapse.

She awakened with a cry and found herself sitting straight up in bed, her body trembling and her heart thudding in fear. As nightmares went, it had been a humdinger. According to all the dream specialists, dreams were ways of working out problems, but if that was the case, what did the fire signify? Julee pondered the question for at least an hour before falling back to sleep. This time her rest was deep and dreamless, and she awoke to the bright sunshine of a new day, another day that brought the hope of locating Brice.

Donning the robe that matched her pajamas—the pajamas she could have sworn Cain peeled from her shoulders at the fence the evening before—she headed barefoot for the kitchen.

While the coffee dripped, Julee dialed Trixie's number. Her eccentric neighbor had analyzed some of her dreams before and her reasoning had made a lot of sense, so why not let her take a crack at this newest one?

Trixie answered on the third ring, sounding as bright and chipper as the blue jay chattering outside Julee's open back door.

"Hi, Trix. You up?"

"Am I up?" The question was accompanied by a throaty laugh. "Of course I'm up. These old bones of mine won't let me be a slugabed. What's happening your way?"

"I was wondering if fire in a dream has any significant meaning."

"It's hard to say, darlin'. I'd need to know the context."

Julee hesitated, not wanting to admit to dreaming of making love with Cain on the beach.

"There's something you don't want to tell me," Trixie said, her intuition on alert when Julee didn't answer immediately. "I'll be right over. I'm more intimidating in person."

The phone clicked in Julee's ear and she set the receiver back on the hook. There was no use calling and telling Trixie not to come over or that she was about as intimidating as a ladybug. Trixie would just pooh-pooh her excuses and come anyway.

Julee got two mugs from the cabinet and cubed enough ham to double the size of her omelet, wondering how she could tell Trixie about the dream without mentioning Cain's name. One thing was certain, the older woman wouldn't leave until she'd worn down Julee's every argument and weaseled all she could from her.

The front doorbell pealed, and Julee went to let her neighbor in. Trixie, wearing a flowing caftan of bright tropical birds and a *tignon*, preceded Julee to the kitchen, leaving behind a wake of perfume and disgusting cheerfulness.

Spying the omelet makings on the cutting board, she smiled. "Mmm. Western omelets. My favorite. Is there anything I can do to help?"

"Just pour yourself a cup of coffee and keep me company," Julee said, turning the heat on under the skillet. Trixie complied and settled herself at the table, her chin in her thin hand. "I've been thinking about it, and I came to the conclusion that the only reason you might not want to talk about your dream is if it was a little, um...risqué? Am I right?"

Julee pinned her neighbor with a stern look. "I don't know about your cards and your horoscopes, but you're pretty sharp about human nature."

"It comes from living a long and full life," Trixie said, with a serene, satisfied smile. "So I'm right, and the dream was about you and a man. It was probably Cain, since—"

"Why do you think it was Cain?" Julee interrupted, a look of exasperation on her face.

Trixie snapped her fingers. "Elementary, my dear Watson. He's the only man in miles you have any contact with, and probably the only one in that radius with enough sex appeal to stir up a decent dream—'' she smiled wickedly ''—or maybe that's an *in*decent dream.''

Julee felt herself responding to Trixie's smile. ''You're incorrigible.''

''But not boring.''

''Never.''

''Now that we've established what a rare and wonderful person I am, how about telling me about the dream you had about Cain?''

Keeping her attention glued to the omelet she was watching, Julee said, ''Actually, I've been having this dream at least once a week since I moved in here. I didn't realize until last night that the man is Cain.''

Without going into all the salient details, Julee gave Trixie a condensed version of the dream, omitting the incident that transpired between her and Cain at the fence the night before.

When she finished, Trixie shook her head. ''I don't think that one needs much analyzing. It pretty much speaks for itself, wouldn't you say?''

Julee nodded.

''What I'd like to know is why neither you nor Cain will act on this attraction if it's as strong as it appears and you both feel it?''

''I don't think Cain does feel it.''

''Of course he does. I've watched him watch you for almost a year now.''

That was encouraging, but Trixie might be wrong. She might be imagining Cain's interest because she wanted it so much for Julee. Besides, there was the other problem.

Julee served up the omelets, her mind weighing the wisdom of telling Trixie her concerns about her feelings for Cain. Trixie read the paper, so she knew about their strange, entangled pasts. Still, Trixie could give her another perspective, and maybe admitting her fears would set her free, the way admitting to an addiction was the first step to recovery.

"It would never work between me and Cain," she said at last.

"Why not?"

"You read the article in the paper. His wife and daughter died in a fire in a house Tad was responsible for building, and Cain's brother-in-law is the man who shot Tad."

Trixie's lined face wore a look of tender solicitation. "I knew your husband was dead and that you were trying to keep his business going, and I knew Cain had lost his family in a fire, but I never made the connection until I read Mavis's article." She shook her head. "I must be slipping."

"Don't be silly!" Julee said. "Why would you?"

Trixie shook her head again, a thoughtful expression on her lined face. Then she took a sip of coffee. "Tell me more about the fire in your dream last night."

While they ate their omelets and whole-wheat toast, Julee recounted how the dream had changed and how she'd awakened scared to death. Goose bumps rose on her arms as she felt the insidious fear creeping up on her again.

Trixie pursed her lips and didn't speak for several minutes. "Just taking the dream at face value, it seems to me that the fire represents this blazing attraction between you and Cain. Obviously there's a lot of guilt on both sides. I'd say that you think your feelings for Cain show disloyalty to Tad's memory and even a fear that giving in to these feelings might ultimately destroy the life you've rebuilt, which, of course, is symbolized by the house in the dream. The collapse of the house is the collapse of your old life and your old dreams. It's so obvious, really." She smiled at Julee. "You can't rebuild until you tear down."

Julee felt her last lingering bit of horror slip away. Trixie's explanation made so much sense, she couldn't believe she'd been so terrified. She told the older woman as much, gave her a hug and thanked her.

Trixie pretended not to be moved by the display of affection. "You know you're way off track here, don't you?" she said when Julee released her and went to refill their cups.

"What do you mean?"

"There's absolutely no reason for you or Cain to suffer any guilt or not to act on your feelings. You're both just victims of circumstance. Why should you sentence yourself to a life of blame just because you were married to Tad Sutherland? The law said he was innocent, so why are you carrying around this load of guilt?"

"Cain's family died in that fire, Trixie."

"Did you set it? Did you or Tad deliberately use defective wiring? Did you or Tad want to hurt those people?"

"Of course not!"

"Did Cain pull the trigger of the gun that shot Tad?"

Julee shook her head. "I've never felt the slightest bit of blame toward him. He isn't Lanny Milligan's keeper. As a matter of fact, Cain never cast the least bit of blame on Tad or appeared to hold him responsible in any way. He said it was just one of those freak things a person never expects to happen."

"Exactly," Trixie said with a firm nod. "So do what he appears to have done. Put it behind you. Go on with your life. Stop beating yourself up for something that wasn't your fault, and stop trying to atone for it by killing yourself with work and denying yourself any kind of life beyond building perfect houses and taking care of Brice. You're young—you deserve to be happy!"

The strength of her conviction was reflected in the fierce glow in Trixie's eyes. The idea of letting go and embracing a new life, one free of guilt and filled with the promise of happiness, was not only alien but frightening to Julee. Her future had been so uncertain since the fire that her only sanctuary had been in living in the past, living for Tad and his dream.

"That's easier said than done," she said at last.

"I'm sure you're right, but if you keep shouldering the blame for something you had no part in, it'll send you to an early grave or turn you into a bitter old woman," Trixie said in her characteristically blunt way. "Brice deserves better than that for a mother."

"Assuming they find him before Lanny Milligan does something to him," Julee said, her eyes filling with tears. "You know, I've thought that when Lanny calls again—if he calls again—I'd offer myself in exchange for Brice. Do you think he'd go for it?"

"It's hard to deal with a mad person, darlin'," Trixie said with a shrug of her narrow, bony shoulders. "What you ought to do is ask Cain for help."

"Trixie, you know I don't believe all that extrasensory perception stuff," Julee said, but she knew her denial lacked the conviction it might have held just twenty-four hours earlier. While she couldn't claim to be a believer in ESP or clairvoyance, her encounter with Cain had shaken the foundation of her long-held tenets. But after her behavior the night before, she wasn't sure she could even face him again, much less ask for his help.

"So you don't believe. That doesn't make it not true, does it?" Trixie said. "That handsome Detective Garvey doesn't seem to be getting anywhere. He can't find Lanny. All he can do is send those patrolmen driving around the neighborhood every hour or so."

Julee didn't know if it was weariness or Trixie's way of wearing down her arguments, but she had to admit the reasoning made a strange sort of sense. "Assuming I decide to ask Cain for his help, how do I go about it? He's made it very clear that part of his life is painful, something he'd rather not deal with. What do I do? Just go up and ask for his help?"

"He's had to deal with it. And people who truly have the gift can't help but use it."

Trixie made it all sound so simple, so logical. Maybe she was right, Julee thought, but what could she do? Just walk up to his front door, ring his doorbell and ask for his help?

After Trixie left, Julee called Dylan and was told there were no new leads on Brice's whereabouts and no signs of Lanny Milligan, even though Houma's finest were keeping a close watch on both her house and Cain's, and the county and state boys were patrolling the highways and byways.

Julee sighed. There was nothing to do but go to work. She found her crew hard at it. The outside work was more or less done, and the crew putting up the drywall had finished taping and floating the day before. The walls would be textured by day's end, and she'd have the painters standing by to start tomorrow. The cabinets were in, and the installation of the plumbing and light fixtures was well under way. If all went according to schedule, the house should be finished in time for her to pocket the bonus Rocky Melancon had offered.

Luther told her he'd hired two new men, and Julee finally remembered to tell him about her dripping showerhead. Luther promised to check with the plumbing contractor to see when he could pull one of his men from a job long enough to drive to Julee's and fix it.

As one task and another carried her through the day, Trixie's advice was never far from her mind. Julee was still considering the wisdom of asking Cain for his help when she got back home after a long and muggy day.

She checked with Chantal and was told that the phone lines had been silent and that the police had come up with zip. The only positive thing that had happened was that the plumber had shown up to fix the dripping showerhead. Thank goodness she'd rid her life of at least one thing that contributed to her sleeplessness.

Julee packed everyone off for the day and went to take a shower. She was standing beneath the tepid spray when she glanced down and saw that the plumber had forgotten his wrench. It lay in the wall corner of the tub in a pool of water. If she didn't move it, water would make a rusty place on the granite tub.

Feeling clean and refreshed after her shower, Julee went into the kitchen to start thawing a chicken breast for her dinner.

She was halfway through the preparation of a salad when she decided to call Dylan and feel him out about asking for Cain's help. No, better yet, she'd go down to the station and talk to Dylan in person. She was feeling restless . . . antsy, as Trixie might say, and getting out for a while might do her some good.

She found Dylan at his desk finishing up a last bit of paperwork before going home for the day.

"I won't keep you long," Julee said, sitting down in a cracked vinyl chair. "But I wanted to run something by you."

"Shoot," Dylan said, a frown puckering his forehead.

"Ouch!" Julee said. "Bad pun, Detective Garvey."

The frown disappeared and Dylan laughed. "I guess I've been in the business too long. What did you want to ask?"

Julee took a deep breath and plunged before her courage faded. "I know we've talked before about Cain Collier's supposed psychic ability and how he used to help the New Orleans police. I just wondered if you'd..." Her voice trailed away.

"Considered asking for his help?" Dylan said, finishing the statement for her.

"Yes."

Dylan picked up a pencil and began to doodle stars and crescents on a yellow legal pad. "I guess you'd have to be a believer in that sort of thing to contemplate using it to help crack a case, and I can't actually claim to believe in what he does."

"Do I detect one of those worrisome 'buts' in your voice, Dylan?" Her question was reminiscent of their first conversation, when Dylan had noticed her reticence about Cain.

"Yeah, you do." Dylan leaned back in his chair and crossed his arms over his chest. "You know that I talked to Cain about his alleged gift when the article ran in the paper."

Julee nodded. "Yes."

"I told him flat out that I didn't believe all that crap and told him he was a suspect until his alibi checked out or until we caught the perpetrator—whichever came first. When I left his place, he asked if he could use my pen. I gave it to him, and after he'd held it for a while, he told me some things about me and my dad that no one knows except Chantal."

Julee saw dismay and a look that could only be described as troubled on her new friend's face. "That's...interesting," she said, thinking of her own encounter with Cain's particular brand of magic.

"Spooky is a better description than interesting," Dylan said.

Julee knew the feeling. "So while you're hesitant about saying you believe, you can't deny that there's something there?"

"Right, but even if I believed in Cain's ability a hundred percent, I'd hesitate asking for his help."

"Why?"

"Because even though he seems like a nice enough guy and his alibi checks out, there's a part of me that's still troubled by the fact that he's related to Lanny and that Brice came up missing just days before Lanny made a break for freedom with every intention of harming you and yours."

Julee had played through the same scenario a dozen times since learning of Lanny Milligan's escape. She thought of her conversation with Trixie, who'd said Cain shouldn't be blamed for Tad's death just because he was related to Lanny by marriage. Should he be blamed for Brice's disappearance for the same reason?

"I agree that it's a strange coincidence, but I honestly think that's all it is."

As she spoke, Julee realized that she believed what she was saying. She didn't know if it was the incident with Cain the previous evening and her tumultuous hormones, or the talk with Trixie, but something had tipped the scales in Cain's favor.

"It's your kid, your call," Dylan said.

"I honestly don't know what to do," she said with a sigh. "No reflection on you or the department, but there just aren't any leads. Maybe Cain can give us something to go on, a starting place." Julee gave a self-conscious laugh. "As my neighbor says, just because I don't believe in something doesn't mean it isn't true."

"Good point," Dylan conceded. He drew a small pad from his pocket and began to scribble down a name and number. "Cain's uncle happens to be a cop in Thibodaux as well as a good friend of mine. Why don't you give him a call? Maybe he can shed some light on the situation and you can make a more educated decision."

"Sounds good," Julee said.

Dylan gave her Phil Rousseau's number and told her he'd be waiting to hear from her after she talked to Phil. "I'll abide by whatever decision you make," he said. "You want to consult psychics, we'll consult psychics. You want us to gaze into a crystal ball, we'll be happy to oblige."

"Thanks, Dylan," Julee told him, extending her hand. "You don't know how much your and Chantal's support has meant to me through all this."

Dylan's hand swallowed hers. "If we've helped in any way, we're happy."

Julee stood. "Oh, by the way, I called your father to see if he'd been contacted for ransom money," Dylan said. "He's out of the country for a few days." Seeing the look on her face, he said, "I have to look into every possibility."

Julee smiled sadly. "I know." Without a word she left the room and started back home. Knowing Dylan as she was beginning to, she understood his reluctance to accept Cain at face value. Dylan's ever-questioning and often suspicious mind were just two of many assets that made him the good cop he was. She couldn't fault him for his uneasy feelings about Cain.

At least her feelings for Cain were settled. Her admission of her attraction for him was a major breakthrough, and reaching the decision that he couldn't have had anything to do with Brice's disappearance was like having a heavy load lifted from her shoulders. While she wasn't certain what had brought about the change in her attitude, she *was* certain that if she didn't have a deep, abiding belief in his innocence, no amount of sexual excitement could have swayed her to change her mind.

With that reconciled in her mind, she could concentrate on whether or not to ask Cain for his help in locating Brice.

She phoned Phil Rousseau as soon as she got home. Her lengthy conversation with Cain's uncle was as enlightening as it was chastening. While she still wasn't sure she believed Cain possessed any psychic ability—or even if she believed in such a thing—she did know that Phil Rousseau believed. His account of how Cain's gift had complicated his marriage and his life was sobering.

When Phil explained how Cain was already being inundated by skeptics and people who were asking for his help, she couldn't hide her surprise. And when Phil told her that Cain had been suspended from his job at the high school and that the school board was not renewing his contract for the following year, her heart throbbed with a painful ache.

Detective Rousseau's accounts of how Cain had helped him and the New Orleans police were fascinating and amazing... and more important to Julee, they were documented on a case-by-case account.

She hung up feeling that whatever it was Cain possessed, there could be no harm in asking him to help locate Brice. Even the smallest clue might expedite the investigation, and, at the very least, he might be able to tell the police something about Lanny Milligan's personality that would clue them as to what action he might take next.

She reached for the phone book to look up Cain's number and stopped, overcome again with embarrassment over her behavior the night before.

Don't be ridiculous, Julee, she chided. *Isn't Brice's welfare worth swallowing your pride?*

Of course it was. She looked up Cain's number and went into the kitchen, where she could see the back of his house. Even though it wasn't dark yet, there was a light on in the kitchen. Drawing a fortifying breath, Julee punched in his number. No one answered, and after the fourth ring, his machine kicked in. She hung up without leaving a message, more disappointed than she cared to admit.

Obviously, Cain had gone away and forgotten to turn out the light, or he was working and didn't want to be interrupted. She supposed she could go over and talk to him, but her bravery didn't extend to a face-to-face confrontation—not tonight, anyway.

She ate her solitary meal and went to bed early. The showerhead didn't drip, but she couldn't sleep for thinking about the possibility of Lanny hiding somewhere outside just waiting for her to fall asleep. She jumped at every scrape of a bush, every creak of a board. She tensed every time a cloud crossed the face of the crescent moon.

Outside, the Houma police made their rounds, flashing their lights into the hidden corners of her yard and along the shadow-shrouded places where shrubs made perfect hiding places for anyone who might not want to be seen.

Toward morning, weariness overcame her fears. She slept and dreamed the dream again. This time, there was no fire, except the one Cain ignited in her body wherever his lips and hands touched....

Their bodies fused, they moved together like a clipper ship riding a high sea before a trade wind... easily, effortlessly. Twining her fingers in his hair, she writhed beneath his weight, seeking a closeness she knew would be enough only if he penetrated her very soul.

Soft-lapping waves of sensation undulated through her, swelling, building toward a crest that would shatter on the shore of all her illusions...about love, life and the past. Too long alone, too long empty, she welcomed it....

With a shudder of surrender and a cry of ecstasy, she arched upward, wringing an answering cry of gratification from him while the sea sighed around them and the night bird, accompanied by the soft suspiration of the wind, sang of pirates, plunder and passion.

Afterward, all was still, except for the wild beating of her heart and the fluttering of faraway angels' wings....

The screech of a gull awakened him. The lingering scent of damp ocean air mingled with the heady fragrances of warm woman and a night of making love. Cain rolled to his side, fully expecting to feel the heat of naked flesh beneath his fingertips. Instead, he encountered the smoothness of percale sheets.

He opened his eyes and saw the jeans he'd tossed onto a nearby chair the night before. Disbelief—and disappointment—swelled inside him. He wasn't on a beach at all. Julee wasn't lying beside him replete with lovemaking. He was in his own bedroom, and it wasn't yet daylight.

Groaning in frustration, Cain rolled on to his stomach and wrapped his arms around his pillow, wishing it were Julee. He drew in a deep breath and closed his eyes. In a matter of seconds sleep claimed him once again. His last thought before succumbing to the arms of Morpheus was that the pillowcase held the distinct and unmistakable perfume of ocean air....

When he woke an hour and a half later, the dream was like a sweet and unforgettable melody, filling the corridors of his mind with bits of memory... tantalizing him with a partially remembered kiss, a half-remembered touch.

He was exhausted, as wrung out as if he'd swum the English Channel. He had to start getting some rest. Not only were his dreams wearing him out, the painting of the woman on the beach had kept him busy the past two days and up until all hours the past two nights. The work was coming along extremely well—he thought that perhaps it was the best thing he'd done in years—but the intensity that possessed him while he stood before the easel was taking its toll. He could hardly pull himself away from it to do anything else, including taking time out to eat or answer the phone.

Grunting in weariness, Cain got up and went into the bathroom, where he stood beneath the stinging needles of a cold shower until his teeth started to chatter. Freezing, but awake and feeling seminormal, he drew on a pair of cutoff jeans without bothering with underwear.

He headed for the kitchen and straight to the coffeepot. He poured a mugful and inhaled the aroma of the pungent chicory-laced coffee. Thank God for the automatic-brew setting, he thought, taking his first sip with all the eagerness of a wino too long without a bottle.

He took another swallow and set the cup down long enough to check out the contents of the refrigerator. A cardboard carton held three lone eggs. The bacon had grown some sort of mold that defied imagination, but he found two pieces of thin-sliced deli ham that were only partially dried out.

Smiling, he pulled them from the meat drawer. He'd warm them up after he'd scrambled his eggs—which he proceeded to do while trying to keep from looking at Julee's house every other second. A few minutes later, he sat down to a breakfast that he rounded off with four slices of buttered toast and a bowl of cereal.

Too full for his morning run, he rinsed his breakfast utensils and put them into the dishwasher. Unable to wait any longer, he carried his third cup of coffee out onto the porch and sat down to keep vigil over Julee's house, something he found himself doing when he finally did take a break from the painting.

There had been a constant flow of people out onto Julee's deck and yard lately, workers with the missing-children's group he supposed—women for the most part, though he had seen a man or two wandering around. He thought he recognized a couple of them, probably parents of kids he taught in school.

He took another drink of coffee and sighed. He really should go over and see if there was anything more he could do. The change of pace would do him good, and it would be the neighborly thing. But neighborliness was the last thing he felt for Julee Sutherland. Bewitchment was more like it. Or enchantment.

He wondered if she was awake, what she was having for breakfast... if she ate breakfast. He pictured her in the shower, the washcloth moving over her body with slow languor. He imagined the little triangle-shaped birthmark near her navel that he'd kissed a dozen times in his dreams. Envisioned her standing naked in front of her closet, trying to decide what to wear.

The sudden shrilling of the telephone at his side sent coffee sloshing all over his hand and elicited an irritated curse. Wiping the hot liquid on his shorts, he reached for the cordless phone.

"Hello."

"Cain!"

Julee! And from the sound of it, she was terrified. His gaze slewed to her kitchen window. Even with the distance of their two yards between them, he could see her standing at the sink, the telephone in her hand. He bolted to his feet and moved instinctively down the steps toward the fence, his eyes never leaving her silhouette. "Julee, what's wrong?"

"Can I come over? I need to talk to you," she said in a rush.

"Sure," he said, bewildered both by the panic in her voice and the fact that she was asking for his help. Their eyes locked across the expanse of grass. "Is something the matter? Has something happened to Brice?"

"No," she said, shaking her head. Then she added, "I don't know. He called me again, Cain. Just now."

"Who?"

"Lanny."

His heart plummeted to his toes. "Lanny! Are you sure?" He heard her breath catch on a sob and watched as she changed the phone to the other ear so she could wipe a stray tear from her cheek. She nodded.

"Lanny said he's coming after me, and he means it, Cain. He really means it. Please," she said, her voice fading to a whisper. "Help me."

Though Cain had cursed every person who'd asked for his help since the story of his psychic proclivities had hit the paper, he knew he wouldn't—couldn't—deny Julee anything.

"Come" was all he said.

She disappeared from sight and there was a sudden buzzing in his ears. It took him a few seconds to realize she'd hung up. He hit the off button and started back toward the house. He stopped at the coffeepot and topped off his cup, then started through the house to unlock the door. He'd barely reached the door before the bell rang. Julee must have come at a dead run.

He turned the knob and opened the door. With an anguished cry, her body slammed into his, and her arms went around him tightly, sweetly. The heat of her tears wet the hair on his chest. A surfeit of emotions transmitted themselves from her to him: Sorrow. Hopelessness. Terror.

Cain was certain that this was perhaps the closest to heaven he might get in this lifetime. He cradled her head in his palms and forced her to look up at him. Moisture glazed her red-rimmed eyes. Her misery caused his heart to break into a thousand pieces.

"What's happened?" he asked in a voice rough with concern. "This is more than a phone call."

"H-how do you know?" She hiccuped. A wan smile teased her lips and her off-beat, misplaced sense of humor surfaced as it often did at strange times. "ESP?"

"I know because you said he'd called before, and I've never known you to go to pieces this way. Now, tell me what happened."

"He's been in my house, Cain," she told him, her eyes wide with fear.

Cain felt a shiver of apprehension quake through him as he recalled Lanny's marked lack of remorse for killing Tad. "How do you know?"

"He left me a note in my lingerie drawer," Julee said. She shook her head. "I don't know how I missed it last night. I—"

"Never mind," Cain interrupted. "What did the note say?"

"The same thing he says on the phone. That he's coming."

Lanny woke with a smile on his face. The sharp pain in his gut drew a gasp and forced him into a fetal position, but nothing could dampen his high spirits—not the fact that his vomiting was getting worse or the giant roach crawling on the stained wall of the grubby room he rented by the week. Things were falling into place. Time was getting close.

Getting into her house had been so easy. When he'd overheard Luther Mabry ask the plumber about sending someone to fix her dripping showerhead, he'd just volunteered to take care of it since the plumbers were all busy. The plumber had been grateful, the foreman had called the house to clear it, and thirty minutes later, Lanny had sashayed in like he owned the place. It bothered him that be'd forgotten the wrench, but by the time the cops made the connection to him, it wouldn't matter.

Little Julee had done well for herself, and after checking things out, he'd decided that his first impression was right. Trying to take her at her house was too risky. There were too many cops prowling the streets, and besides, his former brother-in-law lived just behind. He'd seen Cain sitting on his porch and he'd gotten the shakes. The guy was too damned spooky for words.

He knew too well how Cain got into people's minds just by touching them or holding a belonging. One of Lucy's favorite ways to show off had been to trot her friends over to show off Cain's skills. But watching him in action was enough to give a corpse the creeps as far as Lanny was concerned, and trying to nab Julee Sutherland with Cain so nearby was out of the question.

Lanny shivered. All he needed was for Cain to pick up on his thoughts or whatever the hell it was he did. Then his goose would be cooked for sure.

No, he had a better plan. He would lure Ms. Julee Sutherland away from her house, and cook *her* goose. . . .

Chapter Eight

Once Cain got Julee settled down enough that she could speak in coherent sentences, he urged her to talk.

"Tell me everything," he said. "And start at the fire. We've got to have all the information if we're going to be able to work through this." He didn't say it, but what he meant was that they needed all the information if they were going to be able to keep her alive.

Julee nodded and sipped from the mug of coffee Cain had brought her. Though neither stopped to examine why, they both knew the time had passed for keeping secrets from each other. The time had come for honesty and for sharing past heartbreaks and present fears if they were ever to dare spit in the face of fate by contemplating a future together.

She told him about Tad, about moving to Houma after Brice's birth, and about her problems keeping the business going. He told her how the notoriety connected to his psychic abilities had been both blessing and curse, giving him a feeling of having accomplished something worthwhile, yet coming between him and Amy and making him feel that he'd failed her in some inexplicable way.

He told Julee how the move to Houma and Holly's birth had come too late to save his floundering marriage, and explained how his wife and daughter happened to be at the Milligan residence when the fire occurred.

"It was a long time before I forgave myself for not knowing the dream was a real warning and not just some kind of guilt trip my mind had fabricated," he told Julee.

"But it wasn't your fault."

"Not being outside when Brice was taken isn't your fault, either," he said, "but knowing that on an intellectual level doesn't help much, does it?"

Pressing her lips together tightly, Julee shook her head. "How does your psychic ability work?" she asked, leaning forward in her chair, an earnest expression in her eyes. "Maybe if I understood more about the principles that make it work, it wouldn't be so hard to believe."

"I don't know what principles govern it, and I don't know how it works or why it works for me," Cain told her. "I think it's something we're all born with, and some people develop their ability more than others."

"I don't have any psychic ability."

"Sure you do. Have you ever had someone on your mind for no reason and had them phone you out of the blue?"

"Sure, but that's coincidence."

"Is it? What about knowing Brice is into something he shouldn't be or having an uneasy feeling about something for absolutely no reason?"

Julee thought about the unsettled feeling she'd experienced just prior to the fire while she and Tad vacationed in Italy. Had the feeling of foreboding been some sort of psychic foreknowledge? "I thought that was just woman's—or mother's—intuition."

"And it is. What I do works the same way only better. Usually," he tacked on with a smile. "What I do is just—" he paused, seeking the right word "—open myself up, set my mind free and let it...I don't know...*roam* or something. More often than not, I receive things. Pictures. Impressions. Bits of speech. Sometimes it's like I'm in some person's body, or I sort of *become* that person. It can be very...unsettling."

More like terrifying, Julee thought, recalling the look on Cain's face when she'd confronted him out in the street the day Brice disappeared.

Cain offered Julee a thin smile. "The problem is that I never know what to expect or if it will work. It's frustrating."

Julee gave a lift of her dark eyebrows. "I still don't know if I believe all this, but it does sound like both a blessing and a curse."

"That about sums it up," Cain said. He gestured toward her mug of coffee, which was almost empty. "Enough of that. How about a refill?"

"No, thanks."

Cain got some coffee for himself and sat back down. "When did the phone calls from Lanny start?"

"Five or six months ago. I remember because I'd just fired one of my carpenters, and I thought it was him."

"Why did you fire him?"

"He kept making moves on me—not just crude comments and innuendo—and I took it as long as I could. The day he cornered me inside a house and put his hand down my blouse, I'd had enough."

"But is that reason enough for him to threaten you?"

"I don't know. Mel has an ego the size of Texas and an ugly disposition to match," Julee said, her voice thoughtful. "The day I let him go, he got really nasty and swore he'd hound me the rest of my days, that I'd pay for what I did to him. He kept his promise."

"How?"

Julee's mouth turned down at the corners. "It just so happened that Mel's wife's father is on the police jury. He has a lot of friends in high places. Ever since I fired him, it's been the health department or one inspector or another giving me grief. When the calls started, I figured it must be Mel. I had no idea it was Lanny until he called after the escape." She frowned. "Could Lanny have called me from prison?"

"Absolutely," Cain said. "Things aren't like they used to be. Prisoners have a lot of privileges now. I imagine that calling you once a week was as easy as setting up someone on the outside to take Brice."

A sudden thought occurred to her, and she looked at Cain, her eyes questioning. "When did Lucy die?"

"Six months ago."

Julee shuddered and rubbed her hands over the gooseflesh on her upper arms. "It all makes sense. Why don't the prison officials maintain tighter control? How do they expect innocent people to live normal lives when locking up the bad guys doesn't stop them from committing more crimes?"

"I don't know," Cain said with a shake of his head.

"Do you think he started planning the kidnapping... and to come and get me after Lucy died? As a revenge thing because he'd lost all his loved ones?"

"That might have triggered it, but who knows? Lanny's weird. He might have been just sitting back, letting you get settled into your new life so that when he upset it, it would hurt that much more. It isn't as if he has anything else to do."

"He sounds sick."

"That goes without saying." Cain surprised her by changing the subject again. "How do you think he got inside the house?"

The question was one she'd wrestled with ever since she'd found the note. "I don't have any idea. There were people in and out all day."

"I know." Cain rubbed his lower lip thoughtfully. "I saw a couple of guys out in the yard yesterday afternoon. It's nothing but a wild hunch, but do you think one of them might have been Lanny? Giving a false name and volunteering to help would be easy."

"It's a thought. I guess I can call Chantal and see who was scheduled to work and have her give the list to Dylan."

"Do that," Cain said. "Are you sure no one else had access to the house?"

A sudden light-headedness washed through her. "I forgot. I went out late yesterday afternoon. He could have come then."

"How long were you gone?"

"About an hour. I drove to the station to talk to Dylan."

Seeing the question in Cain's eyes, she said, "I couldn't decide whether to ask for your help or not. Dylan gave me your uncle's number and told me to have a talk with him. I did. Afterward, I decided to call you, but you weren't answering the phone."

"I was working," Cain said. "I'm sorry."

Julee accepted his apology with a short nod. She couldn't shake the feeling that things were coming to a head. She knew she had to ask for Cain's help. Every day that Lanny Milligan went free, she and Brice were one day closer to whatever version of hell he had planned for them. She refused to dwell on the possibility that he might have already exacted his revenge on her baby.

"I'm frightened, Cain," she said, and heard the quiver in her voice. "If he can get inside my house with the police patrolling the block, how can I feel safe there?"

He didn't answer.

She twined her fingers together and lifted her tortured gaze to his. "Maybe it's unfair for me to ask you, to use you this way, especially considering my feelings about your...ability, but can you help me? Will you?"

His smile was sweet; his nod was slow. "I'll try."

Relief and an unaccountable feeling of calm flowed through her. Somehow, she felt that now everything would start falling into place.

"I'll take that refill now," she said, a smile blooming on her face as she reached for her empty mug. "We'll toast our new alliance."

Smiling, Cain took her cup and went to the kitchen.

Alliance. The two of them standing together. Working together. It sounded good to him, Cain thought as he went into the kitchen for more coffee. The pleasure her soft entreaty evoked had filled his heart to the point of bursting. He'd have crawled through an acre of fire ants if she'd just said the word.

And that smile! Seeing a true smile on Julee's face was like the sun breaking through the clouds after a storm. The instant he'd seen it, Cain knew there was no more fooling himself. Somewhere over the course of the past few months his feelings for Julee had changed from liking and admiration to something stronger, more abiding. He was in love with Julee Sutherland, no matter how she might feel about him. He knew something else. His feelings were as inevitable as night following day.

Smiling at the unexpected "rightness" the knowledge brought, Cain returned to the living room. Julee was no-where to be found. For a heartbeat, panic gripped him, but then he realized he was being unnecessarily paranoid.

"Hey! Where are you?" he called.

"In here!"

She was in his studio. Halfway there, Cain's footsteps faltered. She'd see the paintings he done of her. He cursed himself for not putting them away from prying eyes . . . but he liked looking at her too much to hide them in a closet. Besides, how was he to know she'd visit? He wondered if this manifestation of his obsession would end their alliance before it began. He entered the room, his footsteps heavy.

Julee turned, a canvas in her hand. There was no anger on her face. There was nothing but a question in her eyes. "These paintings . . . so many of them are of me," she said, obviously trying to grasp why.

Cain held her eyes with his. "You're a favorite subject of mine," he told her, opting for the truth instead of fabricating a lie.

"But why?"

He shrugged, the gesture conveying his uncertainty. "I don't know. Sometimes I see you out in the yard with Brice or walking across the deck or lying in the hammock, and I feel this urge to capture you on canvas."

Miraculously, she smiled, a hesitant but pleased curving of her lips that was echoed in her eyes. "I'm flattered. You're very good."

"Thank you. I hope the Calliope Gallery's clientele in New Orleans thinks so. I'm working toward a one-man show by the end of the year."

"That's wonderful!" Genuine excitement filled her voice. "What else have you done?" she asked, starting around the easel that faced the bank of windows to the north.

"Don't!" he said. His brusque command halted her in her tracks.

"I'm sorry. I didn't mean to intrude," she said, a sudden stiffness in her tone.

"You aren't!" He set the glasses on a table covered with jars of turpentine and tubes of paint. "I'm sorry I was so short. I don't mind showing you what I've done, but I have this quirk about letting anyone see a piece before it's finished. It's bad luck."

"Oh."

Cain was pleased to see that the tension in her face had disappeared. He went to a stack of paintings leaning against the far wall and picked up the one of the Italian villa he'd finished just days before. He faced her, holding the painting at chest height for her inspection. "I just finished this one."

He could almost see the picture through her eyes: The villa of creamy white stucco accentuated by heavy wooden shutters and a terra-cotta tile roof aged to a soft peach. A table with two chairs sitting on a balcony overlooking a garden with date trees and flowers.

In contrast to the intense colors, the peaceful, somnolent scene was glazed with late-afternoon sunlight that glinted off the water trickling from a fountain and shone through the branches of a eucalyptus tree whose bronze leaves echoed the hue of the rooftop.

He watched the expression on Julee's face turn to surprise. "That's one of the villas near Palo Laziale."

"It is?" Cain said with a lift of his eyebrows and a shrug. "Could have fooled me."

"Are you saying you didn't know that?"

"How could I know when I've never been to Italy?"

"You've never been to Palo Laziale? Never set eyes on this villa?" she queried.

"No," he said, shaking his head. "Never."

"But...how could you paint it if you've never been there?"

Cain shrugged again. "I saw it in a dream."

"You saw it in a dream?" Julee echoed. She shook her head and clasped her hands behind her back, circling him and eyeing the painting from various angles. "It might have been painted from a photograph," she murmured to herself, and cut her eyes to his in query.

"I don't have a photograph. I don't even subscribe to *National Geographic*. I'm telling you I dreamed it."

"Amazing." She stopped and stood staring at the painting for long, silent moments. A soft, dreamlike light entered her eyes. "The villa was the last place Tad and I vacationed before...the fire and...everything."

It was Cain's turn to be surprised. "You and Tad stayed here?"

Julee nodded and pointed to the balcony. "In that very room."

Stunned himself, Cain put the picture on the table next to the mugs of coffee. His careful gaze moved over the picture, taking in the woman standing just inside the door. Julee? he wondered. His fingers moved over the woman in the painting and he felt the same warmth he'd experienced when he'd touched the flyer with Brice's image on it. It *was* Julee.

"You conceived Brice while you were there," he said, his voice soft and even, almost trancelike.

Julee gasped. "How can you possibly know that?"

He turned to look at her. "Is it true?"

"Yes." The word was a harsh whisper.

Cain looked deeply into her eyes and saw that she was trembling on the brink of belief. He also saw that the idea of doing so was frightening. The only thing he knew that might ease her fears was for her to be a witness to what he did, to see for herself that it wasn't anything magical or frightening.

He held out his hand. "Come on," he said.

It pleased him that she didn't hesitate putting her hand in his. "Where are we going?"

"Back to your house to get Brice's ball, and then out to the street. I'll see if I can pick up anything, something I might have missed before."

Less than ten minutes later, Julee and Cain stood in the same spot she'd found him the previous Saturday. She put Brice's soccer ball in the street at the approximate place Cain had found it.

"It might not work," he warned.

"I know."

He went to a place just around the corner, closed his eyes, emptied his mind and began to jog in place. Immediately, he felt the burning in his lungs that signified the last few blocks of his run.

Hurry. Hurry. Hurry.

Running for real now, he came around the corner. The tires of the brown car screeched as it made the turn. He saw the backs of two men's heads, but nothing that would distinguish them in a crowd. Then he spied the ball in the street and bent to pick it up, taking care to keep himself detached from what had happened and from Brice's fear. This time he wanted to observe, not participate.

It was like watching a movie rerun, as if he hadn't already seen the car drive away. From a distant vantage point, he saw Brice's struggle with the stranger, a swarthy, heavily muscled man with dark hair and a mustache. Something about the man made Cain think he was a foreigner. He watched as the man put Brice in the car, his hand muffling the child's screams. Then the car pulled off with a screech of tires, turned the corner and disappeared from sight.

Cain opened his eyes slowly. His limbs felt heavy, and lethargy enveloped him, as if he were awakening from a deep sleep. Julee stood before him, an expectant look on her face.

He handed her the ball and started back toward her house. He didn't speak until they were inside the front door. "I saw the man this time. I think he was foreign. Dark. Swarthy. Italian, maybe. I don't know."

"That isn't much," she said.

"I know. I'm sorry."

"What about Brice?"

There was no way Cain was going to relate Brice's terror to her. He'd take that knowledge to his grave before he put Julee through that particular hell. He shook his head. "I'm sorry."

Julee's teeth clamped down hard on her bottom lip, and she nodded. Just when he thought she had herself under control, she uttered a fierce "Damn!" and buried her face in her hands.

Cain pulled her into his arms and felt Julee's arms circle his waist without hesitation, the way they had when she'd come to his house just an hour ago. The way her body felt in his arms was so familiar it was uncanny.

"Don't cry," he begged, cradling her head against his chest. "I can't stand it if you cry."

But his gentle admonition wasn't enough to stay the emotions that had been building inside her for days. Heartbreak. Fear for her life and Brice's. Hopelessness.

Holding her, stroking her back, murmuring soft words of encouragement and concern while she wept, Cain began to feel the effects of those emotions on her. He began to understand what a strong woman she really was.

He knew intuitively that winning her independence had been a long and hard-fought battle, and that compromising it in any way—even to ask him for help—was a major concession. He knew Tad had respected and encouraged her independence, which was why their marriage and their love had been so strong.

Gradually, the sobs quieted and the tears stopped, but she didn't move. When she raised her limpid gaze to look up at him, Cain saw acceptance and a tentative inquisitiveness in her red-rimmed eyes.

Drawn by a force he couldn't deny or refuse, he lowered his head and took her quivering lips with his. There was no hesitation in Julee's response. They'd both known it would come to this. Her mouth opened beneath his, and a tortured groan worked its way free of the lips that clung to his with a yearning that matched the hunger devouring him from the inside out.

This was the dream, only better.

She knew exactly what her little moans and sighs did to him, just as he knew when and where and how to touch her. Though he'd never before held her in the flesh, he knew that the whispered brush of his lips over the crest of her eyelids, on the curve of her jaw, in the hollow of her throat, would make her breath catch and her fingernails dig into his back.

He knew the sweetness of her mouth, the boldness of her kisses and the way her tongue felt dueling with his. He knew that her kisses could become as fierce and savage as his, that her need was as strong, and that she was not only capable but willing to give as good as she got. He knew that the merest touch of his breath against her lacy bra caused her breasts to pout and that the flimsy barrier was as much of a turn-on as naked flesh against flesh.

He knew... The same way she knew that the way she pressed her breasts against his chest and rubbed her lower body against his was as explosive as adding a dose of gasoline to a fire...and just as dangerous.

Cain didn't know what it was that brought him to his senses. Some sound she made? A car in the street? He lifted his head and saw Julee staring at him from passion-glazed eyes, a reflection, he was sure, of his own.

"Stop," she said again, so softly it might have been a sigh.

It was that single word that had brought him back from the edge. Neither moved, and bit by bit, Cain became aware of how far things had gone.

Somehow, at some time, he had backed Julee against the wall, half lifting her so that their bodies fitted together like two pieces of an erotic puzzle. His lower body, hard and wanting and straining against the metal of his zipper, was wedged between her slightly parted thighs.

Her hair was mussed; her lips were wet and swollen from their wild kisses. Her blouse was unbuttoned and spread wide, baring a peach-tinted demi-bra that pushed the soft globes of her breasts upward and exposed the top halves of pink areolae. The bra was wet, too, and for a moment Cain allowed his mind to reconstruct the way it felt as his tongue laved her, stroking her to a feverish, heedless passion.

Julee arched against him. Her head fell back, exposing the delicate column of her throat. A soft moan followed by a single pleading "don't" fluttered from her lips.

It was only then that Cain realized he could touch her with his mind as surely as he could his body. The perception was stunning, unbelievable. The look in Julee's eyes told him she felt the same way.

He let her go with more reluctance than he would have ever dreamed possible. What if this changed things again? he asked himself as he watched her button up her shirt.

"Julee—" he started, noting that his voice sounded rusty, as if it hadn't been used in years.

"Shh!" she said, a slight, embarrassed smile flickering across her lips. "Don't say anything. Please, just don't say anything."

Cain nodded and stepped away from her. What was there to say, really? He bent and feathered a kiss to her cheek. "I'll talk to you later. Don't forget to call Dylan to let him know his men slipped up."

She nodded, and he let himself out of the house. She wanted him to go, and he understood the turmoil she was feeling. He felt it himself. The fact that they'd gone from wary neighborliness to almost lovers in the span of an hour was mind-boggling. They both needed time to think, to try and put what had just happened into some kind of perspective.

Julee didn't know what had gotten into her. Never in her life had she behaved so...so wantonly. A simple kiss shared with Cain would have been sufficient to make her question the wisdom of her actions, much less her sanity, but what she'd actually allowed was worse—*much* worse. It was as though once she'd sampled his kisses, she couldn't get enough. The touch of his mouth was like a cool drink of water after days of going without. The taste of his mouth was both familiar and different, but it was that disturbing familiarity that bothered her. It hadn't escaped her notice that Cain knew just what buttons to push to elicit a maximum response from her. It was as if they were longtime lovers who had perfected the dance of desire during countless hours of lovemaking.

The Dream, Julee. You've made love with Cain dozens of times in The Dream.

She shook her head to clear it of the fanciful thought. That kind of reasoning could send a person 'round the bend. She didn't know why she'd responded to him the way she had, she just knew that until she got a handle on her feelings, she'd be smart to keep her distance.

Getting back into his work after the kissing session with Julee was next to impossible. Cain couldn't concentrate for remembering the way she smelled, the way her breath rasped in his ear, the way she felt in his arms—small, and utterly feminine. Warm, and incredibly sexy.

When he took a mid-morning break, he saw Trixie out in the yard. She told him Julee had headed off to work soon after the telephone workers arrived.

Cain sighed and ran his hands through his hair. He'd hoped to see her, hoped she'd call to say...what?

A sound drew his attention, and he looked over at Trixie, who was regarding him with a smug look. "'Bout time," she snapped, sashaying back across her yard before Cain could rally. Good Lord! Were his feelings so obvious?

He didn't hear from Julee at all that day. His male pride was the only thing that kept him from picking up the phone and calling her. Knowing he wouldn't be able to sleep, he worked far into the night, finishing the picture of the woman on the beach at 3:00 a.m.

When he shucked out of his shorts and crawled into bed, it didn't take him long to fall asleep.

As usual, a dream was waiting for him. But this dream was different. It wasn't about making love with Julee or of arriving at a burning house too late. This dream was about another house and Brice.

Brice was staying somewhere near the sea; Cain heard the crashing of the waves and the screeching of the gulls. A dense fog prevented him from getting a good look at the house, but the word that came to mind was *massive*.

Brice was somewhere near the house...on the rocky beach, perhaps? The wind carried snatches of childish laughter to him, and he caught the words "pretty yellow hair" and "love forever more."

Cain looked up...up toward the house hidden by the mist, and, cupping his hands around his mouth, called out to Brice. The chanting stopped, replaced by the sound of heart-wrenching sobs and a cry of "Cain! Come get me."

Cain awoke with a start. Breathing heavily, he pushed himself to a sitting position and leaned against the head-board of the bed, his elbows resting on his raised knees, his face buried in his hands.

As dreams do, this one fled the moment he awakened. All he remembered was the sea and Brice calling out to him, begging for him to come after him. Cain's fingers clenched the rumpled sheets. Why couldn't he *see* more? Why was he being tantalized with just enough information to drive him crazy?

He flung off the sheet and rummaged in the hall closet for the atlas he'd used in his experiment a few days before. This time, maybe he'd be able to pinpoint where Brice was. This time, he was certain the place Brice was being held was along the coast.

"Piece of cake," Cain muttered, carrying the book to the kitchen. He flipped the on switch to the coffeemaker and sat down at the table. He stared at the map, trying to psych himself up to make a second stab at getting Brice's location, while the fragrance of fresh-brewed coffee wafted throughout the room.

Finally, Cain put his fingertips at the top of the line that marked the East Coast. Slowly, so slowly he seemed not to be moving them at all, his fingers slid down the page—was that a little warmth near North Carolina?—around the Florida peninsula, up and around the Gulf shore.

Sweat beaded his forehead, and his breathing rasped in his throat. The tendons of his neck stood out with his concentration. He jumped his fingers over Mexico and picked up his search near the Baja peninsula, moving upward along the California coast to Washington State.

Nothing.

Not the slightest feeling that he was getting a vibration from anywhere. Not a hint of warmth. That insidious fear he'd felt before, the feeling that something had happened to Brice, crept through him, chilling him to the bone.

With a cry of impotent rage, Cain swept the atlas onto the floor. He rested his elbows on the table. The heels of his hands dug into his burning eye sockets.

"*...Love forever more...pretty yellow hair...forever more...*" The litany sprang into Cain's mind and his tortured thoughts came to a sudden stop. Those words came from the dream. He shook his head. Something wasn't adding up here. First, he'd dreamed that Brice was calling for him to come after him, and second, now that he was consciously thinking about it, he remembered the distinct feeling in the dream that Brice missed his mother. Third, some child had sung those nonsensical words. If all this was true, Brice must be alive. So why couldn't he get a reading?

"Like I've been saying for years, it's fallible," Cain said to himself, rising to pour himself a mug of coffee. But he didn't want to believe that. He wanted to believe the information in the dream was real. While it was true that he didn't have a one-hundred-percent success rate, he was inclined to put his trust in the dream more than the map gimmick.

He contemplated telling Julee about the dream and the feeling that Brice was all right. But he didn't want to get her hopes up in case he was wrong again. He'd play it cool and concentrate on helping the authorities find Lanny, so he could keep Julee safe. Once the police had Lanny in custody, Cain was certain they had ways of getting him to tell them what he'd done with Brice.

In the meantime, he'd be sure and ask Julee again what "love forever more" and "pretty yellow hair" meant.

Just before daybreak, Lanny stashed the cans of gasoline at the edge of the woods near the house Julee's crew was building. The smell of the gas made his stomach churn and he wrestled with the urge to throw up. After a few moments, the feeling passed. He wiped his perspiring face with a red bandanna and set off through the woods and around the pond, the way he'd come. His footsteps were slow and faltering.

Tomorrow was Saturday, and the carpenters would all be at home with their families. There wouldn't be a soul around. Lanny's pleased laughter shattered the stillness of the evening.

Tomorrow.

Chapter Nine

Julee awakened Saturday morning to the sound of a blue jay's chatter outside her window. Filled with contentment, she arched her back in a lazy, catlike stretch. It was Saturday, she had the whole weekend off, and—

Her euphoria vanished like a melody on the wind, and a rush of hot tears spurted into her eyes. It was Saturday, and Brice had been missing for a full week. She watched enough television to know that if the police hadn't located a missing child within a week, the odds of ever doing so dropped dramatically.

Julee forced back the tightness in her throat. Giving in to her misery was a futile investment of time and energy. She'd be much better off calling Dylan to see if the description of Brice's abductor Cain had passed on the day before had turned up any suspects and if they had any leads to Lanny's whereabouts.

She swung her legs over the side of the bed and got up. She felt a tug on her left hand and saw that her diamond engagement ring was snagged in the eyelet trim of the sheet. As she worked to free the raised stone, a single word entered her mind.

"Julee."

"Tad?" she said aloud, her gaze drawn to the door. But there was no one there. Feeling suddenly breathless and more than a little confused, Julee lowered herself to the edge of the bed. She remembered now why she'd felt so happy when she'd awakened. She'd dreamed about Tad.

She moved her thumb over her wedding rings in a gentle caress. In the dream, he had looked tan and fit, the way she remembered him from their days in Italy and the Caribbean. They'd sat at their favorite sidewalk café holding hands and talking, and she'd felt as nervous as she had on their first date. Tad had squeezed her hand and told her not to be afraid, that it was all right; he wasn't angry.

"What's all right?"

His smile was tender. "Cain," he said.

"How do you know about Cain?" she asked, unable to hide her surprise.

"I just do."

Tears stung behind her eyelids, and Tad squeezed her hand. "Don't cry, sweetheart. It's okay. It's your time now."

And then he was gone, vanished, and she was on the beach making love with Cain again.

Now, sitting in the bright sunlight flooding her room, Julee knew she wouldn't have to call Trixie for a dream interpretation. Its meaning was clear. Tad had come back to say goodbye and to give her his blessing.

Bittersweet tears filled Julee's eyes as she lifted her left hand. The diamond solitaire captured a shaft of sunshine and flung it into her eyes. She could almost see Tad's familiar wink.

Smiling a shaky smile, Julee lifted her hand to her lips and pressed a kiss to the cold stone and metal. Then she brushed away the tears clinging to her eyelashes, drew off the rings and put them in her jewelry box for safekeeping.

Tad was right. It was time for her.

It was too early to call Julee about the strange words from the dream, and Cain knew he needed some physical activity to cleanse him of the frustration gnawing at him. As the past had proved, there was nothing like a long run to anesthetize the emotions. He pulled on his running shorts and headed out the door before the sun got too hot.

When he got back an hour later, he showered, ate breakfast and dialed Julee's number, unable to wait another second before hearing her voice. A part of him wanted to go to her house so he could see her, but another part of him, the raw and vulnerable part that couldn't take a straight-out rejection, told him a phone call would do just fine.

She answered the phone with a breathless "Hello."

"Good morning."

"Hi."

Was it his imagination, or did her voice hold a note of shyness? "Did you manage to get a good night's sleep?" he asked. *After the kisses. After you left me.*

"I slept pretty well," she said, deftly avoiding the personal side of his question. "At least my dripping shower didn't keep me awake."

"That's good. How's work?"

"Fine. It's all downhill on the house. We're actually ahead of schedule, so I gave the crew the whole weekend off."

The words came out in a rush, a sure sign that the nervousness churning his stomach was affecting her, too. He strove for a neutral tone and asked, "Do you have any big plans for the day?"

"Actually, yes. I'm going to a Sutherland family reunion with my in-laws. They thought it might be good for us all to get away."

"I think they're right," Cain said, missing her already. "Did Detective Garvey come up with anything from the description I gave him yesterday?"

"No," Julee said. "He said that it wasn't much to go on. He's going to check the mug books and have you take a look at them if he comes up with anyone fitting the description. He was pretty upset to think that Lanny got into the house. He's going to step up the surveillance."

Knowing he'd exhausted his meager repertoire of small talk, Cain took the plunge. "I know I've asked you this before, and you couldn't think of anything, but I keep hearing the words 'yellow hair' or 'pretty yellow hair.' I thought it had something to do with the kidnappers, but after yesterday, I don't think so."

"Pretty yellow hair," Julee repeated in a thoughtful tone. "I'm sorry," she said after a moment. "Nothing comes to mind right off."

"What about 'love forever more'?"

She laughed softly. "They sort of sound like words to an old ballad, don't they?"

"Yeah." Cain raked a hand through his hair. "Well, maybe it'll come to you when you least expect it."

"I hope so."

"I'd better let you go," he said, "but I want to ask you a favor."

"What's that?"

"Do you mind leaving me a key to your place so I can go in while you're gone and see if I get a feel for Lanny?"

"Do you think that's possible?"

"It's worth a shot. I'd come over now, but I'd really like to be alone when I try. The fewer people there are around, the easier it is to pick up on things." When Julee didn't say anything, he said, "I know it's presumptuous of me, since you hardly know me, but—"

"No, it isn't," she broke in. "And actually," she said in a wry voice, "I think we know each other pretty well."

It was the first mention of what had happened between them the morning before. Cain was glad to have the episode out in the open. "Should I apologize?"

"Don't you dare!" Her laughter was shaky. "It just . . . took me by surprise, you know?"

"Me, too," Cain admitted. He was glad her droll, unexpected sense of humor was intact.

"I just need some time to sort out my feelings," Julee told him. "I mean, with our . . . backgrounds and everything, this . . . might be a dead-end street."

"Only if we let it be," Cain said. "We can't change our pasts, Julee, but we can exert some control over our future."

"Maybe. But right now the most important thing in my future is finding Brice."

"No. Right now, the most important thing is for you to go to that family reunion and try to forget all this for a while."

"Yeah." She cleared her throat. "I'll leave the key to the back door under the flowerpot at the edge of the deck."

"Thanks. I'll be sure and put it back," he told her. "Have fun."

"I'm going to do my best, but that might be hard with plainclothes cops around."

"Garvey is sending cops with you?"

"Yeah. Crazy isn't it?"

"Not crazy, Julee," Cain countered. "Smart."

While Cain waited for Julee to leave, he sketched in another painting with a thin turpentine wash. There was no hurry. Dylan had called to give his okay and whatever—if anything—waited for him would be there whenever he showed up. Julee was safe with her in-laws and her police escorts. For the moment his world was in balance. Meanwhile, an idea for a new painting had taunted him all morning. It came as no surprise that it was another picture with a beach setting, a house set high on a rocky cliff, overlooking a small cove.

Cain smiled to himself. He recalled a time during his college days when he'd been in his Impressionist period. When that passed, he'd painted nothing but nudes for a year or so. Now it appeared that he was in yet another stage—his ocean-dream phase.

He thought about Julee while he worked, and pictured her walking along the white sands, laughing and happy. He wondered if this was another place she'd visited with Tad and hated himself for the sharp shaft of jealousy that pierced him.

When Cain's stomach started growling, he looked up from the painting and realized that he hadn't stopped with just a sketch. He'd actually started painting the picture, which had so engrossed him that he'd forgotten everything. The hands of the utilitarian clock on the far wall pointed to ten minutes after twelve. No wonder he was hungry.

He fixed himself a quick sandwich and a glass of iced tea and ate while he prowled the studio, studying the painting from various angles and trying to decide what he should do next. He sketched in a couple walking on the beach, their arms wrapped around each other's waist.

Then he sat down in the office chair he'd found at a secondhand store, assumed the position of *The Thinker* and contemplated the painting while he finished his sandwich and battled the sudden sleepiness that usually accompanied his noon meal....

The night was awash in moonlight. It danced on the ripples undulating across the face of the water, reflected the pure white facade of the house across the bay, and made the tips of Julee's eyelashes appear as though they'd been dipped in silver.

She was soft and pliant beneath him. Lifting her arms, she looped them around his neck and drew him down until their lips touched. Her mouth was as hot as Hades, as sweet as Heaven. Tongues danced in an age-old ritual of desire: advance, recede, parry, thrust, adding fuel to the building, fiery sensations.

A sharp crackling sound brought his head up, like an animal who senses danger. Somehow, he was standing, and Julee and the ocean were gone. The house on the far side of the pond was no longer a pristine white, but cedar. He knew he was dreaming then, the dream he'd had before. The dream where Amy and Holly and Julee had called out to him from inside a burning house and he'd arrived too late. Knowing it was a dream didn't lessen his terror.

Hurry. Hurry. Hurry.

The chant from the morning Brice had been kidnapped filled his mind. Maybe if he hurried, he could make it this time. Running as fast as he could, he circled the fringe of trees surrounding the pond. The taunting voice called out to him, its menacing tone mingling with the crackling babel of the fire and the terror underscoring a feminine cry for help.

A few yards from the house, he stopped, his breath a harsh rasp in his throat. Julee stood in the window, her eyes filled with sorrow, her palms pressed against the glass. He had just enough time to wonder why he hadn't heard Amy's or Holly's voice this time, before the house came crashing in upon itself and the thunderous sound of splintering wood and breaking glass filled the night....

Cain woke, bathed in sweat. It took him several seconds to realize that he was not on the shore of some pond, or even in his bed. He was in his studio with a broken glass lying next to his chair. He had fallen asleep holding his glass of iced tea. The shattering of the glass on the floor had awakened him. He looked at the clock. The entire episode couldn't have lasted more than a couple of minutes.

He got to his feet, his limbs feeling as old and stiff as Trixie claimed hers were. He reached for a paper towel and wiped the perspiration from his face. No wonder he chose painting over sleep. He never knew what pleasure or torture his dreams might bring.

Cain didn't go to Julee's house until early evening. Instead, he painted until the odor of turpentine and oil seemed to have penetrated his pores and permanently damaged his olfactory senses. Painted until his eyes burned, his head throbbed and his shoulders ached. Until his hand cramped so badly he couldn't hold the thick, bevel-edged piece of glass that served as his palette.

He was literally so tired he couldn't see straight. He cleaned his brushes, covered his palette with cling wrap and stuck it in the freezer. After devouring a microwave pot pie, he downed a couple of aspirin and watched a few innings of baseball, pondering the possible meaning of the dream and wondering if the absence of Amy and Holly in this dream held any significance.

Feeling somewhat more human after a rest and some food, he let himself out the back door. The fewer people who saw him pilfering Julee's house, the better. He jumped the fence separating his yard from Julee's and found the key where she said it would be. He stuck it in his pocket and scanned the backyard, uncertain of what he was looking for.

Nothing seemed out of place. There were no footprints in the flower beds, no broken branches on the bushes around the house, no bits of fabric clinging to the sharp points on top of the fence. Of course, Dylan's men would have already scoured the area. His mouth curved in a grim smile, and he wondered why life couldn't be more like the movies where the hero gets the glory.

He did notice that Julee's caladiums and begonias were dry, their colorful leaves and vibrant heads drooping in the evening heat. He started across the lawn to the outside spigot. Watering plants was probably the farthest thing from her mind these days.

When he bent over to turn on the water, the ground started to recede, and a swell of menace seemed to rise up and slap him in the face. *Lanny.* Fighting the sudden dizziness, he straightened and reached out a hand to the wall. He felt as if he were standing on a beach where the incoming waves shifted the sand beneath his feet.

Lanny had been here. When? Cain pinched the bridge of his nose and closed his eyes. He remembered seeing a couple of men in the yard the day Lanny managed to get inside her house. At the time, he'd blown it off, assuming they were people with the Missing Children group. Now it seemed not only possible, but probable, that one of them had been Lanny, who'd managed to change his looks. The question was, why?

Cain shook his head and took the key from his pocket, unlocking the back door and letting himself in. Maybe he'd find something in the house to give him a clue of what was going on inside Lanny's warped and twisted mind.

The house was quiet except for the muted ticking of the antique mantel clock in the living room. The scent of tea roses floated on the cool breath of air blowing from the overhead ducts. The nostalgic aroma was no doubt due to the potpourri pot sitting on the counter.

Cain toured the kitchen slowly, running his hand over the cabinet tops, letting the essence of the room pervade his senses. Other than a vague sensation of another presence, there was nothing.

He worked his way through the house, repeating his actions in the dining room, living room, Brice's bedroom and the loft Julee used for a home office, closing his eyes and opening himself up for whatever vibrations Lanny might have left behind. Nothing.

Then he stepped through the door to Julee's bedroom, and the hair on the back of his neck stood up. Evil had stood where he was standing, and it had left behind a residue of malevolence so distinct, Cain didn't see how Julee or anyone else could not be aware of it.

He followed the sinister trail through the bedroom to the bed, and ran his hand along the cutwork duvet cover. A shiver went through him, and his fingers tightened on the soft cotton. Lanny had sat on Julee's bed...perhaps had lain on her bed.

Cain did the same and let his eyes drift shut.

"Ha. Ha. Ha."

Cain's eyes flew open. The eerie laughter made his blood run cold. He sat up. A fine film of perspiration broke out on his upper lip. Rising, he went to the dresser. Even though he knew there was nothing sexual about Lanny's obsession with Julee, someone as sick as his former brother-in-law would delight in handling her personal things with his bloodstained hands.

The second drawer, the one where Julee had found the note, was scented with lavender and filled with frothy underwear. Lanny had definitely been there, but other than the note, he'd left nothing behind to indicate his intentions.

Cain slid the drawer shut. Intuition told him the others would yield nothing, either. Turning, he went into the bathroom. Waves of wickedness assaulted him the instant he stepped over the threshold. He wondered again how Julee hadn't known Lanny was there before she found the note.

The phone in the bedroom rang, shattering the stillness and jangling Cain's nerves. He stood unmoving, as if he were afraid that whoever was on the other line might see him. After four rings, the answering machine kicked in, but the caller didn't leave a message. Cain let out his breath in a long sigh. He was beginning to think Lanny hadn't left any messages, either.

"Come on. Talk to me, Lanny," Cain said softly through gritted teeth.

He checked the drawers of the vanity and the contents of the medicine chest. Finding nothing there, he opened the linen closet, where neatly folded sheets resided next to stacks of fluffy white towels that smelled of fabric softener.

He was about to give up and close the door when something stopped him. Something was amiss. What? Cain took a mental inventory. Towels. Washcloths. Sheets. Blankets on the bottom shelf. Cleaning agents on top where Brice's curious eyes couldn't see them, and if they did, his little hands couldn't reach them.

As Cain studied the items on the top shelf, something tugged at his mind like a kid pulling at his mother's skirt to get her attention. What was out of place? There was a generic brand of soft-scrub cleanser that claimed to be environmentally friendly. Glass cleaner. Extra bars of soap and shampoo. Pipe wrench. Toilet tissue. Drain—

Cain's tally came to a halt. Though he didn't know why, his gaze was drawn unerringly to the wrench. He reached up and closed his fingers around the cold, smooth metal.

"Hahahaha. Burn, baby, burn. Hahahahahahaha!"

In a sharp flash of perception, Cain knew that Lanny hadn't sneaked into the house while Julee was visiting Dylan. Lanny was the plumber. Cain barely had time to wonder how his former brother-in-law had learned about the faulty shower and to realize that he must have left the wrench behind, when the familiar mist swirled around him, and he found himself standing back, watching Julee's tormentor work on the dripping showerhead.

Lanny didn't look the way Cain remembered him. He was thin to the point of emaciation, and his hair was dark instead of light brown. But Cain had heard the sinister chuckle often enough in the past whenever Lanny's peculiar sense of humor took the upper hand.

"You think you're so cool, Miss Hoity-Toity rich man's wife. Think money can buy your way out of everything. Well, let me tell you somethin' baby. You're gonna burn. You're gonna burn just like my babies did. And then your hubby's gonna know what it's like to be alone."

"He's dead, Lanny!" Cain cried, icy shards of fear pricking his heart. His angry words bounced off the gray tiles and echoed around the room, but there was no one to hear except the haggard man who stared back at him from the mirror.

Cain looked down at the wrench gripped in his hand. "Tad Sutherland is dead," he said, as if Lanny might also be able to receive a message via the heavy object. "He's dead, damn you, and you can't punish him by hurting his family.''

When there was no answer, Cain put the wrench back on the shelf and sagged against the vanity. It was all beginning to take shape in his mind. He didn't know how Lanny knew Julee needed a plumber, but Cain figured out that he must have been someone working for Julee. Lanny had worked as a plumber's helper when he and Lucy first married, so he volunteered to do the work. But why?

"Because he's sick, and he'd get some sort of perverted thrill by prowling through her house while she was gone," Cain said out loud.

Feeling Lanny's presence near the outside water spigot made perfect sense now. That's where he'd gone to turn off the water supply to the house before he started working on the shower.

"Elementary, my dear Watson," Cain said with a perfect British accent.

Feeling drained and unutterably weary, he made his way back through the house and let himself out, but instead of putting the key back, he slipped it into his pocket . . . just in case Lanny decided to make a return visit.

His dream about the fire made perfect sense now. After hearing what Lanny had said in Julee's bathroom, Cain knew that the fire in his dreams wasn't another version of the dream that had warned him about Amy and Holly. This was another warning, and this time the victim was Julee.

Julee lay in her narrow cot at the lodge, wooing sleep.

It had been a pleasant day. When she'd pulled through the gates at Hodges Gardens, she'd felt as if she was leaving her troubles behind, at least until the following day.

They'd seen a plethora of woodland creatures during the winding drive to the dormitory-style lodge, including a brave doe and her two fawns that stood transfixed while Julee pulled the Explorer to a stop and shot several photos to show Brice when he came home.

The lodge itself consisted of two wings—one for the Sutherland men, the other for the women—along with a well-stocked kitchen and a common room with a piano and a massive fireplace. Not, Julee thought, that they'd be needing a fire in the ninety-degree weather.

They had started the yearly ritual with an afternoon of outdoor games—croquet, badminton and volleyball—while those who weren't up to such physical pursuits had held Scrabble, checkers and chess tournaments. There was a lot of talking and laughing and teasing while the Sutherland clan caught up on who was doing what.

In spite of the plainclothes cops breathing over her shoulder, Julee had felt herself relaxing for the first time in a week, secure in the love and support of the Sutherland clan.

After cooking chicken, sausage and ribs outside in the early evening, they had hand-cranked homemade ice cream and sung songs around the piano. Everyone had fallen into their beds around midnight, and presumably gone to sleep. A huge breakfast in the morning would be followed by a lunch of sandwiches before everyone loaded up and started the long trek back home.

An owl hooted outside the window, a lonely, forlorn sound that echoed in Julee's heart. Her eyes clouded with tears as she recalled her talk with Loretta Sutherland earlier in the day.

Loretta had wanted to tour the four-acre formal gardens, but Gene claimed weariness, so she and Julee had gone alone. A wedding had been in progress in front of the waterfall, and pretty young girls wearing floppy, flower-bedecked summer hats and long gowns whose hems brushed the close-cropped grass had giggled and flirted as if they didn't have a care in the world—which, Julee had thought, they probably didn't.

"Do you ever feel cheated for not having had a formal wedding?" Loretta had asked as they sauntered past.

"Not at all," Julee said with a shake of her head. "I've seen my friends spend thousands of dollars on lavish weddings and have the marriage end up in divorce court in less than a year." She took Loretta's hand in hers. "Tad gave me everything I ever wanted or needed, Loretta. He was a wonderful husband, and he would have been a wonderful father, and all because of you and Gene."

A single tear slid down Loretta's plump, rouged cheek. "Thank you for saying that, honey."

"It's true."

"Gene and I consider ourselves very lucky to have a daughter-in-law like you. I know it sounds corny, but you really are the daughter we never had."

Julee's heart warmed with pleasure at the praise. "It doesn't sound corny to me."

"Good." Loretta smiled and drew in a deep breath. "Which is a rough sort of segue to something I've been wanting to talk to you about for a long time—especially since that picture of you and the teacher came out in the paper the other day."

Julee's heart skipped a beat. "What's that?"

"Your falling in love again."

Julee's lips parted in surprise, and she knew her eyes held the astonishment she felt. Ever since she and Cain had shared that bout of stormy kissing, she had wondered if it was just a hormonal thing or a prelude to love. She'd also wondered what her in-laws might say about another man entering her and Brice's life.

Julee wondered if it was a coincidence that Loretta had chosen to broach the subject the day following her dream of receiving Tad's blessing, or if her timing had something to do with that psychic stuff Cain seemed so keen on.

"That picture was totally out of context," she said.

Loretta gave a dismissive wave of her hand. "It doesn't matter whether or not there's anything between you and Cain Collier, though I've seen many a longing look in your eyes whenever he's in his backyard."

Julee felt her face flame. Loretta squeezed her hand. "It's all right, Julee. You're young. You deserve to be happy. You deserve to fall in love again."

Julee met her mother-in-law's steady gaze. "What if the man I fell in love with *was* Cain Collier?"

"Why shouldn't it be?"

"Because of the fire, and Lanny...shooting Tad."

"I don't see what that has to do with you and Cain. He isn't even related to Lanny Milligan—not really. To put any blame for Tad's death on Cain makes about as much sense as Lanny blaming Tad for something a subcontractor did while he was in another country. It's carrying responsibility a little too far, in my book."

Loretta smiled. "That's why I wanted us to have this little chat. Gene and I have talked it to death, and we want you to know that whomever you choose is all right with us as long as you don't cut us totally out of your life."

Julee's eyes had filmed with moisture, and she'd hugged Loretta close. "As if I would," she'd said, around the tightness in her throat. "As if I could."

Now, as she lay in bed watching the clouds play peekaboo with the moon, she felt the tears prickling behind her eyelids again. She had Tad's blessing; she had his parents' blessing. Now all she had to do was figure out what her real feelings for Cain were.

She closed her eyes and conjured up a picture of him in his cutoff shorts, a runnel of sweat trickling down his bare chest and over the flat planes of his abdomen. She drifted off into sleep, thinking about capturing that drop of perspiration on her tongue and tracing the whorls of hair on his chest with her fingertips.

She was unaware that Cain was pacing the floor and calling her house every fifteen minutes. Unaware that danger lurked in the woods, waiting.

Lanny was sick of waiting for her to come home. If he'd called once, he'd called a dozen times. Where the hell was she, anyway? he thought, as he paced his small room on legs that felt weak and trembling. Why wasn't she at home where she belonged?

He stopped and picked up the phone to call again. It had to happen soon. He needed a doctor, and bad. If it didn't happen this weekend, he was afraid it might not happen at all.

Chapter Ten

Cain paced the floor all evening, wondering where Julee was, fearing something had happened to her and telling himself that his fears were unreasonable because Dylan Garvey's men were watching her. Even so, he put in a call to the detective at the Houma police station, only to learn that Dylan was off for the day.

Cain even considered calling Dylan at his Thibodaux home, but talked himself out of it. Dylan had okayed Cain's foray into Julee's house, but he still wasn't sure the hard-nosed cop would believe he'd actually heard Lanny's voice, or that he would treat a nightmare with the seriousness it deserved.

Cain decided that there was nothing he could do but wait and watch for Julee to get home. At midnight, he made a pot of coffee and checked the *TV Guide* to see what late movies were showing. At around three he fell asleep at the kitchen table, his head cradled on his arms.

For once his sleep was deep and dreamless, and he woke up just past seven the next morning to the sound of one of his neighbors mowing the grass. As he rubbed his eyes and looked around him, wondering why he was asleep in the kitchen, memory came hurtling back.

Leaping to his feet, Cain went to the window. There was no light on, no sign that Julee was home. He picked up the phone and called her. Her answering machine picked up after four rings, and he hung up without leaving a message.

He poured himself a cup of cold coffee, nuked it in the microwave while he put some fresh coffee on to brew, and scalded his tongue on the first sip of the stale coffee.

His mind churned with possibilities: First, Julee had stayed with the Sutherlands overnight; second, they'd decided to do a little sight-seeing instead of rushing home; third, she'd had car trouble; fourth, Lanny had somehow managed to get his hands on her.

Cain ground his teeth in frustration and uttered a curse that would have done the saltiest sailor proud. After getting no reply at the Sutherlands, he made another trip across the backyards and used the key to let himself back into Julee's house. She wasn't there, and it didn't look as if she had been. As he was leaving, he heard her phone ringing, but he didn't hang around to see who it was.

He locked the door behind him and crossed the yards to his house. While he agonized over what to do next, it occurred to him that Julee might have confided her plans to Trixie. He thought of jumping the fence and knocking on her back door, but figured he'd probably give Trix a coronary if he sneaked up unannounced. Rather than chance it, he went around to the front and rang her doorbell.

Trixie answered the door wearing an orange-and-blue exercise outfit. Her fiery curls were plastered to her damp forehead. She was breathing hard and her makeup was a little smudged from her efforts, but Cain had to hand it to her for caring about her looks at her age.

"I don't mean to interrupt, Trix, but—"

"Please interrupt!" she cried, throwing her hands up in a gesture of surrender. "That Gunther isn't human. Thirty minutes of pure torture and he doesn't even break a sweat."

Cain smiled. Gunther was the Nordic giant who hosted an early-morning exercise program. Cain had caught parts of the program a time or two and had come away with the suspicion that Gunther's chest measurement was larger than his IQ.

"I bet he's kin to that Hannibal the Cannibal guy," Trixie rushed on, a naughty, speculative glitter in her eyes. "Bet his pulse never gets above sixty no matter *what* he does." She put her finger to the side of her mouth and cocked her head in a gesture of thoughtfulness. "Then, there's always the chance that he's a humanoid or android or one of those Terminator kind of things."

"Trixie—"

She spied her newspaper at the edge of the lawn. "Mind gettin' that paper for me, darlin'?" she interrupted with a flutter of her ring-laden fingers.

Cain went to fetch the paper, wondering when and how he was ever to get a word in edgewise. He thought about the garrulous woman whose tire he'd fixed the previous weekend and decided that talkativeness must go hand in hand with loneliness.

Biting his tongue and telling himself this was a lesson in patience, he handed Trixie the paper without a word. She peeled the rubber band off the newsprint and onto her wrist, glanced at the headlines and shook her head. "Same old garbage," she said. Then she lifted a wide smile to Cain. "Now! What can I do for you?"

"Julee," he said without preamble. "Do you know where she is?"

"Of course I know where she is. She went with the Sutherlands to a family reunion."

"I know that, but I thought she'd be home by now."

"Oh, no, it's a two-day affair," Trixie said in a breezy offhand manner. "Come on in. I'll fix us some breakfast."

"No, thanks," Cain declined. "I—"

"Have to eat," Trixie said, interrupting him again. She crooked her arm around his. "Come on. You'll be a new man with some bacon and eggs in you." She gave a throaty laugh. "Though there's not a darn thing wrong with the old man."

Cain knew better than to argue, and now that she mentioned it, he was getting hungry. With a sigh, he followed her through the living room and down the hall into the kitchen.

Decorated with a hodgepodge of mismatched styles and the bright colors she favored in her clothes, the house was a true reflection of Trixie's personality. The amazing thing was that it all came together in a cheerful, eclectic whole that few people could pull off.

Trixie poured him some coffee and set about cooking their breakfast while demanding that Cain check their horoscopes. After reading that she should concentrate on the small details and that Cain should listen to what his inner self told him and not be too proud to accept help from those in authority, Cain broached his concern about Julee.

"Are you sure you don't know where the reunion is? I really need to talk to her," he said, watching as Trixie beat the farm-fresh eggs with a fork.

Trixie abandoned the fork and laid her finger next to her mouth, an orange-red nail tap-tap-tapping while she searched her mind for an answer. "I'm not rightly sure she ever said where she was goin'. Now, why don't you tell me what's goin' on?"

Cain looked into the old woman's keen brown eyes. Should he confide his fears to her or keep his concerns to himself? "I don't want to worry you."

"Look, if you're afraid I'll go to pieces—don't be," Trixie said in a sharp voice. "I may be old, and I may not be as strong as I was a few years back, but I'm not senile, and I've never been the kind who's subject to the vapors. Now, if something's wrong with Julee, you'd best tell me. I just might be able to help." As usual when she was agitated, Trixie's Cajun accent was as thick as ribbon cane syrup.

"I'm sorry."

"You ought to be," Trixie chastised. "You think I'm not worried about that girl, too? Lord knows, I haven't had a good night's sleep all week. Now, stop beatin' around the bush and tell me what's got you so stirred up."

Cain told her about dreaming of Brice, the childish words he'd heard, and how Brice had seemed all right. Then he told her about trying to locate Brice on the map and how that failed avenue seemed at odds with his dream. He told how he and Julee had tried to re-create the scene of the kidnapping on Friday.

"I got a description this time," he said, "but the police haven't come up with anything yet."

He cast a troubled look at Trixie, wondering how she'd handle the next part. "Then, yesterday, with Julee's permission, I went over to see if I could pick up on any vibrations Lanny might have left behind."

"What do you mean 'left behind'?" Trixie asked. "Don't tell me that lunatic broke into her house and she never told me?"

"Not exactly. There wasn't a forced entry." Trixie was obviously more upset about Lanny getting into Julee's house than she was about Cain picking up vibrations. He explained about Julee finding the note in her lingerie drawer and that she'd had no idea how Lanny got inside.

He told Trixie how he'd felt Lanny's presence out by the water spigot.

"Lanny pretended to be a plumber so he could get into the house," Trixie said in amazement.

"Right." Cain told her that Lanny must have left the wrench behind by mistake and how finding it on the shelf in Julee's bathroom had helped him to visualize Lanny and his scheme. When he told her what he'd heard Lanny say, Trixie's face grew white.

"It all ties in with a dream I've been having about a fire," he said, winding up his tale.

"Laws a mercy, Cain!" Trixie said through stiff lips. "You've got to find that girl and warn her. I think that madman means to take her to Brice and burn them both up!"

Trixie might be a talker, but she definitely wasn't senile.

Something nagged at Trixie's memory all day, some nebulous, worrisome tidbit that made her want to bite her nails—if they hadn't been acrylic. She'd told Cain the truth; she didn't know where Julee had gone, but there was something she should know, something she should be able to tell him....

"Pay attention to details," she said aloud, recalling the horoscope Cain had read to her that morning.

She did a tarot reading for herself and couldn't find a single thing to help. She considered getting out the Ouija board, but a couple of hair-raising experiences in the past made her loath to unearth the wretched thing—which she suspected was *not* the tool of good psychic forces—from its hidden nook in the hall closet. It was pure-dee hell getting old.

She shook her head in disgust. There was nothing to do but keep trying to remember. While she was doing that, she might as well clean out her drawers. Lord knew the little fairies weren't going to come and do it for her while she slept.

Julee and the Sutherlands started home soon after lunch. The excitement and confusion as well as trying to sleep in a strange bed had tired Gene until all he could talk about was getting home. But even his weariness didn't stop their reminiscing about the people they'd seen and how much fun they'd had. The miles flew by, and not even the sight of the white Ford sedan tailing them diminished their exuberance.

Julee had looked through photo albums and watched home movies. There were innumerable pictures of Tad. But this year, they brought no real sorrow, only a quiet feeling of losing something dear while still having a wellspring of beautiful memories. She would always love Tad, but he was truly a part of her past.

North of Lake Charles, Julee got behind a poky bread truck. Unfamiliar with the roads and uncertain whether or not there was passing room on the two-lane highway before the next hill or curve, she took the safe route and followed behind it for several miles.

When she finally passed the truck, a group of cars coming from the opposite direction kept the plainclothes detail from following. Julee met Gene Sutherland's gaze in the rearview mirror.

"I think we've ditched our tail for a mile or so."

The words had no more than left her lips when she glanced in the rearview mirror and saw red plastic bread racks, complete with bread, tumble from the back of the truck onto the highway.

"Oh, my gosh!" she said, hitting her brakes and slowing the Explorer to a crawl. "That bread truck is losing its load."

Gene and Loretta turned around to see what was going on. Julee snatched quick glimpses in the mirror while trying to keep her own vehicle on the road.

The police car cut to the left, trying to avoid a collision with the shelves, but even though the move looked like a quarterback dodging a block, there was no way to avoid the rack that flew smack-dab into the windshield of the unmarked car.

"Oh, dear!" Loretta moaned as loaves of bread fell to the ground like manna from heaven.

Gene's comment was a terse "Damn!" as the driver of the unmarked police car swerved across the centerline, just missing an oncoming pickup, then slewed to the right, where the car skidded in the soft dirt of the narrow shoulder and landed nose down in a ditch. The driver of the bread truck, who must have noticed what was happening, eased to the side of the road.

"Should we stop to see if everyone's all right?" Julee asked, pulling to a stop.

"Nah!" Gene said. "A couple of other people have stopped and both the cops are out of the car walking around. They're fine. Just get me home to bed."

Despite a feeling of uneasiness at leaving her protection behind, one look at Gene's gray face told Julee that maybe he was right to want to get home. The last thing she needed was for him to have a spell with his heart while they were a couple of hundred miles away from his doctor. Stifling a sigh, she increased the Explorer's speed to the conventional fifty-five miles per hour.

* * *

Cain thought that the day might possibly be the longest he had ever lived through. He kept watch on Julee's house and called at least once an hour, just in case he missed seeing her get home. He was too nervous to watch television or work outside. He tried going back to the painting, but it was hard to be creative when his mind was a million miles from any beach house.

A little before five, he'd had about all he could take of pacing the house. He changed into shorts and pulled on his battered running shoes. It was too hot to take a long run, but if he didn't get out of the house for a while he'd go stark-staring crazy.

He hit the front door running, filled with frustration and a growing concern. Where was Julee, and why hadn't she come home?

After Julee helped the Sutherlands unload their things and made sure they were settled in for the night, she decided to check her messages from her car phone—something she hadn't done since she'd left the day before. The last thing she wanted to do was drive all the way home only to find that Dylan Garvey needed her to come to the station, or that she wasn't to go back into the house for any reason, or that Trixie needed her to pick up something from the store. Once she stepped through the door, all she wanted to do was crash.

There were several dozen hang-ups on the machine. More than she could ever remember getting in such a short time span. She frowned, wondering who on earth could have called so many times without leaving a message.

"Hello, Julee."

Those two softly spoken words were her answer. Julee clenched the receiver with a white-knuckled grip. The caller was Lanny Milligan. "Where are you, Julee?" Lanny's voice asked via the airwaves and her answering machine. His pleasant, conversational tone was more terrifying than threats.

"I've been trying to get hold of you for two days," the disembodied voice said. "It's real important, see, and I didn't want to leave a message. I needed to talk to you in person. But you haven't been home, so-o-o-o..."

He dragged the word out, and Julee knew she wasn't imagining the malicious, teasing note in his voice. This was all just a game to him. A deadly game of cat and mouse, hunter and prey.

"I finally decided that maybe I ought to leave a message after all, so here it is. If you want to see your little boy, meet me at the house we've been working on, say... around six-thirty this evening. And Julee, you know the drill. Come alone. No cops. Et cetera, et cetera, et cetera," he droned.

"Gee, I was really hoping to talk to you in person so that I could impress the importance of you showing up. I sincerely hope you get this message in time to make it...if you know what I mean."

A chilling chuckle followed the comment, and then a click signaled that he'd hung up. Julee did the same. A shiver of apprehension slithered down her spine. Of course she knew what he meant. She looked at her watch and saw that it was just twenty after five. That gave her plenty of time.

"Meet me at the house we've been working on."

"We've?" Julee said aloud. Her heart leaped into her throat. Had Lanny Milligan been working for her? If so, he had to be one of the two men Luther had hired this week.

Julee gripped the steering wheel and drew a deep breath to steady her nerves. She had to think! She needed to decide what she was going to do. Lanny said not to call the police. Julee had seen enough movies to know that it was daring, if not downright risky, to play the game by Lanny's rules, but she intended to do just that. She was a mother, and the police wouldn't understand that she was willing to offer herself to save Brice. She would go to the meeting alone, but she'd be careful. She wanted to hold Brice in her arms again, and if that meant jumping through Lanny Milligan's hoops, that's what she'd do.

She put the Ford in gear and backed out of the driveway, her weariness forgotten in a rush of adrenaline and a surge of hope.

"What do you mean, you were ambushed by a bread truck?" Dylan demanded when one of his men phoned him from a convenience store in Lake Charles. He listened in amazement while Kyle Lattimer told him about the driver of the bread truck—a new man—not latching the door securely and the shelves spilling out onto the highway.

When Dylan was assured that no one was hurt, he asked the question he most feared hearing the answer to. "Where's Julee Sutherland?"

"She kept going," Lattimer told him.

"Why doesn't that surprise me?" Dylan muttered almost to himself. "When did this fiasco take place?"

"About three."

Dylan cursed. It was nearing five-thirty. "Why did you wait so long to call?"

"When the rack hit the windshield, it shattered into a jillion pieces. Prothro and I both had to have some stitches."

"Stitches!" Dylan exploded. "I thought you said you were all right!"

"We are, other than a few cuts. Thank God, we both had on sunglasses."

Yeah, thank God, Dylan thought, recalling horror stories of crash victims who hadn't. The realization that two of his best men might have suffered permanent sight damage made him ashamed of his outburst. He offered Lattimer a faltering apology.

"It's all right, Lieutenant. What do you want us to do?"

Dylan raked a hand through his hair. "See if you can get the car towed in and arrange for a rental to come home in. We'll pick up the other one when it's fixed."

"What about Julee Sutherland?"

"Maybe a patrol can pick her up at this end when she drops off her in-laws or something."

"Okay. I'm sorry, Lieutenant."

"Nothing to be sorry for, Lattimer. It was just one of those things. One more thing, Lattimer. Where's the house Julee Sutherland's building?"

"Rocky Road."

"Thanks."

Dylan hung up and went to the window, where he planted his hands on his lean hips. This was just dandy. He had a woman with a known killer after her, a killer who'd finagled his way into her house while it was full of people and with the police crawling all over the place, a killer who, according to the phone tap, had recently left a chilling ultimatum on her answering machine, and she'd driven off and left what little protection he could offer her sitting in a ditch.

Dylan swore. Where was she? Knowing Julee as he was beginning to, he had little doubt that she'd make tracks to the rendezvous spot without bothering to contact him.

He contacted a plainclothes unit and told them to make tracks for Rocky Road. It wouldn't hurt to have someone in place.

There was a deserted shack about a quarter of a mile from the turnoff that led to Rocky Melancon's house. Julee pulled off the highway and drove around back of the tumbledown house, a half-baked idea forming in her mind. If she hiked to the house and Lanny didn't know she was there, she might be able to do something to catch him off guard and—

Do what, Julee? Knock him unconscious? Wrestle him to the ground? You aren't some tough, female sleuth. You aren't even Nancy Drew.

What she was was a mother whose child was in danger. And like any mother, she'd fight for her cub to the bitter end. Still, her determination didn't keep her knees from knocking or her hands from shaking as she locked the doors of the Explorer and stuffed the keys into the pocket of her denim shorts.

She started down the driveway, certain that what she was about to do was insanity. She *wasn't* a cop, and she couldn't pull off any acts of derring-do. Despite Lanny's warning, she should have called Dylan. He was a trained professional. He would know how to handle the situation. She stopped a few yards from her vehicle and gnawed her lower lip in indecision.

Maybe she should at least call Cain or Trixie so someone would know what was going on. She retraced her steps back to the Ford and unlocked the door. She wouldn't call Trixie. Though her neighbor was a ball of fire, she was a long way from youth's blush, and knowing that Julee was walking into certain danger might be too stressful.

Besides, there was a part of Julee that wanted to hear Cain's voice, to be reassured that everything was going to be all right and that he'd be there for her, that her white knight would come rushing to her rescue. Her mouth twisted into a wry smile. So much for women's lib.

She thought of the way Cain's mouth had warmed hers with such insistency and the way it felt to be held in his arms, and she knew that if—no, *when* she got out of this mess, she would do whatever she could to hold on to those feelings and him.

She looked up Cain's number in the phone book she kept on the seat and dialed his number. His phone rang four times.

"Hi, this is Cain. I can't come to the phone right now...."

She started to hang up and then remembered him saying that he seldom answered the phone these days because of the steady influx of undesirable calls and his devotion to his painting. Even so, he must check his machine at regular intervals just in case there was a legitimate call coming through. Julee waited for his message to end and listened for the beep.

"Hi, Cain," she said. "This is Julee...."

Cain finished his run just short of five-thirty. The heat was a killer, he thought, peeling off the sleeveless worse-for-wear T-shirt and heading straight for a lukewarm shower. The run had accomplished what he'd set out to do: It had purged his mind of every troubling thought, at least for that short half hour. The only problem was that now all those thoughts were all rushing back, stronger than before.

He pulled on a pair of clean jeans and started for the kitchen and a glass of iced tea. The phone rang as he passed the living room, and he saw the light blinking on the answering machine. Against his better judgment, he picked up the receiver with a terse "Hello."

"Cain! Thank God you're back!"

"Trixie! What's wrong?" Cain asked, his heart leaping in fear. "Is it Julee?"

"No-o-o. Well, not exactly, but something's been nagging at me all day, something I should have remembered. Well, I was cleaning, and I finally figured out what it is."

"What?"

"Julee has a phone in her car," Trixie said. "A mobile phone. I swear, I don't know what they'll think of next. Back when I was a young lady, we were lucky to even have a phone, and now they put them in cars! Can you imagine?"

Cain ground his teeth. He wasn't in any mood for Trixie's babbling. "Do you know the number?"

"Of course I do." There was no disguising the affront in her voice. "I found it when I was cleaning out the kitchen-junk drawer. That's why I called."

Cain closed his eyes. "Why don't you give it to me and I'll see if I can reach her."

"Sure 'nough, darlin'."

He wrote down the number she rattled off, thanked her and hung up. He started to dial, but the red light of the answering machine kept winking at him. He had listened to the messages just before he left, so chances were that it was some jerk wanting a tip on the lottery. But what if it was Julee? On that off chance, he pressed the button to rewind the tape.

"Hi, Cain. This is Julee."

Cain's heart leaped in relief and happiness.

"In case you're wondering what happened to me, we stayed overnight at the reunion. In case you're wondering where I am, I'm getting ready to go to the house we've been building.

"I got a call from Lanny while I was gone. He wants me to meet him at the house so I can see Brice. He said to come alone and not to call the cops, but I thought maybe I should tell someone where I am, just in case." A nervous giggle followed the statement.

"Anyway, don't be mad." He heard her sigh. "And Cain, just if something...happens, I want you to know that I think I'm falling in love with you."

"Bad timing, baby," Cain said as the message ended and the machine beeped three times. "Real bad timing." He reached for the mobile number Trixie had given him and punched it in. "Come on, Julee, answer," he begged. "I want to hear you say you love me in the flesh."

After half-a-dozen rings, Cain slammed down the receiver, thought better of it and dialed Trixie's number. "Where's the house Julee's building?" he blurted when Trixie answered.

"What?"

"There was a message on my machine from Julee," he explained. "She's going to meet Lanny at the house she's been working on. I've got to get out there!"

"Oh, dear," Trixie said. "Let me think."

Cain could almost see her tapping her finger alongside her mouth.

"I think she said it was out Highway 311. A couple of miles past a little grocery store. It's for that fancy lawn man—what's his name? You know, he's always in the paper."

"Rocky Melancon?"

"That's the one," Trixie said. "It's out there on a road they named after him."

"Melancon Road?"

"No," she said with a giggle. "Rocky Road."

"You're sure."

"Well, of course I'm sure. I'm not senile, I just—"

"Thanks, Trixie," Cain interrupted. "Do me a favor, will you?"

"Anything for you, darlin'."

"Call the police station and ask for Detective Garvey. Tell him what's happened and have him send out some help."

"Will do. And Cain, be careful, won't you? It wouldn't do for Julee to lose you, too."

"I will," Cain said, and hung up. He thought about taking a weapon, but knew he'd never be able to use one. He had his fists, and his brain. That would have to be enough. He grabbed his truck keys and headed out the door. As the kidnappers had just a week before, he left the house with a screeching of tires.

He was almost out of the subdivision when he had a thought that gave him a marginal sense of relief. Dylan Garvey had a team of men following Julee. No matter where she went they wouldn't be far behind. For the first time since he'd met the young detective, Cain was thankful for the man's thoroughness.

Situated at the end of a half mile of winding gravel road and nestled between a large pond and a grove of trees, the cedar-and-rock house Julee's company had been working on was impossible to see until you entered the twelve-acre clearing.

Despite the fact that she'd walked the last half mile, she was early. There was no car in sight. Maybe she'd managed to beat Lanny. Good.

Julee's nerves were stretched to the screaming point. She heard a crackling noise and looked over her shoulder. A rabbit scampered through the tangle of brush. She squeezed her eyes shut and forced herself to take deep, slow breaths. When she opened her eyes again, she felt a little calmer.

As she neared the house, she kept a cautious eye out for anything that looked out of the ordinary. This was the first time she'd been to the site when there wasn't a crew of men around, hammering, sawing, laying the rock work around the foundation or doing the hundred-and-one things necessary in building a house.

She eyed the scrap lumber, the scattered shingles and the empty windows. They hadn't reached the cleanup stage yet, and the house looked almost forlorn. It might just have easily been abandoned as one that had yet to be filled with people.

Julee's gaze scanned the area around the house. Seeing nothing out of the ordinary, she took a set of keys from her pocket and let herself in the front door. Dusk was fast approaching, aided by the shade from the thick trees that bordered the edge of the soon-to-be lawn.

Julee found a length of two-by-four with a nail in the end. As a makeshift weapon, it would do. Moving as quietly as possible through the gathering gloom, she checked out each of the downstairs rooms. There was no sign of Lanny.

She paused in the doorway of the kitchen and let her gaze roam the room. She saw nothing but the cans of sealer and mineral spirits the painters had left behind. Leaving the kitchen, Julee went upstairs and checked the two bedrooms and baths. Still no sign of Lanny.

As she had been since they began work on the house, she was drawn to the master bedroom, where a giant balcony hung over the edge of a huge Olympic-size swimming pool, forming shade in an area where there weren't any trees.

Rocky Melancon, a highly successful landscape artist from Baton Rouge, had inherited the acreage from his family several years before and designed the house himself. He spent several weekends a year at the property, staying in a small travel trailer so he could work on the grounds.

He wanted the house to be a showplace, and it looked to Julee as if his wish was coming true. The perfection of the landscaping was a testimony to his huge success, a *House Beautiful* dream come true.

Rocky had finished the pool the summer before. It was kept in swimming readiness throughout the summer months so that he and his ladylove could take a dip whenever the heat from all his digging and planting and tending became too much.

Leaning over the edge of the upper deck, Julee peered down at the crystal-clear water. She wondered if Brice was old enough for lessons and if Cain liked to swim.

The flash of something across the pond at the far edge of the pasture interrupted Julee's wandering thoughts. She straightened from the balcony railing, her heart breaking into a faster rhythm. Was it Lanny she'd seen at the edge of the woods across the way, or just one of the many deer that roamed the place? An uncontrollable shiver whispered down her spine. Whatever she'd seen, it was time she stopped daydreaming and found herself a place to hide and wait for Lanny.

As she started to turn on one rubber-soled Keds, she heard a sound like a grunt of pain, and then a thousand fireworks exploded inside her head and everything went as black as a moonless night.

Consciousness returned in slow degrees. Julee tried to lift her head and found that it weighed twice its normal weight. As a matter of fact, her head hurt so badly it felt as if she'd drunk a bottle of sangria all by herself—no, make that two bottles—and her stomach was cramping with that unmistakable pain that usually preceded upchucking.

She opened her eyes in slow increments and realized she was sitting against the wall in Rocky Melancon's master bedroom. With a moan of distress, she tried to get up and discovered that her ankles were bound together and her hands were tied behind her back. *Great, Julee,* she thought groggily. *What would a female cop do in this situation?*

She was still contemplating that question when she heard a noise and lifted her head. Lanny Milligan stood in the doorway, his evil face wearing a smirk of satisfaction, a gun in his right hand. He didn't look anything like the man she remembered from the trial. If she'd passed him on the street, she'd never have known him. The gun was his only give-away.

"You woke up, I see."

"You hit me," she accused him.

"Just a light tap to the back of the neck to incapacitate you for a little while. I had a—" he grinned that diabolical grin again "—burning desire to take care of some unfinished business, and I didn't need you distracting me."

"Where's Brice?" Julee demanded. The breeze that blew through the open French doors held a hint of wood smoke.

"Brice?" Lanny looked perplexed for a second.

"You said I could see him."

"Oh, yes. Brice," he said, rallying. "Your little boy. I wouldn't worry about him if I were you. The little angel is doing just fine, I'm sure."

"You said I could see him!" Julee shouted, the effort setting up a din inside her head. She drew her legs up against her chest.

Lanny tsk-tsked. "Don't be such a worrywart."

The smell of smoke grew stronger.

He moved closer to Julee and leaned down until his face was mere inches from hers. "You'd be wise to worry about yourself, not the boy. You're about to burn for what you and your husband did to my little girls."

Burn? Julee looked into his cold blue killer's eyes and felt her heart shrivel up inside her. It *was* smoke she smelled. Her eyes grew wide and her heart set up a wild stampede. It all made perfect sense now. Lanny had lured her here so that he could kill her. He'd never had any intention of letting her see Brice. She prayed to God that he hadn't hurt him.

"You can't fight face-to-face," she said in a hushed, venomous voice. "You have to ambush your victims and take out your revenge on innocent children."

"An eye for an eye," he quoted.

"Please," she said, shaking her head and closing her eyes to block out the sight of him. "Don't try to justify your behavior by quoting Scriptures. You're nothing but a despicable coward!"

Lanny leaned over and the back of his hand caught her across the face. Julee didn't stop to question the wisdom of her actions; she didn't think. She just reacted with the only weapon she had. Giving a scream of rage, she kicked both feet out with all the force she could muster. They contacted solidly with Lanny Milligan's middle and sent him staggering backward onto the floor.

He screamed, a sound of agony. Julee expected anger, not pain. He rolled to his side, and she heard him retching.

"Lanny!" she cried. His only answer was an agonized moan as he curled into a fetal position. She waited for him to move. To get to his feet and use the gun to kill her.

After what seemed like an eternity, Julee called out to him again. Lanny didn't answer, didn't move. Tendrils of smoke rose up the stairway and drifted into the room—the fire was gaining strength with every minute. Julee tried to get to her feet, but couldn't get her balance with her bound ankles and wrists.

Pushing herself with the toes of her tennis shoes and moving like a snake, she inched her way along the floor to the doorway. When she saw the roiling smoke coming up the stairs, she knew that even if she managed to get down the stairs without breaking her neck, there was little chance of surviving the fire.

Defeated, Julee turned her cheek to the floor and prayed while tears ran down her cheeks. She thought of the phone in the Explorer that had rung and rung as she'd walked away, the phone she hadn't answered because she was filled with that damnable Eldridge pride and didn't like to depend on anyone else. It occurred to her that pride was a terrible price to pay for a life.

Chapter Eleven

By the time Cain reached the turnoff, his nerves were in tatters. As he'd driven toward the Melancon place, breaking every speed and traffic law in Louisiana, the same litany he'd heard just a week before whispered through his mind: *Hurry. Hurry. Hurry.*

He switched on his signal and made a right turn onto a narrow gravel road. Branches arched overhead, and gathering shadows imprisoned the sunlight that was rapidly being swallowed by the encroaching night.

Fearing exposure by sight or sound, Cain pulled his car to the side of the road. If he walked in, anyone who might be watching would be less likely to see him. He eased the door shut and was about to turn around when a no-nonsense voice ordered, "Hold it right there."

Cain froze, his hand still gripping the door handle, the hair at the nape of his neck standing at attention. So much for his attempts to play the hero.

"Put your hands on top of the car."

Cain did as he was instructed. The voice didn't sound like Lanny, but neither did it sound like anyone Cain wanted to tangle with...especially since he had a vivid mental picture of the hand connected to the voice holding a snub-nosed revolver.

"Pat him down."

Relief eddied through him. If all his television watching counted for anything, he suspected these two were police, not murderers. Satisfied that he wasn't carrying a weapon, the owner of the first voice ordered him to turn around. Slowly.

Cain complied.

A burly middle-aged man in an off-the-rack gray suit stood a few feet away. His partner, a tall, thin black man who looked several years younger, stood with his hands on his hips. The first man reholstered his weapon and flashed a badge. "Joe McClellan. Houma P.D. What's your name and what are you doing out here?"

"Cain Collier. Julee called me. What's this all about, officers?"

"Collier. Oh, the psychic. Lieutenant Garvey instructed us to come out here and watch for Ms. Sutherland and Lanny Milligan. So far we haven't seen either of them."

Cain frowned, and a sick feeling lodged in the pit of his stomach. "I thought your men were following Julee."

A look of embarrassment crossed McClellan's face. Lancaster spoke up. "They had a minor accident, and she got away from them."

Cain swore. "So there's no one watching her?"

The policeman shook his head. "We thought we got here early enough to intercept her, but she didn't come down the road, and this is a big place. We've already called for backup."

"How did you know Julee was meeting Lanny?" Cain asked.

"Phone tap," McClellan said.

"She didn't know her phone was tapped."

"She wasn't supposed to."

Cain checked his watch. "They have to be here—probably in the house. Julee was supposed to meet Lanny at six-thirty, and it's almost that now."

"I know. We were heading in when you arrived," Lancaster said. "So why don't you get back in your truck and let us handle it? We've got lots more experience, and more help is on the way."

Cain recalled the horoscope he'd read that morning, something about accepting assistance. But he didn't care what his horoscope said. Julee needed him. "Like hell," he said with a shake of his head. "I'm going in. Lanny's here, and he's going to burn down the house with Julee and Brice in it."

A shocked expression crossed Lancaster's bland features. "How do you know that? Did Milligan tell you his plans?"

"No," Cain said. "I dreamed it." At that point he didn't particularly care whether the Houma policemen believed him or wanted to try him for heresy. He just wanted to get to Julee.

"Dreamed it? Oh, yeah," the black cop said. "That psychic stuff, right?"

"Right," Cain said with feigned patience. "Now will you just get out of my way and let me do what I came to do before it's too late? I can't be too late again."

"What do you mean?"

"I mean that I dreamed about a fire once before, but I didn't realize it was a warning until it was too late to save my wife and daughter. I can't be too late with Julee."

Cain would never know what shifted things in his favor. Maybe they saw the truth in his eyes. Maybe they thought they could use his help until backup arrived. Or maybe they recognized the torment there, a torment they were familiar with and appreciated. They understood too well what being too late could mean.

"Let him go," Lancaster said.

McClellan nodded. "We'll be right behind you."

Hurry. Hurry. Hurry.

"Thanks." Cain started off at a fast jog. He stopped and turned. "Call the fire department. Unless I'm badly mistaken, we're gonna need them."

The cops nodded simultaneously and Cain sprinted forward. A breeze rustled the leaves and fanned his heated face as he ran along the winding road. He thought he caught a whiff of smoke, and increased his speed. *Hurry.*

After almost a quarter of a mile, he rounded a curve and came to an abrupt halt. Here the trees ended and the road took a sharp curve to the right, running along the top of a dam that held back the waters of a large pond. The pond sat in the middle of several cleared acres that was fringed with more trees. Beyond the pond sat the pool and the house that Julee had built.

The house that Lanny Milligan was destroying.

A goodly portion of the bottom floor was already ablaze, and greedy tongues of flame licked the dry cedar with a hunger that wouldn't be appeased until there was nothing left but skeletal remains.

An undertow of fear swirled around Cain, pulling him closer and closer to a spiraling abyss. The dream rushed back with sickening clarity. Julee at the window. Calling. Too late.

"No-o-o!" he screamed in perfect re-creation of the dream. He turned and started to run, but a heavy hand gripped his shoulder. He turned in surprise. Lancaster stood in front of him, sweat running in rivulets down his ebony face.

"See him?" Lancaster cocked his head toward the house.

Cain looked and saw a man sidling into the woods. He walked doubled over, as if he was in intense pain. "Lanny," he said, in no doubt that it was his former brother-in-law.

"Joe and I'll take care of him. You get your lady." Cain nodded. "Stay off the road," Lancaster advised. "Stay close to the trees and don't do nothin' crazy. But if you can't help doin' something crazy, for God's sake be careful."

Cain nodded again. He felt a supportive squeeze on his shoulder, and then he was off, running strongly, steadily, sticking close to the perimeter of the woods, while the underbrush snapped beneath his feet and a voice taunted him from inside his head.

"I'm going to get you, Julee. Hahahaha!"

Cain shook his head to rid himself of the sound of Lanny's voice and the dream. As he sprinted the last long yards to the house, his troubled gaze searched the area. Lanny had vanished, intent on making his getaway. But Lanny wasn't the foe Cain feared. The fire would be the true test of his courage.

Screaming Julee's name, he circled the house. There was no getting in the French doors of the dining room. The heat was so intense it took only a matter of seconds before he gave that up as a lost cause. Gaining entry on the living room side of the house was impossible, too. Cain edged around the house to the pool side. One glance through the doors beneath the second-story deck showed an impossible situation. The fire had spread to the bottom of the stairs and was licking its way up tread by tread.

Julee was on the second floor.

A quick appraisal of the situation told Cain that the only avenue up was the latticework that formed a sheltered nook beneath one side of the overhanging deck. It was also the only way down.

"Don't do nothin' crazy.... Be careful." Lancaster's admonition played through Cain's mind as he checked the strength of the lattice. Thank God, Rocky Melancon wanted, and could afford, only the best. The lattice was the pricey, one-inch-thick kind that was not just stapled, but glued at every junction.

A closer inspection showed him that Julee's workmanship was a worthy companion to the materials used: the lattice was screwed into the treated lumber framework, not nailed. It might not hold, but Cain knew that if he'd had the opportunity to put in his order, this was better than anything he ever could have dreamed.

Without waiting another minute, he pulled off his sneakers. The toes were too wide to fit into the small openings of the lattice. As it was, he'd have to hook a couple of toes in and rely on the strength of his arms to pull his weight.

He looked up. Smoke was swirling out the open French doors in oily gray billows. Thankfully, he only had about a twelve-foot span to climb. "Hold on, Julee!" he yelled over the noisy crackling of the fire. "I'm coming up!"

Reaching as high as he could, Cain grasped the lattice and wedged his toes into the small opening. He pulled himself up, got another toe- and fingerhold and inched up another foot or so. He thought he heard sirens screaming in the distance, but couldn't be sure. A gust of wind blew straight at him, carrying a blast of heat that almost caused him to let go. The other side of the house was going fast, the cedar boards a perfect conduit for the ravenous flames. Even if the sirens belonged to a fire truck, there was no way the blaze could be extinguished in time to save Julee's life.

Cain stretched, and his fingers curled over the smooth, eased edge of the railing. Pushing with his feet, he took a tighter hold and heaved himself over the side. He paused for a couple of seconds to catch his breath, and then fought his way through the smoke toward the doors and into the bedroom, calling Julee's name as he went.

"Cain!" she screamed. "Over here...by the door!"

He turned toward the sound of the hoarse, panic-stricken cry, but thick gray smoke obscured everything. He lowered himself to his belly where the smoke wasn't quite so dense and crawled along the floor army-style toward the sounds of Julee's sobs. The plywood felt hot to his touch.

Finally, when he was beginning to think he'd never reach her, his fingers encountered the warmth of her skin. Relief, so sweet and poignant he wanted to gather her in his arms and shout from the rooftops, swept through him. But there was no time for rejoicing. Not yet. He could see the angry flames thrashing their way closer and closer.

"Can you walk?" he yelled into her ear. His throat was raw from smoke. He could only imagine what Julee's felt like.

"My hands and feet are tied."

Cain swore. There was no time to untie her. The fire was getting closer, slurping up the fresh air coming through the open doors and exhaling thick acrid smoke. They had to get out. He took a deep breath and squatted next to Julee. Grabbing her around the waist, he hoisted her to his shoulder. Then he stood, the muscles in his runner's legs holding him in good stead.

"Hold your breath," he gasped, heading toward the small patch of darkening sky outside the open doors.

Though smoke roiled out behind them, the air on the balcony seemed fresh and sweet in comparison. Cain lowered Julee to the deck. Even knowing that time was at a premium, nothing on the face of the earth could have stopped him from making sure she was all right. He framed her soot-smudged face between his hands, and her red-rimmed eyes filled with tears.

A mighty groan rent the air. Cain turned in time to see part of an outside wall collapse, sending a geyser of sparks high into the sky. He reached into his pocket and pulled out the small penknife he'd carried since he was a boy. Dull from years of misuse and neglect, he had to saw at the ropes binding Julee's hands and feet.

Hurry. Hurry. Hurry.

When he pulled the last rope free, Julee reached up and laid a palm against his cheek. Her eyes were filled with love and thankfulness.

"Your timing stinks, Julee," he said in a bleak voice, but there was the barest glint of laughter in his eyes that she answered with a faltering smile.

He hooked his arm around her waist and hauled her to her feet. "Let's get out of here."

Julee grabbed his wrist in a tight grip. "Cain, did you see Brice?"

He shook his head. He didn't need to tell her that if Brice was on the lower floor, the chances of his survival were zero. The light in Julee's eyes dimmed, and she seemed to grow older in the span of a few seconds.

"Come on, baby. Let's go."

"I don't think I can," she said in a faltering, tear-thickened voice. "My legs and arms are asleep."

The house gave another mighty groan, like the agonized moan of a dying dinosaur. Cain knew there was no way he could carry her down, even if the lattice was strong enough to hold their combined weights.

"We'll have to take our chance in the pool." He dragged her to the railing. The water looked clear and inviting and a long way down. "Do you dive?"

Julee's eyes widened in terror. She shook her head.

"Me, neither." His smile was wry and fleeting. "I guess we'll just cannonball."

"Cain, I—"

His gaze bored into hers. "Get up on that rail and jump, Julee, and be damned glad Rocky Melancon built his pool first."

Julee nodded. She eased her legs over the rail. Cain was beside her in a second. He squeezed her hand and brushed her cheek with a light kiss, then they pushed off the edge of the high deck together and fell through the endless sky....

Azure water rushed toward him and then he hit with a splash that sent him rushing down, down, down, into the turquoise depths. Somewhere on the way, he lost his grip on Julee's hand. He opened his eyes but didn't see her. Then his feet hit the bottom of the pool, and he shoved himself upward.

When he broke the surface, he trod water, looking for Julee, screaming her name over the sound of half-a-dozen sirens. He saw two fire trucks pull to a stop as part of the house trembled, creaked and collapsed in an explosion of sparks and smoke.

Simultaneously, it seemed, Julee came shooting to the surface like a missile from a submarine. The sight of her gasping, eel-sleek head was the sweetest sight Cain had ever seen.

For the next three hours, paramedics, police and firemen swarmed Rocky Melancon's place, which had been cordoned off by the familiar black-and-yellow crime-scene tape. Julee, who was naturally overwrought and crying for Brice, was given a mild sedative and taken to the hospital, while Cain, who insisted that he was all right, stayed behind to help sort out what had happened.

Lanny, who was in so much pain from Julee's well-aimed kick that McClellan and Lancaster had apprehended him with minimal effort, was taken to the hospital, where he would undergo extensive questioning, and where he would stay under constant guard until he was well enough for transportation to Angola.

Rocky Melancon's dream house had literally gone up in smoke, and now lay in a smoldering heap of rubble. Rocky, who had been notified of what had happened, had voiced extreme disappointment, but had projected a healthy optimism when he'd said he'd been down before and pulled himself up. He also expressed gratitude that the pool was full.

The doctors decided that Julee should spend the night at the hospital. By the time Cain finished making his statement to the police and got cleaned up, the charge nurse suggested that he wait until morning to see her. He had no choice but to settle for a late dinner with Trixie, who pampered him like a long-lost son and listened to his tale with an expression of interest that bordered awe.

That night, for the first time in more than a week, Cain's sleep was deep and dreamless. There were no more messages . . . at least for now.

The dawning of the next day might have been the brightest Monday in the history of the world . . . or at least the century. Cain got up, took a quick shower and called Chantal Garvey to tell her to keep the phone workers away until they were further notified. Julee needed rest, not a house full of people.

He was headed out the door to pick Julee up from the hospital when the phone rang. It was his uncle Phil with the news that the firemen had found no evidence that Brice died in the fire.

"What does that mean?" Cain asked.

"That Lanny didn't bring him and probably that he had no intention of letting Julee see Brice," Phil said. "That was just a classic con, the dangling-carrot scam. Lanny knew that the best way to get Julee to the house would be to tempt her with the promise of seeing her son."

"So where is Brice?"

"I don't know. This isn't my case, so I'm not privy to all the inside information. I only found out he wasn't in the fire because the Houma fire chief and I bowl in the same league. I imagine Dylan will be giving Julee a call any time. He'll fill in the blanks and this will all be over."

"I hope so," Cain said. "I'm not sure how much more Julee can take."

"I know what you mean."

"Look, Phil, I appreciate your calling, but I've got to run. I'm picking Julee up at the hospital."

"Sure. Give me a call when you find out something, okay?"

"I will."

Cain hung up and drove to the hospital, where he found Julee sitting on the edge of the narrow bed waiting for him. When she saw him standing in the doorway, she slid off the bed and walked straight into his arms.

He held her tightly, drinking in the clean scent of her hair, trying to absorb her into his very soul. She was small and delicately formed, but not, he knew, delicate. She was tough, as only someone who's found their back against the wall can be tough, and sensitive as only those who've suffered a great pain can know true sensitivity.

She was his.

After long moments, she leaned back in the circle of his arms and looked up at him with weariness and defeat in her eyes. "Take me home."

"Just as fast as I can."

She started for the bathroom to change, and Cain spoke her name. She turned, a question in her eyes.

"The fire department found no evidence that Brice died in the fire."

Her dark eyebrows drew together in a frown. "Lanny didn't bring him, then?"

"Evidently not."

The heaviness in her demeanor lightened the slightest bit as the frangible tendrils of hope took a new hold. It vanished almost immediately. "Then where is he? Do you think Lanny..."

Her voice trailed away. Cain knew she was contemplating the worst. Cain shook his head. "Maybe Lanny's talked to Dylan by now. We'll know more soon."

She nodded and went into the bathroom. When she'd changed into the clean clothes he'd brought, they walked out of the hospital into the blinding May sunshine, their hands clasped together.

"Your house or mine?" Cain asked when he turned into their subdivision fifteen minutes later.

"Mine. I just want to be around my own things, you know?"

He did. There was comfort in the familiar, and comfort was what Julee needed most now, what she would need until the police found Brice.

Cain pulled into her driveway and helped her inside. He was about to leave when she said, simply, "Stay."

"You should rest."

"I can rest better if you hold me," she said. Cain put his hand in hers and let her lead him to the bedroom, where she lay down and pulled him down beside her. Wrapped in his embrace, she buried her face in his neck and burrowed as close as possible.

"I'm tired," she murmured. "So very tired."

"Then sleep," he told her. "I'll be here."

There was so much to say, so much to tell. So many things to set straight. But now Cain knew, there was time.

They awakened to the chiming of the doorbell. Cain went to answer it and saw Dylan Garvey standing on the front steps looking very somber, very official.

"Is Julee awake?"

"Barely," Cain said, feeling a little self-conscious that the detective had caught him half-asleep. He ran a hand through his rumpled hair. "I'll get her."

"I'm up," Julee said from the middle of the living room. She covered a yawn and gave Dylan a wan smile. "I could use a cup of coffee. How about you?"

"That sounds great, thanks," he replied with a smile.

While Julee set the coffee to dripping, Dylan asked Cain how he thought Julee was doing.

"Physically, she's exhausted. But the truth is, I'm worried about her. She really thought she was going to get Brice back when she agreed to meet Lanny."

"I know." Dylan shifted, as if he couldn't get comfortable in his chair, and finally brought his gaze to Cain's. "I owe you an apology for thinking you were involved."

"No, you don't," Cain said, meaning the words. "Being suspicious is just part of what you do, and I wasn't exactly the most cooperative person in the world."

"I owe you an apology for doubting in your...gift, too."

Cain saw that apologizing didn't come easy for Dylan and that the detective wasn't going to be happy until he'd cleared his conscience.

"Both apologies accepted," he said. "Now, can we forget it?"

"We can drop the subject," Dylan said, "but I doubt I'll ever forget it."

"The coffee will be ready in a little while," Julee said from the doorway. She padded across the room and sat down next to Cain.

"Good. I wanted to stop by and take your statement," Dylan said. "And to give you an update on what we know."

For the next half hour, Julee told about her trip back from the reunion, how she'd received Lanny's message and called Cain. Cain told Dylan about his recurring dream of the fire and how he hadn't known until he found the wrench in Julee's house that fire was Lanny's preferred method of murdering Julee. He explained how he'd tried to reach Julee for two days while she was at the reunion, how Trixie had remembered her mobile phone too late, and how close he'd come to not listening to the message she'd left on his machine.

"Thank God you did," Dylan said. "Even though I knew what was happening because of the phone tap, Lancaster and McClellan couldn't have pulled it off without you."

The look in Julee's eyes said she knew exactly what Dylan meant.

Julee told about her arrival at the house and what had transpired from the time she arrived until she heard Cain calling out to her, finishing with the statement that when Lanny had roused after his brief stint of unconsciousness, he'd staggered down the stairs, leaving her to the hell he'd devised.

"I've never seen anything burn so fast," Cain said.

"The house was cedar," Julee said. "It burns easily, like pine."

"That's true," Dylan said, "but it had a little help. Lanny admitted to dumping gasoline around the lower floors. After Julee kicked him in the stomach and he passed out, he was lucky to save his miserable hide."

"I know the kick must have hurt, but I didn't kick him hard enough to make him pass out, did I?"

Dylan grinned. "I know you're a tough lady, but no. Lanny has a history of bleeding ulcers, which is why he was in the hospital instead of a prison cell when he escaped last week. According to the doctors, he's in pretty serious condition."

"Did he say why he decided to extend his vendetta to Julee and Brice?" Cain asked.

"When he lost Lucy, he felt as if Tad Sutherland had cost him his entire family. He decided to repay Tad in kind. It didn't matter that Tad was dead and wouldn't know. Lanny spent months perfecting his plan...making the calls, growing a beard and losing the weight so no one would recognize him."

"Why did he break into my house if he planned to lure me out to Rocky's place?" Julee wanted to know.

"Ego," Dylan said. "Pure and simple. He just wanted to see if he could get that close to you without getting caught— and to scare you, of course."

"Ego," Cain said with a shake of his head.

"Thank God for it," Dylan told them. "If Lanny hadn't wanted to put one over on Julee, you'd never have found the wrench, and you might not have figured out the dream in time."

"I've thought about that," Cain said, his eyes solemn. "A lot."

"What about Brice?" Julee asked, now that most of the questions about the fire had been asked and answered to everyone's satisfaction.

"That's another reason I came," Dylan said. The troubled look Cain had seen in his eyes earlier was back.

Julee's hand crept into Cain's. "What about Brice?"

"It's sort of an unexpected wrinkle in the whole episode," Dylan said. He rubbed his blunt index finger against his nose in a gesture that betrayed his chagrin. "We thought that when we got Lanny we'd have our hands on Brice in a matter of hours. But Lanny swears on the graves of his kids and his wife that he doesn't have Brice. Never did."

Unable to stand being in the house any longer, Julee and Cain went to a fast-food restaurant for lunch. Julee was quiet while she picked at her food. She'd been wrapped in a cloak of depression ever since Dylan had left.

Dylan's conclusion was that if Lanny's story was the truth—and they'd check more closely with a lie-detector test—then Brice's disappearance could have only been a random kidnapping.

"Can't you do something?" Julee blurted out of the blue. She sat with her hands wrapped around her chocolate milk shake. "Can't we try again like we did the other day with the ball?"

"I have tried." Julee's eyes questioned; Cain's eyes held an apology. "I haven't been completely honest with you."

"What?"

"I tried something my uncle told me about, something he'd read about another psychic doing. I tried locating Brice on a map. Two maps, actually. One of Louisiana and one of the United States. I didn't get a sense of anything."

"And that's... bad?"

"I don't know. I'd never used that technique before, so I don't know if it just doesn't work for me, or if..." He let his voice trail away, unwilling to verbalize his fears.

"Or if Brice is dead," she finished for him.

Cain nodded. "I didn't say anything because I didn't want you to worry any more than you already were. And then I had another dream that made me think Brice was okay, and I didn't know what to think."

"You have a lot of dreams," Julee said. "Which one is this?"

"Remember the morning I asked you again about 'yellow hair' and 'love forever more'?" She nodded, and he continued. "I dreamed that Brice was somewhere along the coast. There was a house, but I couldn't see it for the dense fog coming off the water. I had the feeling that he was all right, maybe even happy, except for missing you."

"So what does that mean?"

"I'm not sure. I'd like to believe the dream and say that the map trick just doesn't work for me, but I just don't know."

Cain watched her struggle to digest this new and contradictory information, and wanted to hold her close and offer her the comfort of his love. He could be more of a support to her if she'd let him, and he knew that she'd let him when she was ready, but just now the pride and strength that enabled her to keep going after Tad's death was still intact.

On the other hand, he understood that she was trying to deal with the knowledge that Lanny didn't have Brice, and that she was making whatever internal adjustments that might be necessary to her emotional survival if he wasn't found.

All he could do was wait and take his cue from her.

* * *

Cain and Julee spent the rest of the day watching television and getting to know each other as friends. It was a necessary part of the dating ritual, he knew, just as he knew that as lovers, they had a long and glorious history through the dream.

Trixie came over at mid-afternoon, with a chocolate pie and Julee's horoscope—don't fly off the handle, and consider options that seem impossible. Then she demanded a blow-by-blow account of what had happened out on Rocky Road. After relating the episode yet again, Julee hugged her friend and thanked her for all she'd done.

"Buck up, girl," Trixie said as she rose to leave. "You'll find Brice. I just know it."

After Trixie left, Cain checked his messages and was surprised to find that one was from Mark Hightower, the high school principal. When Cain called to see what Mark wanted, he was told that a Detective Garvey had contacted the school board and said that Cain was innocent of any wrongdoing and that it would be a shame to deprive the students of such a capable, caring, talented teacher. The board had reviewed the case and decided to let him come back in the fall, providing he got a proper haircut.

Cain decided that Detective Dylan Garvey might be an all-right fellow, after all.

Julee asked Cain how his work was progressing, and he told her that he'd been painting like a madman the past two days and it was the best work he'd ever done. When she teasingly asked him if she could see the picture, he told her no and changed the subject.

Talked out, Julee took Cain's hand and drew him down on the flokati rug in the middle of the living room floor. "Hold me," she said. Cain complied and for long moments they simply lay on the floor while the music of Yanni's *Reflections of Passion* CD spun a magical web around them.

Finally, Julee raised herself on one elbow and kissed him. At his instant response, she pushed him to his back and lowered her body on top of his. She'd never been aggressive in lovemaking, and she wasn't now. But she led the way, did the encouraging, until Cain took the initiative from her and began to unfasten her buttons. In a matter of minutes, their clothes were scattered across the room.

Cain's mouth traveled over her breasts and her stomach to the little birthmark near her navel.

"I've always loved your birthmark," he said, pressing his mouth to it in a tender kiss.

"How can you have always loved it? You've never seen it," Julee said with a smile.

"Yes, I have," he said, as his hand moved up her rib cage. "You and I have made love dozens of times in another place."

"Another place?" she asked with a smile, but deep inside her heart, she knew he was right. "Where?"

"On a white sandy beach in..." He paused and shook his head. "I'm not sure where. Wherever my dreams have been..."

A disbelieving look entered Julee's eyes. "It was real, then?" she asked, acknowledging with the question that she'd shared the dreams, too.

"As real as dreams can be. But this is better."

His body moved over hers, and he began a gentle stroking like the soft lapping of the water against the shore.

The white rug wasn't sand, but it wasn't a bad substitute.

Later, sated with loving, they watched the sun go down in a blaze of glory. Julee knew that she was lucky to have found Cain and that she was lucky to be alive. She also knew that as long as there was life in her and Cain believed that Brice was alive somewhere, she would never stop looking for him. She made the tearful announcement wrapped in Cain's embrace.

"Me, neither," Cain said, drawing her nearer. When Julee had gained control of her emotions again, he pronounced that he would fix dinner.

"If I'd known you could cook, I'd have snagged you long ago," Julee said, blinking back her tears and trying her best to match his lighthearted mood.

"If I'd known it mattered, I'd have told you," he countered.

After checking the contents of her spice rack, Cain asked if she minded going to his house to get his Greek seasoning—something he simply couldn't make this dish without—while he cleaned the vegetables. "Or you can clean the vegetables and I'll go."

Julee made a face. "I'll go. The walk around the block will do me good."

Darkness wasn't far away, and the heat of the day was waning as Julee let herself into Cain's house. She found the spice exactly where he said it would be and was on her way out when her curiosity about his painting got the best of her. Feeling like a thief and doing her best to reassure herself that he'd never know, she slipped down the hall to his studio.

The room lay in accumulating shadows, and she flipped on the light so she could see better. The back of the easel faced her, and she circled it stealthily, as if she was afraid someone might jump out and grab her.

The house in the painting sat high on a rocky hill at one side of a cove. Sunlight splashed the sea and glinted off the roof of the house.

Julee's eyes widened in shock. Clutching the seasoning in one hand, she lifted the other to her lips to stifle an agonized cry. She didn't know how long she stood staring at the painting, trying to resolve the implications in her mind and finding no answers.

Fury replaced the pain in her heart. Damning the consequences, she grabbed the painting from the easel and stormed toward the door. At that moment she didn't care about the repercussions. She was going to confront Cain, and this time she was going to have the truth.

Chapter Twelve

Julee found Cain in the kitchen, slicing eggplant. He turned when he heard her, a smile on his face. When he saw the fury in her eyes, his good humor faded. When he realized she was carrying his painting, his own temper flared.

"What the hell do you think you're doing?" he asked. "I've told you I don't want you seeing my work until it's finished."

"And why is that, Cain?" she demanded, her face flushed with anger. "Were you afraid that if I saw it, I'd figure out what you were really up to?"

Cain put down the knife and faced her, crossing his arms over his chest. "I don't know what you're talking about," he said. "And I didn't mean you specifically. I don't like anyone looking at my painting until I'm finished."

"Is that right?" She turned the face of the picture toward him and held it out at arm's length. "Well, why don't you try explaining this, anyway."

Cain looked at the picture he'd been working on and back to her. "What about it?" he said with a shrug. "It's a picture of a house on a cliff with a beach. There must be thousands of places like it along the coastlines of the world."

"Places like it, sure. But not places exactly like this one."

Cain held his hands palms out, as if to stay any more of her accusations. "Wait a minute. Are you saying that this is a real place?"

"That's exactly what I'm saying, but since you've done such an excellent job reproducing it, I'm sure you already know that."

A feeling of déjà vu came over Cain. He and Julee had had this conversation when she saw the painting he'd done of the villa in Italy. He thought he'd explained things to her satisfaction. Obviously not. He blew out a long, exasperated breath. "I don't know that. I've never been there, Julee, I swear. I dreamed it."

"Oh, come on, Cain!" Julee snapped. "I fell for that line once, but it's wearing pretty thin the second time around."

"It's the truth!"

Julee laid the painting on the bar and turned a stony face toward him. "I want to know how you met him and what he had to do to get you to weasel your way into my life." She hated herself for the tears that filled her eyes and slipped down her face in silence. *"I want to know how much it cost him to... make you pretend to care about me."*

Cain's face held a pained look, but Julee wasn't buying it, not just now.

"No one paid me to pretend anything," he told her in a weary voice. "And I don't know who you mean."

He was good, she thought, her anger fading before a rising feeling of defeat. Very good. "I'm talking about Cyril Eldridge," she said. "My father."

Stunned didn't begin to describe the shock of Julee's accusation. Cain felt he could have been knocked over with the proverbial feather. There was a short in their communication somewhere, because it looked very much as though she thought he was in the employ—if that was the right word—of her father. But for what reason remained a mystery.

Anger and hurt warred inside Cain. It took considerable effort to keep his voice calm and steady. "I don't know him, and I can't begin to imagine why you think he'd have to pay me to get involved with you."

"Because he's a control freak."

Like everything else she'd said, the statement made little sense in the context of their conversation—if that's what they were having. It was beginning to feel more like an inquisition.

"All right," Cain said in a steady, sensible tone. "He's a control freak. What does that have to do with me? With us?"

"Because he'd like to hurt me the way he claims I hurt him. He'd love nothing better than for me to fall in love with someone and then have me find out that person was just stringing me along, that it wasn't real . . . none of it."

Cain closed the few feet between them and put his hands on her shoulders. The starch and the fight had gone out of her. "Look at me, Julee." She didn't move. "Look at me!"

She raised her head, albeit with reluctance. There was a residual anger in her stormy green eyes, but it was the long-festering pain that cut his heart to the quick.

"It is real," he told her. "All of it."

She wanted to believe him. The need to trust him was there in her eyes along with the agony of her uncertainty. He pulled out a bar stool and guided her toward it.

"We're adults. Capable of talking through our problems. So sit down and tell me what you mean about your father, and how this house fits into the scheme of things, and why you think I've hooked up with him to hurt you. We're going to get to the bottom of this if it takes all night."

Julee sat. Cain leaned against the countertop and listened.

She began falteringly, telling Cain how Cyril had always controlled her and her mother with an iron will, about how she'd done her best to break away before she became swallowed up in his strong personality and lost every bit of what made her Julee Eldridge.

She told him about meeting Tad and how her father's disapproval of her marriage had ended in an irreparable rift in their relationship. She explained how she'd contacted Cyril at Brice's birth and how her father had never acknowledged his grandson. She told him that she'd had no communication from her father since her marriage, except when he sent his attorney to pick up her car.

"Sounds like a real jerk," Cain said when she finished. He inclined his head toward the picture. "What about the house?"

"The house in the picture belongs to my father. It's on a Greek island called Folégandros. I spent a lot of time there as a child." There was nothing left in her voice but the bittersweet memory of happier times and broken dreams.

"I've never been there, Julee," Cain told her. "And I don't know your father."

Her lower lip trembled. "I'd like to believe that."

"I'll swear it on a stack of Bibles and write it in blood if you want."

Julee pressed her lips together and didn't say anything. He understood her hesitation. The evidence against him was strong, at least in her mind, and she'd been through a lot the past week . . . the past four years.

He picked up the painting and stared at it. How could such an innocent endeavor cause such a ruckus? He thought of the intensity of his feelings as he'd painted, and recalled how he'd pictured a carefree, happy Julee walking along the beach. He remembered how he'd jealously wondered if she'd been there with Tad.

As he gazed at the picture, he heard from far away the laughter of a child and the words "love forever more."

Cain closed his eyes and saw Brice running along the water's edge, his brown legs pumping, his feet churning up the white sand while an old woman in a black dress watched with an indulgent smile on her face.

"Come and get me, Clio," Brice called. *"Come and get me."*

"Come and get me...." Cain murmured. "Come and get me...." *Clio.*

"Cain!" Julee said sharply. "Are you all right?"

Cain's eyes snapped open and the image faded from his mind like words drifting away on the wind. Confusion filled his mind and his eyes as he tried to focus on Julee.

"You saw something," she said, hope shining in her eyes. "You saw Brice. You kept saying 'come and get me.' You know where he is, don't you?"

"Brice is here," he said, gripping the painting. Conviction laced his voice.

"Here? Do you mean he's in Greece?"

Cain nodded abstractedly and cut his gaze to Julee's. "He was talking to someone named Clio. Does that name mean anything to you?"

He saw the blood drain from Julee's face. Her whole body began to tremble.

"Clio watched me when I was a child and we stayed at the house in Folégandros," she said, her voice a wisp of sound. "She used to read nursery rhymes to me. She and her husband Dimitri have worked for my father for as long as I can remember."

Cain let the implication of her statement sink in. It opened up a whole new realm of ugly possibilities.

"It never was Lanny," she said, raising her anguished gaze to Cain's. "It was him all along. My father took my baby."

When Julee was empty of tears, empty of everything but a burning anger directed at her father, Cain called Dylan and asked him to come over.

Cain had a hard time believing anyone could be so cruel to his own daughter or his own grandchild, but Dylan was less trusting. He'd seen too many remarkable things during his tenure as a policeman to be surprised by much. Still, he was interested in motive.

"He wanted me under his thumb," Julee said. "When I refused to listen to him and married Tad, it was as if I'd broken some sort of unspoken covenant. He wanted Tad to be everything he claimed he was—a gold digger, a failure— so that I'd come to my senses and come back home...and back under his rule. But Tad was none of those things.

"Then, when Tad was killed, I'm sure Cyril expected me to come crawling back, but I didn't. It never even occurred to me. Instead, I aligned myself even more with Tad by putting everything I had into keeping Sutherland Construction going."

"But you said you contacted him when Brice was born."

"I did," Julee said, nodding. "But he was probably still angry with me for not approaching him sooner. I know him," she said, shaking her head as she paced back and forth across the kitchen.

"The birth announcement wasn't an apology. It wasn't a plea for help. It was just a piece of paper announcing the birth of my son. Tad's son. Something else I'd managed to do without him.'' She stopped and pinned Dylan with a look of conviction. ''He didn't acknowledge Brice because he wasn't through punishing me yet.''

''Sounds like a real sensitive guy,'' Dylan said. ''So why wait until now to get back at you?''

''Who knows?'' she said, throwing her hands into the air and resuming her pacing. ''Maybe it was Thursday and he had a hangnail. Or maybe the stock market was down, or he was bored. Or maybe he saw that Sutherland Construction was doing well, that I was relatively happy, and that the odds were looking slimmer every day that I'd ever come back. Maybe he arranged to have Brice taken so he could show me once and for all that he could still control my life.''

''Do you think he actually believed he could keep Brice a secret forever?'' Cain asked.

''Money can buy a lot of things,'' Dylan said. ''Including silence. It would have been harder—but not impossible—if he'd had to leave Brice in the States. Keeping him out of the country, leaving him on an island where he'd see few people, was an ideal situation. He could tell everyone it was his grandson whose parents had been killed, or they didn't want him, or half-a-dozen other stories. Who's not going to believe a guy with his kind of clout?''

''What do we do next?'' Julee said.

''I'd say we get hold of the Greek authorities and see if we can verify that there is a child at the house. If there is, and we know for sure it's Brice, we'll notify the authorities and have them issue a warrant for your father's arrest. Then I guess you can fly over to Greece and pick up your little boy.''

''How long will that take?'' Julee asked.

''As long as it takes,'' Dylan said.

*   *   *

It took almost a week for the Greek police in Piraiévs to confirm that a child matching Brice's description was indeed staying at the house near Agkali that belonged to Cyril Eldridge.

During that six days Julee and Cain went through the necessary red tape for travel to Greece. After much discussion, they took the plunge and made a quick trip to a nearby justice of the peace. Cain's argument was that he wanted her to have the protection of his name.

Julee knew that even though their falling in love seemed to have happened fast, in reality, the feelings between them had been growing ever since she'd moved into the house behind his. The bond they felt was right and strong. With no doubt in her mind that it would grow even stronger, she said yes to his proposal. The Sutherlands stood up for them at the justice of the peace and Trixie treated them to a quiet, elegant dinner afterward.

The day Dylan brought the snapshots that had been sent from Piraiévs by overnight courier, Julee took one look and burst into tears.

"That's Brice," she whispered in a choked voice. She raised her pain-ravaged face to look at Dylan.

"I'll call the police in L.A. and have them issue the warrant. I'm sorry."

"Don't be," Julee said. "This is his doing, not yours."

"Yeah." Dylan rose and went to the door.

"Dylan!" He turned. "I want to see him when they pick him up," Julee said. "I want to ask him why."

Dylan nodded. "Once we get him, I'll arrange it. But why don't you go get your son first."

The arid, northerly winds that swept the Aegean Sea made the sunshine in the Cyclades Islands so bright it hurt

the eyes and threw everything into sharp relief, intensifying
the colors and deepening the shadows. After the darkness
that had hung over them while they were waiting to find out
about Brice, the bright sunlight seemed like a promise.

Learning that Cyril was at his home in California, the
L.A. police had picked him up at his downtown office.
Three days later, they'd arrested the two men who had actually taken Brice. Julee had been shocked to learn that the
"wrong number" calls she'd received the morning Brice was
kidnapped were actually the men in Cyril's employ, who'd
made the calls from a cellular phone. One kept her busy
trying to locate the elusive, fictitious Carla, while the other
snatched Brice. Julee had to admit that it was a clever plan.
One that almost worked. Would have worked had it not
been for Cain.

Julee's loving gaze found her husband's profile. He was
absorbing his surroundings as the ferry from Piraiévs carried them and their small delegation of Greek policemen to
Folégandros. She smiled, knowing he was storing up memories to paint when they got back home.

Cain murmured in pleasure as they passed the small hill
town perched at the top of a seven-hundred-and-fifty-foot
cliff and the quaint tavernas and squares that cascaded from
the Venetian bulwarks that edged the old, restored houses
in the hills.

They disembarked at the small port of Karavostasis and,
after taking a light refreshment, piled onto the backs of the
police motor scooters to negotiate the two-plus miles between the hamlet and her father's house.

Cain had painted it accurately. The house was massive, a
spectacular whitewashed structure with weather-aged tiles
and a profusion of flowers tumbling down the sloping yard
that melded into the rocky incline to the white sands of the
secluded cove of Agkali.

As the motor scooters chugged up the drive, Julee saw two people step out onto the covered porch. Dimitri and Clio. She disembarked from behind Cain and unwrapped the scarf from around her head. A small figure ran out the door and hid behind Clio's skirt. Brice!

She started forward, but Cain's hand stopped her. "Let's do this all legal and proper," he said as the three policemen marched with military precision to confront the couple. Julee's Greek was minimal, but gestures alone said enough.

The police chief told Clio and Dimitri that they had papers demanding that they give up the child who had been taken illegally from his mother in the United States. Clio gasped and her shocked gaze found Dimitri's.

Cyril Eldridge, their employer and the man responsible for taking the boy, was in jail in America, and the boy's mother had come for him.

Clio raised her eyes to Julee's. Julee wasn't so far away that she couldn't see the torment there. Both Dimitri and Clio began talking at once, Clio to say she was sorry, Dimitri swearing their innocence and saying that Cyril had told them another story about how he came to have the boy.

The police chief waved his hand for silence and continued, stating that Dimitri and Clio, acting only under the orders they'd received from Mr. Eldridge, would not be held responsible for any wrongdoing, provided they complied with the demands of the police and the boy's mother.

Clio bent over and said something to Brice. He peeked out from behind her, his gaze looking Julee over from head to toe. Slowly, almost shyly, he stepped forward.

"Brice!" Julee called. The single word was all it took.

Brice ran across the porch and through the flowers, his chubby legs carrying him toward Julee's arms. She knelt, bracing herself for the impact of his small body. Even so, he almost knocked her over. It was the sweetest pain she'd ever felt, she thought as her arms closed around him and she buried her face in the hollow where his neck and shoulder met.

He smelled like dates and sunshine and small boy. And his stocky body felt like heaven. She covered his face with kisses while he wriggled like a puppy longing to be free. Thankful, delirious with joy, she smiled at him and said, "Let's go home."

Brice frowned. "Where my sandbox is?"

"Yes."

"And Power Rangers are on TV?"

"Yes."

"Okay!" he yelled, tightening his hold on her neck. It was then that he saw Cain standing back, his hands in his pockets, smiling.

"What are you doing here?"

Cain riffled Brice's hair. "I came to take you home, tiger."

Brice smiled as if the idea made him happy.

While Cain put Brice in the sidecar of a motor scooter, Julee looked up and saw tears streaming down Clio's withered cheeks. Telling Cain she'd be just a minute, Julee walked onto the porch and took the old woman's frail body in a loose embrace.

"He told us you were dead," Clio sobbed. "He said the boy was with his father who was no-good."

"It's all right," Julee whispered, and the old woman cried harder. "I don't blame you or Dimitri. I want to thank you for taking such good care of Brice while he was here."

The old woman nodded. "Will you come back?"

"Someday," Julee promised. "Someday."

* * *

Brice told his tale during the ferry ride back to Piraiévs. He recounted how the man Cain had described had slipped into the backyard and snatched him from behind.

"That man had his hand over my mouth. I was scared," he said, his brown eyes wide as he divided his attention between his mother and Cain. "I kept calling for Mama," he said to Cain. He pointed to his temple. "I was calling inside here."

Julee's heart broke. It would be hard forgiving her father for what he'd stolen from Brice...that sweet, pure innocence of childhood that once it's taken can never be replaced or replenished.

As the ferry cruised the calm waters, Brice began to sing. "Bobby Shaftoe's got silver buckles on his knees...pretty Bobby Shaftoe."

Brice didn't know all the words and he wasn't in tune, but Julee noticed that something about the song had piqued Cain's interest.

"What's that?" he asked.

"It's a nursery rhyme my mother used to sing to me."

"Clio sang it to me," Brice said, and launched into a garbled second verse. "Bobby Shaftoe's hmm, hmm, hmm, combing back his yellow hair..."

Memory came surging back. Julee's eyes met Cain's and she began to sing in a clear soprano. Brice followed where he could. "Bobby Shaftoe's fat and fair, combing back his yellow hair. He's my love forever more, pretty Bobby Shaftoe."

Cain smiled. Julee smiled back.

"You were picking up on Brice singing the nursery rhyme, except I didn't recognize it, because I didn't have enough of the words. The dream was trying to tell you that Brice was on Folégandros."

Brice was listening intently. He propped his elbow on Cain's knee and said, "Sometimes I dreamed you were calling me, Cain. I always called back." He grinned. "Mama says always answer, so she'll know where I am."

"She's right," Cain said. "And I'm glad you did call back, because I heard you."

Brice smiled and scrambled up into Cain's lap.

In a day or two, when things settled down and Brice was secure again, Julee would tell him that she and Cain were married and that he had a new dad. It would be all right. She knew it as certainly as she knew that everything between her and Cain would be all right.

Why, he's just an old man, Julee thought when the guard ushered her father into the small room divided by mesh-covered glass. Old, and sick. He'd suffered a heart attack when the police had stormed his L.A. office with their warrant. Julee was surprised to learn that it was his third heart attack, and by far the worst.

"So I had to get thrown in jail for you to come to me, huh, Jules?" he said, calling her by the nickname he'd favored when she was a child. The sarcasm was familiar, too; she recalled it well.

"You're the one who cut me out of your life, Daddy," Julee reminded him. "And you don't know how much it hurt."

His nostrils flared in the way she remembered when his temper was on the rise. "You think it didn't hurt me when you married that redneck carpenter?"

"He wasn't a redneck carpenter! He was a small-town guy who was a brilliant architect and builder."

"Whatever," Cyril said. The dismissive wave of his hand reminded Julee of the way a person might flick away a troublesome insect, which was all Tad had ever been to her father.

"Why did you take Brice?" she demanded, refusing to soft-soap the wrong he'd done her.

"He's my grandson."

Julee knew that the statement had more to do with possession than it did emotion. "If you wanted to see him, all you had to do was ask."

"Eldridges don't ask, they act!"

"Cut it out, Dad," Julee said, fed up with his attitude. "You can't bluster or boast or bribe your way out of this one. You kidnapped my child and you'd have kept him away from me forever if it hadn't been for Cain—wouldn't you?"

"I don't have to explain myself to you."

"No, but you're going to have to explain your actions to your Maker, and if I were in the shape the doctors claim you're in, I'd be doing my best not to add to my list of sins."

"We never did see eye to eye," he said. The expression in the eyes so like Julee's was unafraid and unrepentant.

"No," Julee said. "We never did." She stood. There was no talking to Cyril. No reasoning with him. She'd heard her mother say it a thousand times. She picked up her handbag and clutched it to her breast. "I won't be back."

"Suit yourself."

Julee felt the sharp sting of tears and dropped her head. The sound that came from her lips was a strange cross between laughter and a sob. She shook her head slowly, and raised her gaze to his. "You're a real piece of work, Daddy," she said. "But that old saw is true—blood is truly thicker than water. I want you to know that I forgive you for what you've done to me and Brice. And for what you did to Tad."

Cyril's face flamed. "I don't want your damned forgiveness."

"Maybe not, but you have it. I've learned something you never did. Life is too short and too unpredictable to be miserable for a single second. Carrying around any bad feelings for you would rob me of more joy than any satisfaction I might get from my hate." She drew a deep breath and offered him a faltering smile. "And in spite of everything, I want you to know that I still care about you."

Without another word, Julee turned and indicated to the guard that she was ready to go.

Cain and Brice and the sunshine of Disney World were waiting for her.

Epilogue

The breeze coming off the sea was warm and moist and smelled of salt and adventure. But no adventure could equal that which Julee had experienced during her year-long marriage to Cain, she thought, showering his face with kisses.

The primal beat of the gently lapping waves kept time with the beat of her heart and the passion pulsing inside her. The sorrows that had been a part of her life for so long were bittersweet memories as distant from her present happiness as the sound of a faraway gull's cry. She wondered now, as she often did, how she had ever managed to live without Cain.

She strung a series of kisses as delicate as sea foam across his chest and over his hard stomach. His groan of pleasure was an aphrodisiac and she covered his mouth with hers in a slow, drugging kiss. Taking the initiative, he tumbled her onto her back and she cradled his weight between her thighs, acutely, thankfully, aware that she was a woman.

For a long moment as he lay poised above her, there was no movement, no sound but the unmistakable rasp of their breathing and the soft sighing of the sea. He brushed his thumb across the wetness of her bottom lip.

"Uh-oh!" a childish voice cried. "Mom and Dad are wrestling again."

"So I see."

Cain gave a groan of agony and let his hot gaze roam Julee's face. "You're gonna get us into trouble yet."

Julee brushed back the hair he let grow too long during the summer and spread his fingers over her gently rounded stomach. "Too late. We're already in trouble."

"This isn't trouble. It's heaven."

Julee lifted her eyebrows. "I'm going to remind you of that after we've been up five nights in a row with a colicky baby. Now let me up, you animal."

Cain grinned and helped her to her feet.

"You promised you'd build me a sand castle," Brice said, clinging to Julee's bare leg.

Julee grimaced.

"You did," Cain said.

"All right. Get your bucket and shovel."

Julee sent Trixie back to the house to rest until dinner. Then she sat beneath a red-and-white striped umbrella and guided Brice's hands while Cain worked on a seascape, struggling to capture the sharp brightness of the Aegean Sea and the clear cerulean sky before the light failed him.

Cyril had died eight months before, succumbing to his fourth heart attack. Julee had been stunned to learn that he'd left her everything he owned. Maybe he'd had a change of heart, or maybe he just felt guilty. She'd never know.

Cain had gone back to teaching, and the one-man art show in New Orleans had been a success. At Julee's insistence, he'd decided to take a year off and concentrate on his painting.

Julee had rebuilt Rocky Melancon's house, but even though the business was going well, she'd decided to sell a half interest to Luther. He'd keep up the high standards she expected, and she could be a silent partner and stay at home for a change.

Brice would start preschool in the fall, and he'd soon be gone all day. Julee didn't want to miss a minute more of his growing up, or to be deprived of the things she had missed out on with Brice when the new baby came—the first smile, the first tooth, the first step, small things that Loretta Sutherland had experienced first, while Julee worked. As she'd told Cyril, life was too short. She wanted to live every moment to the fullest, to savor every sweet drop of time she had.

As she'd known they would, she and Cain grew closer every day. He was sometimes temperamental, but his moods didn't last long and they were never too severe. He continued to help Dylan and Phil on a selective basis, but maintained the promise he'd made to himself not to let his gift disrupt his life.

"Where's Brice?"

Julee looked around and saw that Brice had lost interest in the sand castle and was climbing the rock steps up to the house. She'd been so lost in her reverie, she hadn't noticed his disinterest.

Cain sat down in the sand beside her, put his hand on her stomach and closed his eyes.

"What do you see?" Julee asked.

"Another boy."

"Are you serious?"

"'Fraid so."

"Darn!" Julee said. "Trixie says the cards show a boy, too. I wanted a girl."

Cain stretched an arm across her and kissed her pouting lips. "Hey, I know you're disappointed, but I don't mind trying until we get it right."

Laughter bubbled up from a never-ending wellspring inside Julee.

"What?" Cain asked, wanting to be let in on the joke.

Julee wrapped her arms around his neck. "I love you."

"I know."

"Oh, yeah?" she teased, tickling his ear with her tongue. "How do you know?"

Cain looked into her eyes, his own alight with love and happiness. "Because I've been where dreams have been. And you're always there with me."

Julee smiled and opened her mouth for his kiss.

The crooning of the sea accompanied the steady beating of her heart, and Julee acknowledged that this was good and somehow destined to be.

* * * * *

MONTANA Mavericks™

Stories that capture living and loving
beneath the Big Sky, where legends live
on...and mystery lingers.

This April, unlock the secrets of the past in

FATHER FOUND
by Laurie Paige

Moriah Gilmore had left Whitehorn years ago, without
a word. But when her father disappeared, Kane Hunter
called her home. Joined in the search, Moriah and
Kane soon rekindle their old passion, and though the
whereabouts of her father remain unknown, Kane comes
closer to discovering Moriah's deep secret—and the child
he'd never known.

Don't miss a minute of the loving as the passion
continues with:

BABY WANTED
by Cathie Linz (May)

MAN WITH A PAST
by Celeste Hamilton (June)

COWBOY COP
by Rachel Lee (July)

Only from **♥ Silhouette®** where passion lives.

MAV9

A MAN FOR MOM
Gina Ferris Wilkins
(SE #955, May)

Struggling to keep a business afloat plus taking care of the kids left little room for romance in single mother Rachel Evans's life. Then she met Seth Fletcher. And suddenly the handsome lawyer had her thinking about things that were definitely unbusinesslike....

Meet Rachel—a *very* special woman—and the rest of her family in the first book of THE FAMILY WAY series...beginning in May.

"The perfect Mother's Day gift...for your *very* special mom!

♥ *Silhouette* ROMANCE™

Arriving in April from Silhouette Romance...

Bundles of JOY

Six bouncing babies. Six unforgettable love stories.

Join Silhouette Romance as we present these heartwarming tales featuring the joy that only a baby can bring!

***THE DADDY PROJECT* by Suzanne Carey**
***THE COWBOY, THE BABY AND THE RUNAWAY BRIDE*
by Lindsay Longford**
***LULLABY AND GOODNIGHT* by Sandra Steffen**
***ADAM'S VOW* by Karen Rose Smith**
***BABIES INC.* by Pat Montana**
***HAZARDOUS HUSBAND* by Christine Scott**

Don't miss out on these BUNDLES OF JOY—only from Silhouette Romance. Because sometimes, the smallest packages can lead to the biggest surprises!

And be sure to look for additional BUNDLES OF JOY titles in the months to come.

**Five unforgettable
couples say "I Do"...
with a little help
from their friends**

*Always a
Bridesmaid!*

Always a bridesmaid, never a bride...that's
me, Katie Jones--a woman with more taffeta
bridesmaid dresses than dates! I'm just one of
the continuing characters you'll get to know in
ALWAYS A BRIDESMAID!--Silhouette's new
across-the-lines series about the lives, loves...and
weddings--of five couples here in Clover, South
Carolina. Share in all our celebrations! (With so
many events to attend, I'm sure to get my own
groom!)

In June, **Desire** hosts
THE ENGAGEMENT PARTY by Barbara Boswell

In July, **Romance** holds
THE BRIDAL SHOWER by Elizabeth August

In August, **Intimate Moments** gives
THE BACHELOR PARTY by Paula Detmer Riggs

In September, **Shadows** showcases
THE ABANDONED BRIDE by Jane Toombs

In October, **Special Edition** introduces
FINALLY A BRIDE by Sherryl Woods

Don't miss a single one--wherever
Silhouette books are sold.

▼ *Silhouette*®
™

AAB-G

the exciting new series by
New York Times bestselling author

The MacKade Brothers—looking for trouble,
and always finding it. Now they're on a collision
course with love. And it all begins with

THE RETURN OF RAFE MACKADE
(Intimate Moments #631, April 1995)

The whole town was buzzing. Rafe MacKade
was back in Antietam, and that meant only one
thing—there was bound to be trouble....

Be on the lookout for the next book in the
series, **THE PRIDE OF JARED MACKADE—**
Silhouette Special Edition's 1000th Book!
It's an extraspecial event not to be missed,
coming your way in December 1995!

THE MACKADE BROTHERS—these sexy, trouble-
loving men will be heading out to you in alter-
nate books from Silhouette Intimate Moments
and Silhouette Special Edition.
Watch out for them!

NRTITLE

Silhouette

SPECIAL EDITION™

And now for the powerful conclusion to the trilogy

This Time, Forever

by Andrea Edwards

It began with A RING AND A PROMISE (SE #932), continued with
A ROSE AND A WEDDING VOW (SE #944) and finally,
in A SECRET AND A BRIDAL PLEDGE (SE #956),
a last pair of star-crossed lovers hope to be reunited.

U.S. Marshal Mark Miller was endangered witness Amy Warren's only
protection. The trouble was, Mark made her feel as unsafe as a woman could
be! But there was also something strangely familiar and compelling about
how he made her feel.... Could this be her chance at a forever?